I

MURDER AT
MADAME TUSSAUDS

By Jim Eldridge

MUSEUM MYSTERIES SERIES
Murder at the Fitzwilliam
Murder at the British Museum
Murder at the Ashmolean
Murder at the Manchester Museum
Murder at the Natural History Museum
Murder at Madame Tussauds

HOTEL MYSTERIES SERIES
Murder at the Ritz

a&b

MURDER AT
MADAME TUSSAUDS

JIM ELDRIDGE

Allison & Busby Limited
11 Wardour Mews
London W1F 8AN
allisonandbusby.com

First published in Great Britain by Allison & Busby in 2021.

Copyright © 2021 by JIM ELDRIDGE

A CIP catalogue record for this book is available from
the British Library.

First Edition

ISBN: 978-0-7490-2775-9

Typeset in 11.5/16.5 pt Adobe Garamond Pro by
Allison & Busby Ltd.

The paper used for this Allison & Busby publication
has been produced from trees that have been legally sourced
from well-managed and credibly certified forests.

Printed and bound by
CPI Group (UK) Ltd, Croydon, CR0 4YY

To Lynne, as always, for always

CHAPTER ONE

London, 1896

The dense, slimy tendrils of green and grey acrid fog, a real 'pea-souper' in the local parlance, floated along Marylebone Road, as it did through the rest of central London, choking everything in sight. The few people who'd braved it held handkerchiefs or cloths to their mouths and noses and blinked to clear the burning tears from their eyes. The fog had held London in its grip for three days now. It was so thick that no horses were on the roads for fear of them stumbling into something – people, other horses, buildings. There were no wagons, no omnibuses, no hansom cabs, no carriages, just people shuffling along with their faces masked and their heads down, trying to spot where the pavement ended and the road began.

Safe from the fog inside the Chamber of Horrors in Marylebone Road's Madame Tussauds, Daniel Wilson and Abigail Fenton stood alongside the manager of the museum, John Theodore Tussaud, a great-grandson of Madame Tussaud, as he pointed a trembling finger at the guillotine; the centrepiece of the French Revolution tableau.

'Eric's body was found right there, his head lying by the blade,' he told them.

The fog had stopped the usual flow of visitors to the famous museum. Though even if any had attempted to call, they would have found the Chamber of Horrors closed to the public as a result of this particular real-life horror: the discovery of the headless body of one of the museum's two nightwatchmen, Eric Dudgeon.

Daniel and Abigail took in the scene, the guillotine and the unnervingly lifelike wax figures which stood around looking at the deadly wooden machine and its vicious blade, the sharp edge smeared red. Most of the figures' faces bore the bloodthirsty expressions of rabid revolutionaries from the time of the French Revolution. Others represented members of the royal family and other aristocrats standing in positions of horror beside the guillotine, their faces showing such vivid fear and revulsion at what awaited them that Abigail had to remind herself they were just wax models and not real people.

At first sight, the two appeared a mismatched couple. Daniel was a former detective at Scotland Yard, a stocky muscular man in his thirties whose north London accent betrayed his working-class roots. Abigail was tall, slender and elegant with an air of confidence that came with gaining a first-class Classics degree at Cambridge. She also had a reputation as one of the world's leading archaeologists and Egyptologists. But those who knew them soon discovered that despite their apparent differences, there was a strong bond between them – not just as private investigators, but in life. All that remained, they constantly reminded one another, was to marry, and they'd frequently drawn up serious plans to execute this, but somehow things seemed to turn up and force a deferment.

'Are we doing this for us, or for society's demands of respectability?' Abigail had asked on one occasion.

'For us,' Daniel had replied.

But then something had intervened, as it usually did. This time, it was a headless body discovered in the Chamber of Horrors, which led to a call from John Tussaud.

'Is the blade really sharp enough to slice someone's head off?' asked Daniel, perturbed.

'No,' said Tussaud. 'It's been blunted to avoid accidents.' He was a very precise man in his late thirties, formally dressed in frock coat and black tie, and whose usual precision had been turned into unhappy agitation by this tragic turn of events.

'But there's blood on its edge,' Abigail pointed out.

'We believe whoever killed Eric daubed his blood on it after they'd cut his head off, to create the impression he'd been guillotined,' said Tussaud.

'I assume the police took the body away,' mused Daniel.

Tussaud nodded. 'A Superintendent Armstrong was here. From Scotland Yard. We contacted the police as soon as we discovered the body.'

'When you say "we". . . ?' enquired Daniel.

'Myself and the cleaners. I like to open the museum and let the cleaners in.'

'At what time?'

'Eight o'clock. They work for an hour and a half, and we open to the public at ten o'clock. I come in to inspect everything in case there's been an accident or something during the night.'

'And does that often happen?' asked Abigail.

Tussaud shook his head.

'No. We've had problems in the past with thrill-seekers trying to break in, or hiding in the museum just before we close, in order to spend the night here. Some people have this desire to boast that they spent the night in Madame Tussauds' Chamber of Horrors, but we usually find them hiding in the conveniences and turf them out with a warning that they'll be prosecuted if they try it again. That usually does the trick. And our watchmen have always been alert for any intruders.'

'Except for last night,' murmured Daniel. 'Mr Dudgeon was one of your watchmen?'

'He was,' confirmed Tussaud. 'Along with Walter Bagshot.'

'Who you say has disappeared.'

'Yes,' Tussaud nodded unhappily. 'Superintendent Armstrong said it was obvious what had happened: Eric and Walter must have had an argument. Walter killed Eric, then fled. He said this was backed up by wounds to the back of Eric's head indicating that he'd been struck with a heavy metal object. Also by the fact that the keys to the museum had gone. He said Walter must have taken them with him.'

'Is that likely?' asked Abigail. 'The argument?'

Tussaud shook his head.

'No. Absolutely not. Eric and Walter were as close as any two people could be, like brothers.'

'Brothers have been known to fall out,' commented Daniel.

Tussaud bristled at this.

'If you're suggesting that myself and my brother Louis . . .' he snapped, glaring at Daniel.

'No, no,' Daniel assured him hastily. 'I was just mentioning the possibility that Mr Dudgeon and Mr Bagshot may have had some sort of disagreement.'

'It would have to be something especially serious for Walter to do something as hideous as this.'

'Indeed.' Daniel nodded. He looked apologetically at Tussaud. 'And I do assure you, Mr Tussaud, that I intended no reference to anything to do with your family. To be honest, although I'm obviously aware of Tussauds waxwork museum, I'm not acquainted with your family's history. Except for the fact that your great-grandmother was the one who established the museum here in London, after she left France.'

'*Many* years after she left France,' stressed Tussaud. Seeming slightly mollified, he enlarged. 'She sought refuge in England when things became too dangerous for her after the revolution. She was forced to make wax models of the heads of people she had known and who were dear to her, including the queen, Marie Antoinette and the king, Louis XVI. When she saw that the insatiable guillotine was taking the lives of many around her, she brought her wax models across the Channel and toured with them around England, Scotland and Ireland, before settling in London.'

'How long did she tour for before establishing herself in London?' asked Abigail, keen to keep the conversation amicable, determined to repair any damage Daniel's comment

11

may have caused. It didn't do to upset a client.

'Twenty years,' said Tussaud.

'What can you tell us about Eric and Walter?' asked Daniel. 'How long had they been working for you?'

'Not long at all,' said Tussaud. 'Barely two weeks, now I come to think about it.'

'How did you find them?'

'I didn't, they found me. Our previous nightwatchmen, Donald Bruin and Steven Patterson, suddenly announced they were leaving the next day.'

'Did they tell you why?'

'They said they'd been offered an opportunity to make more money.'

'Doing what?'

'They didn't say. I must admit, I was too stunned to enquire further. I asked them how much more they'd been offered, because I was prepared to meet the sum. They'd both shown themselves responsible and reliable . . .'

'Until they left,' murmured Abigail.

'Yes. But they said their minds were made up, and they'd be leaving after they'd finished their night shift.'

'It could have been worse, they might have just not turned up.'

'True, but – as I say – they'd always struck me as responsible men. The next morning when I arrived for work and to let the cleaners in, they took the wages they were due, shook me by the hand, and left. As you can imagine, I felt absolutely helpless. I'd still hoped they might change their mind.'

'Had there been any ill-feeling between you? Or them and anyone at the museum?'

'No, absolutely not. Everything had been amicable right from the start.'

'How long had they been with you?'

'Almost nine months, which is why it came as such a shock.'

'And how did Mr Dudgeon and Mr Bagshot enter the picture?'

'They called later that same morning and asked if we had any vacancies.'

Abigail and Daniel exchanged intrigued glances, Daniel saying blandly, 'That was very opportune.'

'Indeed,' said Tussaud. 'I did wonder afterwards if perhaps the two watchmen who'd left hadn't informed Eric and Walter that they were leaving.'

'It's certainly possible,' said Daniel. 'Did Eric and Walter mention the previous watchmen at all?'

Tussaud shook his head. 'No. And I must admit, I was so relieved that I didn't ask. I asked for their references, of course, and they had excellent ones from their previous employers.'

'Where had they worked before?'

'On the railways, as labourers. They told me there'd been a cave-in while they were digging a tunnel in which some of their fellow workers had been seriously injured, which made them decide to look for something less dangerous.'

'Where was the tunnel?' asked Abigail.

'I don't know,' admitted Tussaud. 'To be frank, I was so relieved to find them that I hired them on the spot.'

'And had there been any difficulties with them since they started working for you?'

'None at all. Their timekeeping was excellent, so was their attitude. No complaints.'

13

Abigail gestured at the guillotine. 'I understand that the guillotine is an original, brought by your great-grandmother from France.'

'Yes,' said Tussaud, 'and not just the machine, but the figures of the French royal family, Louis and Marie Antoinette and her sister. And of the revolutionaries, Danton and Robespierre and the others.' He looked admiringly at the waxwork images, his voice full of pride. 'Can you imagine the responsibility on the shoulders of a relatively young woman at that time, to transport all of this from country to country, town to town? And this was before the advent of the railways, so everything had to be hauled in wagons across what were often very poorly-constructed roads. All while continuing to expand the exhibition. She was an astounding woman!' He gestured at the figures on display, all unnervingly lifelike. 'Burke and Hare, the bodysnatchers. William Marwood, the hangman. Charles Peace. Mary Ann Cotton. Any one of them capable of sending terror through any visitor.'

'Hence the challenge to spend a night here, I imagine,' observed Abigail.

'I suppose so,' said Tussaud. 'Charles Dickens was a great admirer of my great-grandmother and her work,' he added. 'She was the model for Mrs Jarley, the waxworks owner in *The Old Curiosity Shop*. And he was a frequent visitor to her exhibitions. It is said that the display you see before you of the guillotine and the revolution in France was the inspiration for his *A Tale of Two Cities*. We have an incredibly lifelike mannequin of the great man in our literary gallery. I do urge you to see it.'

'We will,' Daniel assured him. 'But to return to the two previous nightwatchmen, Donald Bruin and Steven Patterson.

Do you have their addresses? And those of Mr Dudgeon and Mr Bagshot?'

'Those last two I can certainly give you, but I'm not sure if Bruin and Patterson will still be at the address they gave us. I got the impression their new appointment meant them travelling further afield. If we go to my office, I'll let you have all the details on file.'

CHAPTER TWO

Armed with the address of Dudgeon and Bagshot at a house in Marylebone, and one for Bruin and Patterson at a house in Somers Town, Daniel and Abigail left the museum, promising John Tussaud they'd be in touch as soon as they had any news.

'The fog appears to be lifting,' observed Daniel.

Indeed the thick, green mass had risen from the ground and was now at head height, which meant they were able to watch their step, provided they moved slowly and kept their heads down. They both pulled their scarves over their mouths.

'A bit suspicious, don't you think?' asked Abigail as they made their way carefully down Baker Street. 'Bruin and

Patterson leave with barely a moment's notice, and within a few hours, two men turn up looking for work.'

'Very suspicious. I think we need to look into both pairs of men.'

'We also need to be careful of what we say. That was a sticky moment when you mentioned his brother, Louis.'

'I didn't mention him! I was just talking about brothers in general. Many do fall out, Cain and Abel being the best-known example. I didn't know there was bad feeling between him and his brother.'

'We're not sure there is.'

'Well, he certainly acted as if there was something there,' Daniel grumbled. 'I think we need to find out more about the family. I obviously touched on a nerve when I mentioned brothers falling out, and I don't want to do something similar again because of my ignorance and put this case at risk.'

'Can I suggest you leave that to me,' said Abigail. 'I can look into the background of the Tussaud family, while you dig into the lives of the two nightwatchmen.'

'That's a good idea. Especially as it could involve going into pubs in the Marylebone area where they lived, and women tend to get viewed with suspicion in those sort of pubs. They're usually taken to be prostitutes or religious do-gooders spreading the gospel of abstinence from alcohol. But before we do that, I suggest calling on John Feather at Scotland Yard to tell him we're on the case, and swap information.'

* * *

By the time they arrived at Scotland Yard, the fog had lifted further, although it still hung in thin grey strands just above their heads.

'It is definitely thinning,' said Abigail. 'Let's hope this is the last we'll see of it.'

'We said that yesterday,' said Daniel. 'And the day before.'

'It can't stay this way for ever,' said Abigail.

'I remember a few years ago we had thick fog for a month,' Daniel told her. 'The city was the quietest I've ever known it. No sound at all. Everyone stayed indoors, with their coal fires on, throwing out even more foul-smelling smoke to add to the mix.'

They entered the reception area and Daniel was relieved to see that someone he knew, Sergeant Riley, was manning the desk.

'Good morning, Sean.' He smiled, and was surprised to see that, instead of the usual welcoming smile in return, the sergeant looked back at him, obviously uncomfortable.

'Mr Wilson.' He nodded, but his attitude and facial expression remained polite but distant.

We have a problem, thought Daniel. But aloud he asked in pleasant tones, 'Is Inspector Feather available?'

'I'm afraid not,' said Sergeant Riley.

'Do you know when he will be?' asked Daniel.

'I believe he'll continue to be unavailable,' replied Riley, and Daniel saw the discontent in the sergeant's eyes at being forced to say the words.

We're barred, he realised. He smiled, nodded, and said, 'I understand. Thank you, Sergeant.' He began to turn away, then stopped and enquired, 'Would it be all right for me to leave a

18

message for him to say that I called?'

Riley hesitated, looked around to see if he was being observed by anyone, before muttering, 'If you give me the note, I'll have it sent to his office.'

'Thank you.' Daniel smiled. He took his notebook from his pocket, tore out a page and wrote, *We're in reception. Yrs. Daniel.* He folded the paper over and handed it to Riley, who passed it to a constable, grunting, 'Take this to Inspector Feather's office.'

As Daniel and Abigail walked away from the desk towards the main doors, Abigail asked, 'What was all that about?'

'We're barred,' whispered Daniel.

'Why?' asked Abigail.

'I have no idea,' he sighed.

Just before they reached the doors, he stopped and crouched down to retie his shoelaces, keeping his eyes on the reception desk. As he finished his second shoe, he saw the constable returning down the stairs, holding a piece of paper in his hand. The constable was about to go to the reception desk, when he caught sight of Daniel. The constable handed him the small, folded piece of paper. 'From Inspector Feather.'

'Thank you,' said Daniel. He unfolded the paper and read: *Freddy's. Ten minutes.*

'Hopefully we'll find out what's going on,' he said as he led Abigail out of the reception area and into the street.

Daniel and Abigail had taken a table at Freddy's Coffee Shop, opposite Scotland Yard and ordered three coffees. Their coffees had just been delivered to their table by the waitress, when Daniel saw the figure of John Feather emerging from Scotland Yard and crossing the road. The fog was thinning and now consisted of light grey fronds hanging in the air just above head height.

'Here he comes,' he said.

He and Abigail both stood and shook Feather's hand as he joined them. Feather sat down, lifted his cup and took a sip. He was a short, slim and genial man in his early forties; clean-shaven, but his dark hair was already turning grey at the sides. The result of having a harsh boss as his superintendent, as well as the responsibility of a large family to provide for.

'I needed that,' said Feather.

'So, going on?' asked Daniel. 'Are we persona non grata again at Scotland Yard?'

'Superintendent Armstrong's orders,' said Feather. 'If he knew I was here with you I'd be getting a rocket.'

'Why?'

'There was an article in one of the cheaper tabloids a couple of days ago, *The Whistler*. I don't know if you saw it?'

Both Daniel and Abigail shook their heads.

'It questioned how much of Scotland Yard's success in recent murder cases at museums in London was actually due to you two, or "The Museum Detectives", as it calls you.'

'That was nothing to do with us,' said Abigail.

'We have no control over what the papers say,' added Daniel.

'Be that as it may, the super was furious, so he's given an order that neither of you are allowed into Scotland Yard, and no one in the police force is to have any contact with you. Not in a positive way, at least. I expect he'd be quite pleased if someone arrested you.'

'That's ridiculous!' said Abigail. 'Aren't we all supposed to be on the same side? Fighting crime! Catching criminals?'

'The super doesn't see it that way,' said Feather. 'As far as he's concerned you're competition, and he's compared unfavourably to you.' He sipped his coffee and looked anxiously at the door. 'I'd better not stay too long in case anyone comes in and reports back to Armstrong that they've seen me with you.'

'What will you do if that happens?' asked Abigail.

'I'll say that I was in here for a coffee, and you two sat down at my table.' He looked at them quizzically. 'So, you must have wanted to see me for a reason?'

'The murder this morning at Madame Tussauds,' said Daniel.

Feather shook his head. 'That's not my case.'

'Why not? You're Armstrong's best detective, and this is a famous museum, so it'll be high-profile.'

'Armstrong wants me on something else that he feels is more important. As far as he's concerned, the Tussauds murder is straightforward. He's sure that Bagshot killed Dudgeon and then did a runner. He's instituted a search for him.'

'What's this case he's put you on that's more important than a murder?'

Feather hesitated, looked around to make sure they couldn't be overheard, then whispered. 'Officially I can't tell you, but I'm fairly sure it's going to made be public very soon. In recent weeks there have been a series of bank robberies where the criminals have broken into the vaults at night, through the cellars of adjoining premises.'

'I haven't seen anything in the newspapers about that,' said Daniel.

'There hasn't been . . . so far,' said Feather. 'The banks and the government have kept it secret because they don't want panic to spread about their security measures. Otherwise people might start to take their money out, which could lead to a run on the banks. But your reporter friend, Joe Dalton, has uncovered the story and I believe it's going to be in *The Telegraph* tomorrow. Armstrong hasn't only got the banks on his back, but the Bank of England and the government as well. Originally the robberies were in the hands of Fred Calley, but he fell off the back of a lorry and broke his leg. He's going to be out of action for a good while. The superintendent put me in charge just a few days ago.'

'So who is in charge of the Tussaud case?'

'Jim Jarrett.'

Daniel groaned. 'Is he still around?'

'Armstrong likes him. Jarrett does what he wants.'

'Badly. What do you know about the man who was killed, and the other nightwatchman – Walter Bagshot?'

'Apart from their names, nothing. Like I said, Armstrong's keeping me away from the case; he wants all my attention on these bank robberies. And he'll want something by the end of the day so he's got some kind of answer when the article comes out.' He finished his coffee and stood up. 'If I do hear anything, I'll put a note through your letterbox at home.'

'And we'll meet up?'

'If we do, I suggest somewhere other than here. Too many coppers calling, eager to pass on things to Armstrong so they can get a leg up the ladder.'

'Like Jim Jarrett?'

'Exactly like Jim Jarrett.'

He tipped his hat to them, and left.

'It looks like we're out in the cold,' observed Daniel.

'We've been here before,' Abigail pointed out.

'Yes, but at least we had someone inside. With John being cut out of the Tussauds case, that's gone.'

'What's this Jim Jarrett like?'

'Inspector Jarrett,' sighed Daniel. 'Narrow-minded. Bigoted. Thick as a brick. Couldn't find his backside with both hands. But he follows orders.'

'Will we meet him?'

'I'm sure we will, sooner or later. But don't expect any scintillating conversation.' He finished his coffee. 'Right now, I suggest we set about our separate tasks. You go and research the Tussaud family.'

'And you find out about the two sets of nightwatchmen.'

CHAPTER THREE

A middle-aged lady wearing an apron opened the door to Daniel's knock at the Marylebone address John Tussaud had given him.

'Mrs Pershore?' enquired Daniel with a smile.

'Yes.'

'I believe this is where Mr Dudgeon and Mr Bagshot live?'

'Yes,' she replied again. 'But they're not in at the moment.'

Daniel hesitated. He'd have expected that the police would have made the men's address their first port of call, but obviously that hadn't been the case. Inspector Jarrett at fault, he suspected.

'Then the police haven't been, I assume,' he asked.

Mrs Pershore gave a worried frown. 'No? Why would the police be calling here?'

'I'm afraid there's been an incident at the museum,' said Daniel. He produced one of his business cards and handed it to the woman. 'My name's Daniel Wilson and I'm a private investigator. I've been asked by Madame Tussauds to look into the tragic death of Mr Dudgeon and the disappearance of Mr Bagshot that occurred some time during the night.'

Mrs Pershore's hand flew to her mouth. 'Dead? Mr Dudgeon's dead?'

'I'm afraid so.'

'What happened? Did he have an accident?'

Again Daniel hesitated before answering; then, sure that the murder would be in the next day's newspapers, he said, 'It appears he was murdered.'

'Murdered?! How? Who did it? Surely not Mr Bagshot!'

'That's something the police are looking into.'

'No!' she burst out. 'I can't believe Mr Bagshot would harm Mr Dudgeon in any way. There must be some mistake.'

'There may be about Mr Bagshot's disappearance, but I'm afraid there's no mistake about Mr Dudgeon being killed.'

'How?' she repeated, more insistent this time.

'Someone cut his head off and left it beside the guillotine in the Chamber of Horrors at the museum.' As Daniel saw Mrs Pershore sway, he said, 'I'm sorry to be so brutal. Please, shall we go inside and you can sit down.'

Dazed, Mrs Pershore walked into the house and down the short passageway to the kitchen, where she stumbled to the table and sat down heavily on one of the wooden chairs.

'Are you . . . are you sure it wasn't an accident?' she asked weakly. 'He might have been playing a joke and the blade slipped?'

'According to Mr Tussaud, the blade has been made deliberately blunt,' said Daniel. 'Can I get you anything? Water? Tea?'

'No, thank you,' she said, still stunned. 'When did this happen?'

'Some time last night. Mr Tussaud discovered it when he opened the museum at eight o'clock this morning.'

'But no one came to tell me!' she said, angry.

'I expect Mr Tussaud thought the police would be doing that. Look, I can see you're upset, so I'm happy to come back later. All I'm trying to find out is something about the two men. What they were like. People they mixed with.'

'They were lovely,' she said. 'Absolute gentlemen. It's not always the way with men who've been in the army, or who is involved in building work, but Mr Dudgeon and Mr Bagshot were two of the nicest men you could ever find.'

'How long had they been with you?'

'Two years, and never a hint of trouble. Always paid their rent on time.'

'You say they were in the army.'

'Yes, although they left it some years ago. Mr Dudgeon took a bad injury to his leg in some foreign place, and got invalided out. He had a limp when he walked, but it didn't stop him working. Oh no, he was a worker, Mr Dudgeon was. As was Mr Bagshot.'

'Do you know which section of the army they were in?'

'The Royal Engineers. They were always very proud of their regiment. They had a little kind of flag from it hung on their mantelpiece.'

'Would you mind if I went and looked around their room.

I'm hoping to find something that might tell us why Mr Dudgeon was killed, and where Mr Bagshot might have gone. I promise I won't make a mess. You can watch me, if you like.'

She shook her head. 'No. You go ahead. I'll sit here and get myself sorted out. It's a lot to take in. It's the first door on the right upstairs.' She went to a dresser, took a key from a hook and gave it to him.

The first thing Daniel saw when he entered the room was the small cloth banner hanging from the mantelshelf bearing the legend *Ubique Quo Fas Et Gloria Ducunt*. He took out his notebook and made a note of it, intent on asking Abigail for a translation later. Then he set to search the dressing table and the wardrobe. One thing was sure, if Walter Bagshot had gone missing of his own volition, he hadn't thought to take anything to carry his belongings in; there were two military-style knapsacks in the wardrobe, one bearing the name 'Bagshot', the other 'Dudgeon'. It also looked as if Bagshot had left his clothes behind as well. Again, like many former army men, they'd had their names inked inside the collars. There were two jackets hanging up, worn but of reasonable quality, which Daniel guessed were the men's best for Sundays and special occasions. There were also two pairs of trousers hanging in the wardrobe.

If Walter Bagshot did a runner, he did it without coming back and picking up his belongings, mused Daniel. *No, something else happened to him. But what?* If whoever killed Dudgeon also killed Bagshot, why didn't they leave his body in the Chamber of Horrors, as they had Dudgeon's? Could Bagshot have given chase to the killers and caught up with them away from the museum, and then been killed? But if so, the same question remained: why didn't they leave his body behind?

He finished his inspection of the room, then went back downstairs.

'Thank you,' he said, handing the key back to Mrs Pershore. 'I'm sure the police will want to do the same.'

She shook her head, still in a state of shock.

'I can't believe it,' she said. 'Who'd want to do such a thing?'

'That's what we're hoping to find out,' said Daniel. 'One last question: was there any particular local pub that Mr Dudgeon and Mr Bagshot used to go visit?'

'Yes. The Railway Tavern. They liked that one because of the name. They used to work on the railways, see.'

'Yes. I was told they were labourers.'

'I think they were a bit more than that. You know, proper building work. It came from them being engineers when they were in the army, I suppose.'

As Abigail walked between the towering Roman columns that fronted the British Museum, she felt that same thrill she'd always experienced. The British Museum, along with the Fitzwilliam in Cambridge, felt like a home to her. Every time she visited, the displays in the Egyptian, Greek and Roman rooms brought back memories of her time before she'd become, almost accidentally, a full-time detective alongside Daniel. All those periods in Egypt, months at a time, exploring newly opened pyramids, joining in the digging of the sites around the pyramids and examining the items unearthed. She felt a tinge of sadness when she realised how long it had been since she'd been 'in the field'. Four years. Too long an absence for any archaeologist. Her time at the Fitzwilliam, curating their exhibition of Egyptian artefacts, had been intended as a stopgap before she embarked on another expedition, but then she'd met Daniel, and her life had changed completely. The newspapers still referred to her as 'the noted archaeologist', but only when writing about her current exploits solving murders with 'Daniel Wilson, famed as one of Inspector Abberline's team of Scotland Yard detectives during the hunt for the notorious Jack the Ripper'. Her career as an archaeologist had been cut short, and she felt sad that it was unlikely to resume, even though that sadness was very much tempered with the happiness of her life with Daniel. *I may have lost a career, but I have found love*, she reminded herself.

It had been on one of those archaeological digs that she'd first made the acquaintance of Erasmus Black. They'd both been part of a team led by Flinders Petrie at Hawara, but with different areas of expertise. For Abigail it had been items made of clay, votive offerings; for Erasmus it had been the wax figurines used in funeral rites and buried with the pharaoh. There was no one else who knew as much about wax figures as Erasmus did. Not just those from ancient Egypt, but throughout history, and right up to the present day. If anyone could tell her about the Tussauds and any family intrigues, it was Erasmus.

The Railway Tavern was nearly empty, just a few drinkers at the tables and the barman wiping glasses behind the bar. Daniel looked at the clock. Twelve o'clock, noon. The pub was close to Marylebone railway station, and Daniel guessed that much of the business would be railway workers. It had all the hallmarks of a pub for working men, rather than one with a middle-class clientele, such as office clerks. There were even spittoons by the bar, and some at the far wall. All it lacked was sawdust on the floor.

Daniel strode up to the barman, who regarded him warily. *They don't get many strangers here*, thought Daniel. *This must be a pub for regulars.*

'Good afternoon. I believe Eric Dudgeon and Walter Bagshot are customers here?'

The barman shrugged and scowled at Daniel while he continued to wipe the glasses.

'Never heard of 'em,' he grunted.

'That's a pity,' said Daniel, 'because I have news of them. Tragic news.'

The barman stopped wiping the glasses and looked at Daniel warily.

'Police?' he asked.

'I was,' said Daniel. 'I'm now a private investigator. I've been hired by Madame Tussauds museum to look into the murder of one and the disappearance of the other.'

The barman stared at Daniel, his mouth falling open in shock. Then he recovered himself and leant forward, keeping his voice low, at the same time shooting an urgent look past Daniel's shoulder towards the tables by the wall. Daniel looked into the mirror and saw a woman sitting on her own, a glass of port in front of her, a vacant look on her face. She was in her forties, Daniel guessed. Her frilled blouse displayed ample cleavage which, along with her dyed hair and excessively-applied make-up, marked her out as a lady of the night, though it was early afternoon.

'Who got murdered?' asked the barman in a whisper.

'Eric,' said Daniel, also keeping his voice low.

'And Walter?'

'Vanished. I'm trying to find out what happened to them, so

30

I need to get some background on them.'

'You're looking for Walter?'

'Eventually. The police are. I'm just trying to find out what they were like and what they were involved in.'

'They're good blokes,' said the barman. 'How was Eric killed?'

'His body was found this morning at Madame Tussauds, next to the guillotine in the Chamber of Horrors. His head had been cut off.'

The barman gave a shudder.

'It can't have been Walter who did it,' he said firmly.

'That's Mr Tussaud's opinion as well,' said Daniel. 'He said they were like brothers.'

'They were.' The barman nodded. 'Rock solid.'

'But brothers can fall out.'

'Not Eric and Walter.'

'How close were they?' asked Daniel carefully.

'What do you mean?' asked the barman suspiciously.

'When Eric had to leave the army because he was injured, Walter went with him. They seemed to do everything together. They shared a room. I get the impression they were . . . particularly close.'

The barman glared at Daniel, angry.

'There was nothing like that!' he snapped. 'If you don't believe me, ask Elsie over there.'

Daniel turned and looked at the woman, sipping at her port. Every now and then she turned to look at the clock, then at the door, before turning back to her drink.

'Whose was she?' asked Daniel. 'Eric's or Walter's?'

'Eric's. That's why she's here. He usually comes in around

this time.' He hesitated, then asked, 'Will you tell her? But be gentle. She was very fond of him. They were almost like a married couple.'

'Almost?'

'Well, she has her own business to look after.'

'Does she have a minder?'

The barman shook his head. 'Eric wouldn't allow it. You know what these minders can be like.'

Daniel nodded; he knew only too well from his time at Scotland Yard. He'd lost count of the number of prostitutes whose bodies he'd viewed at the mortuary, most killed by a client, or more often than not, by their so-called minder.

'Elsie what?' he asked.

'Harkness.'

'What's she drinking? Port?'

The barman nodded. Daniel produced a coin, but the barman waved it away, then poured a port. 'This one's on the house,' he said. 'Eric spent more than enough here.'

Daniel carried the glass of port across to the table.

'Good afternoon,' he said.

She shook her head. 'Sorry, I'm waiting for a friend.'

'Yes, so I understand. Eric Dudgeon.' She looked up at him, concern on her face. Daniel put the glass of port on the table in front of the woman. 'I believe you're Elsie Harkness.'

'You got a message from Eric?' she asked.

'In a way,' said Daniel, sitting down opposite her. 'My name's Daniel Wilson and I'm a private investigator hired by Madame Tussauds wax museum.'

'That's where Eric works,' she said.

'That's right,' said Daniel. 'I'm afraid I've got some bad news for you.'

'Bad news?'

Daniel looked at her and gave a sympathetic sigh. 'I'm afraid there's no easy way to say this, but there's been a tragic accident at the museum. Eric's dead.'

She stared at him, her mouth dropping open in shock, and then she shook her head.

'No,' she said, firmly. 'I don't believe it. I won't believe it until I hear it from Walter.'

'And Mr Bagshot has disappeared,' said Daniel.

'Disappeared?' she repeated, bewildered.

'Eric was found this morning in the Chamber of Horrors, dead. There's been no sign of Walter Bagshot, but I've been told the police are looking for him.'

'No!' she whispered in horror. 'Not Walter! He'd never hurt Eric! Never!' Suddenly she began to cry, her whole upper body shaking as tears rolled down her heavily-rouged cheeks. Daniel produced a handkerchief from his pocket and offered it to her.

'Here,' he said. 'I'm sorry to be the bearer of such bad news.'

She refused his offer of the handkerchief and instead lifted the sleeve of her fur coat and buried her head in it, sobbing, before wiping the sleeve across her face. She looked at Daniel, still uncomprehending, her make-up smeared and smudged. 'He was my Eric,' she said.

'I know,' said Daniel. 'That's why I need to find out as much as I can about him in order to catch the person who did it. Had you known him long?'

'About a year,' she said.

'Before he went to work at Madame Tussauds?'

She nodded. 'When him and Walter were on the railways.'

'Did they work here at Marylebone?' asked Daniel.

'No, they were mainly at King's Cross and St Pancras. They worked on the Gasworks Tunnel.'

'The Gasworks Tunnel?' queried Daniel.

'At King's Cross. I don't know what they did there; they told me but I didn't follow it. I don't know much about that sort of work.'

'Why did they leave the railways and go to work at Madame Tussauds?'

'I don't know.'

'Were the wages better?'

'I can't see how,' said Elsie. 'They were getting good money on the railway. I remember when they told me they were changing jobs, it was about three weeks ago. Walter started to say how there'd be a lot of money coming, but Eric shut him up, then made a joke about it. But I could tell there was something in it. Walter had had a bit too much to drink that night and it had made him a bit merry. It was like he was celebrating something.'

'What?'

She shook her head. 'I don't know. And I didn't ask. They were always coming up with ideas for making money, ideas they'd joke about and laugh at, but really they were happy living the way they did. Earning enough to pay their rent and have a good night out. Though all that changed when they started doing the night job at Tussauds, of course. They had to be at work for nine o'clock at night, so there weren't any late nights boozing any more. But they used to come in after they'd finished their shift. Well, lunchtime, after they'd gone home and got a few hours' kip.'

'Did they ever talk about their army experiences?'

She gave a soft, sad chuckle. 'All the time. I think that was when they were happiest. They went all over the world, you know.'

CHAPTER FOUR

The Boy first encountered the Lady when leaving work. He walked out of Morton's of London Wax Museum and found a smartly-dressed man standing by the kerb next to an expensive-looking carriage. The man moved away from the carriage to join him.

'Someone wants to see you,' he said. 'She's inside.'

'What's she want with me?' asked the Boy, puzzled and also wary.

'She'll tell you that herself,' said the man, and he took the Boy by the arm and steered him towards the carriage.

'Who is she?' asked the Boy, apprehensively, wondering: *what is this? What have I done wrong?*

'She's the Lady,' said the man, and he opened the door.

The Boy looked in, suspiciously. A very well-dressed woman in her early fifties sitting inside smiled at him and said, 'Do come in. You'll find it far more comfortable than walking.'

The Boy climbed in, still wary, then sat on the seat opposite her. The man shut the door and the Boy heard him climbing up to the driver's seat, then the carriage began to roll.

'Where are we going?' asked the Boy.

'That depends on you,' said the Lady. 'I can take you to your home, or we can go to my house where we can have tea and cake.'

'Why?' asked the Boy suspiciously.

'Because I have a proposition to make to you,' said the Lady.

'What sort of proposition?'

'About your work. In wax. I've heard good things about you. I understand they call you the Boy.'

The Boy nodded, but with a scowl.

'How old are you?'

'Thirteen,' said the Boy.

'And you are an apprentice at Morton's wax museum.'

'Yes,' said the Boy.

'What's your real name?'

'Thomas.'

'Which do you prefer to be called: Thomas or the Boy?'

'Thomas,' he said. 'The Boy makes me sound like a pet or something. I think it started as a joke because I was younger than everyone else, and I'm small for my age, but they all started calling me it.'

'And you don't like it.'

'No.'

'Why don't you work somewhere else? Somewhere where they'll call you by your name?'

'Because I've got to finish my apprenticeship. I signed a paper.'

'You can write?'

The boy nodded.

'I've been told that you're an orphan,' said the Lady.

Again, he nodded.

'And you live in lodgings with a Mrs Wicksteed in Paddington.'

Again, the Boy – Thomas – looked at her suspiciously. 'How do you know so much about me?'

'I made it my business, especially after I heard good things about you. So, do you want me to take you to your lodgings, or would you like to come home with me and have tea and cake and listen to my proposition?'

'Your place,' said Thomas.

The Lady smiled. 'Excellent,' she said.

Daniel's last port of call was to the address in Somers Town he'd been given for Donald Bruin and Steven Patterson. As he expected, he was told they'd left two weeks previously, and left no forwarding address.

'A pity to see them go,' said their landlord, a Mr Possick. 'Decent blokes. Always paid their rent. But there you are. That's people for you.'

'Did they give any idea of where they were going?' asked Daniel. 'Or what they'd be doing?'

Possick shook his head. 'No, and I didn't ask. Ask questions and you get a reputation for being nosey, and tenants don't like landlords who are nosey.'

From Somers Town it was just a few minutes' walk home, and Daniel found Abigail already there and with the kettle on the range.

'How did you get on?' she asked.

'Bruin and Patterson seem to have vanished, and I'm not at all sure that Walter Bagshot has run off, as Inspector Jarrett seems to think.' He filled her in on what he'd discovered at the men's lodgings, and at the Railway Tavern. 'It's not just that everyone says how close the two men were, it's the fact he left everything behind. Including a regimental flag.' He pulled out his notebook and read the motto. '*Ubique Quo Fas Et Gloria Ducunt*.' He looked at her enquiringly. 'I'm guessing it's Latin.'

'It is,' she said. 'It means "Everywhere whither right and glory lead".' She frowned. 'But I don't know what it means, in this context.'

'It's the motto of the Royal Engineers,' said Daniel. 'It's obviously precious to both men, so that's another reason I don't think Walter ran off of his own accord. I can't see him leaving that behind.'

'So what do you think's happened to him?'

'I think he was either killed or abducted. What about you? How did you get on?'

'I went to see a friend of mine at the British Museum, Erasmus Black. We met when we were on a dig together at Hawara. He was making a study of wax modelling in ancient Egypt.'

'It goes that far back?'

'Absolutely,' said Abigail. 'Wax figures of the deities were used in funeral rites, and many are on display in museums.'

'They last that long?'

'They do indeed. Beeswax is a wonderful medium. Anyway, as I hoped, Erasmus, who's got a passion for wax modelling, knows all about the Tussaud family and their wax museum. Right from the very early days.'

'Do we have to know about their early days?' asked Daniel apprehensively.

'Yes, we do,' Abigail told him firmly.

'It always takes so long,' complained Daniel.

'The more we know about the past the better we can understand the present,' said Abigail.

'Yes, but . . .' began Daniel. Then he gave a resigned sigh. 'All right.'

'It seems that Marie Grosholtz – that was Madame Tussaud's maiden name – was born in Strasbourg, France on 1st December 1761. Nothing is really known about her father except his name, Joseph. Marie claimed he was a soldier who died two months before she was born. Her mother, Anne Marie, was eighteen years old and in domestic service. Soon after Marie was born, her mother went to work as a housekeeper for a young bachelor doctor, Philippe Guillaume Curtius, who was Swiss. Curtius was also a very skilful maker of wax miniatures. One of his admirers invited him to move to Paris to develop his work in wax, and exploit it. Which Curtius did, taking with him his housekeeper and her young daughter, who was now six years old. She showed an aptitude for also working in wax, and she became Curtius's apprentice. By her teens she was at least as good as he was in modelling lifelike figures. The thing she learnt from Curtius was getting the flesh tones right.'

'This is all very interesting, but I'm not sure how it relates to the murder,' posed Daniel.

'You're the one who's always said we need to know the background of the people involved,' countered Abigail.

'Yes, but there's background and there's ancient history,' Daniel complained.

'Unless you know everything, you won't know which parts to ignore and which bits are relevant,' insisted Abigail.

I can already tell, thought Daniel wearily, but wisely he chose not to say that aloud.

'Curtius's wax displays became the talk of Paris, with all the leading people coming to see them, and sitting for their likenesses to be made,' Abigail continued. 'This included the French royal family; the king and queen and their immediate relatives, and you couldn't get any higher than them. And then came the revolution.'

'With the royal family going to the guillotine,' said Daniel.

'Exactly.' Abigail nodded. 'The revolutionaries decided they wanted the heads of their hated enemies preserved in wax, and so poor Marie Grosholtz was given the job. Which meant handling the bloody originals, with all that entailed.'

'That must have been harrowing for her.'

'Indeed. But she did such a good job that later, when the revolution was over and its leaders – Robespierre, Danton and the rest – were themselves beheaded by that same guillotine, it was Marie who was given the task of preserving their heads in wax.'

'How did she manage to cope with all that bloodshed and

having to handle the mangled heads?'

'By having an iron will and a strong sense of self-preservation, I guess. But she was acutely aware that things in France were politically unstable, and that today's hero was tomorrow's villain, and that could equally apply to her.'

'She was under the threat of execution?'

'Everyone was. It only needed someone to pass an adverse comment about someone, someone who'd been upset and was feeling bitter, or jealous, and that person soon found themselves in a tumbril on their way to the scaffold.

'In 1794, Curtius died, and he left his wax figures and everything to do with his wax model business to his apprentice, Marie, who was now thirty-three years old.

'The following year, Marie married François Tussaud, a man eight years her junior. He was described as an engineer, but by all accounts the only engineering he did was financial.'

'Financial?'

'He wheedled money out of Marie and her waxwork business. Basically, he was a sponger, full of grandiose schemes to make money, all of which failed, and for all of them he used Marie's money.

'The couple had two sons, Joseph, who was born in 1798, and Francis in 1800. In 1802, Marie had the opportunity to take her wax exhibits to England, in partnership with a showman called Philipsthal. I won't go into details because they're too long, but Philipsthal turned out to be another financial parasite, one it took years for her to get rid of ,because he'd got her to sign a contract.

'The bottom line is that in 1802 she left for England, taking her eldest son, Joseph, but leaving her youngest, Francis, behind in the care of her mother and husband. She never returned to France, and it was twenty years before she saw Francis again.'

'My God, this woman's life was one tragedy after another!' burst out Daniel.

'Not completely. She did find success later in life,' Abigail pointed out.

'But look at what she had to endure before she found it! When did she finally manage to open her museum in London?'

'In 1835, and in Baker Street, just round the corner from the present museum site.'

'What about her two sons? They must have been in their thirties by this time.'

'They were. Francis came to England to be reunited with his mother in 1822. In that same year Joseph, now in his mid-twenties, married an English girl, Elizabeth Babbington, and they went on to have three children. Francis married a woman called Rebecca Smallpage and they had their first child in 1831. By the time the wax exhibition opened at Baker Street Marie's family had grown. Eventually she had twelve grandchildren, and all of them came into the Tussaud family business.'

'Any bad blood between the different branches of the family? I'm thinking about Mr Tussaud's reaction when I mentioned brothers falling out.'

Abigail shook her head. 'Not as far as I could find. John Theodore Tussaud is the elder brother, Louis Tussaud the younger. Both worked as wax figure sculptors at Tussauds, but in 1889 the company was sold to a conglomerate of businessmen headed by a man called Edwin Josiah Poyser.'

'Sold? Who sold it?'

'The boys' father, Joseph, Marie's grandson, although by this time they weren't really boys. John Theodore was thirty-one and Louis was twenty.'

'What had happened to Marie, the matriarch? Didn't she have any say in it?'

'She died in 1850, aged ninety.'

'Ah,' said Daniel. 'Yes, I forgot how old she would have been.'

'Poyser appointed John Theodore as chief artist and manager of the museum, and Louis decided to leave and branch out on his own,' continued Abigail. 'He set up Louis Tussaud's waxwork museum in Regent Street . . .'

'I remember it!' exclaimed Daniel. 'It burnt down soon after it opened.'

'It did,' confirmed Abigail. 'Six months after, in fact.'

'Any suggestion of foul play?' asked Daniel.

Again, Abigail shook her head. 'No, it appears it was just an accident. I can't find any reports of accusations of any wrongdoing, and the two brothers still appear to be on good terms, which wouldn't be the case if there was anything doubtful about the fire.

'Since then, Louis has been working on recreating his models, determined to open his own wax museum again. But not in London, from what I hear. I believe he's intending to open in a seaside town. Less competition from the established Madame Tussauds.'

'Why did the boys' father sell it to this business conglomeration?'

'It seems that by 1883 the museum's previous site in Baker Street was getting too crowded, not just with exhibits but the people flocking to see them. So their father decided to move the whole lot to the museum's present site in Marylebone Road. He had a new building constructed, very grandiose, but the cost spiralled so much that he had to look for funding. He formed a limited company to try to raise funds, but it didn't work. So he was forced to sell. Not that our Mr Tussaud here, John Theodore, lost out. As I've said, he retained his roles as chief artist and manager, so effectively the Tussauds are still in charge, setting the tone for the museum.'

The Lady looked on with an indulgent smile as Thomas tucked into a large slice of cake and sipped at the tea, being careful to put the delicate china cup carefully back on the saucer each time. He was the ideal person for what she had in mind. No living relatives, treated dismissively by his fellow workers, and with some experience at working with wax. But not yet known as a wax artist, still just a low-paid apprentice. Bringing him back to her grand and luxurious house was part of her ploy: to show him what sort of lifestyle might await him if he took up her offer.

'I hear you're good at working wax,' she said.

'Better than many of them at Morton's,' he said. 'Most of them are rubbish. One day I'll work at Tussauds.'

'I worked at Tussauds,' said the Lady.

'You?' said Thomas in surprise. He looked around at the elegant furniture, the paintings that adorned the high-ceilinged walls. 'Is that how you got all this?'

'In a way,' said the Lady. 'It's how I started.'

'So I could have all this?'

'There's no reason why not,' said the Lady. 'The thing is, we do unusual things here. Not just the normal wax models.'

'What sort of things?' asked Thomas.

'Later,' said the Lady. 'Does being with dead people bother you?'

Thomas shook his head. 'One of my first jobs was doing death masks. You know, with plaster of Paris.'

'Yes, I know. I did that myself.'

'You have to do it quick before the flesh starts to go rotten,' said Thomas. 'And you have to oil the skin to stop it sticking to the plaster.'

'Yes, you do.' The Lady nodded. 'Would you like to work for me? In wax?'

'I can't,' said Thomas. 'Like I said, I signed a paper. I'm apprenticed to Morton's.'

'How about if I bought your apprenticeship from Morton's.'

Thomas frowned and looked at her, curious. 'Can you do that?'

'You can,' she said. 'It's all very legal. It's done all the time, an apprentice moving on to a different master. It's all a question of money. And I have money.'

'Don't I have to sign something?' asked Thomas.

The Lady smiled. 'You are a very clever and knowledgeable young man,' she said. 'Yes, you do. I'll draw up the documents. All you have to do is sign to say you wish to transfer to me for the rest of your apprenticeship. I take that to Morton's and make an arrangement with them and pay them an agreed price, and you work for me. No longer the

Boy, but Thomas.' She saw that his face suddenly turned into a frown as he thought about it, and she realised that he was calculating how real her offer was. At Morton's he had all the tools of the trade to hand, as well as tuition by experienced wax artists, and in a relatively short time he'd be finished his apprenticeship and could move elsewhere.

'Would you like to see my wax studio?' she asked.

Thomas nodded, his head bobbing up and down energetically.

She stood up. 'This way,' she said, and swept out of the room. Thomas followed her along the long passage and then out through the back door to a brick-built annexe room in the rear of the main house. Once inside, he stood and looked at what surrounded him, stunned. There was everything any wax artist could want here. It made the studios at Morton's look shabby by comparison.

'This is all yours?' he asked, awed.

'It is,' she said. 'Although I retired from the wax business, I like to keep my hand in. Mostly, these days, I prefer to supervise and teach others.'

'You've had other apprentices?'

'I have, and they've all gone on to greater things,' said the Lady.

'How many apprentices have you got at the moment?' asked Thomas.

'None,' said the Lady. 'My last moved on just a couple of weeks ago, which is why I'm looking for someone to replace them. Someone good. Someone who wants to learn.' She gestured around her at the expensive equipment on display. 'Someone who wants all this. Because it would mean staying here.'

'Staying here?'

'There is a very comfortable bedroom off the studio, with everything anyone could want. Including your own indoor bathroom, with its own toilet.' She shrugged. 'Or, if you prefer, you could return to Morton's and your present lodgings. It's up to you.'

'You sure about the apprenticeship?' asked Thomas. 'I'll still be doing it, only here? And Morton's will agree?'

'They will,' said the Lady. 'I'll make them an offer they'll find hard to refuse.'

CHAPTER FIVE

Next morning, after they'd breakfasted, Daniel headed to the newsagent's to get the morning newspaper. 'They were out of *The Times*,' he told Abigail when he returned. 'But I was interested to see what Joe Dalton would be writing in *The Telegraph*. I also got this.' He held out a copy of *The Whistler* to her.

'What's this?' she demanded.

'The newspaper John mentioned, *The Whistler*. I thought it might be interesting to see what they say.'

She handed the newspaper back to him, deftly removing the copy of *The Telegraph* from his fingers at the same time.

'It looks like a semi-literate rag. If you're so interested you can look at that while I check *The Telegraph*.'

'Fair enough,' said Daniel. 'And we'll swap afterwards.'

He settled down and began to scan the paper. 'The Tussauds murder is the lead story in this. "Real-Life Horror in the Chamber", with a rather gruesome drawing of a man's head separated from his body by a guillotine, while a crowd of ghoulish waxworks look on.' He read on, then said, 'They mention us. "We understand Madame Tussauds have brought in the famous Museum Detectives, former Scotland Yard detective Daniel Wilson and renowned Egyptologist Abigail Fenton, to solve the mystery of the murderous phantom of the Chamber of Horrors. Another slap in the face for Superintendent Armstrong and Scotland Yard's detective division following Wilson and Fenton's great successes investigating grisly murders at the British Museum, the Fitzwilliam and the Ashmolean, which Scotland Yard had failed to solve."'

'I hardly think that's fair,' observed Abigail. 'John Feather was a vital part of the investigations.'

'But Armstrong was obstructive, just as he's being now.'

'They missed out our investigation in Manchester,' commented Abigail.

'I doubt if the people at *The Whistler* know where Manchester is,' mused Daniel. 'The paper doesn't exactly have a literary style. Lots of verbose descriptions, especially emphasising bloody decapitations.'

'Any interview with Mr Tussaud?'

'None. "Mr Tussaud promised to speak to us later, when more is known." It then goes on to say that the dead man was Edward Dungeon, and that his fellow nightwatchman, William Bagstaff, is being hunted by the police for this horrific murder. They say that Inspector Jarrett from Scotland Yard is in charge of the investigation.'

'At least they got some of the names right.'

'What's *The Telegraph* say about it?'

'Not a great deal, just the bare bones. Mr Dudgeon, a nightwatchman at Madame Tussauds, was found dead, apparently decapitated by means of the guillotine in the Chamber of Horrors. Scotland Yard, under the direction of Inspector Jarrett, are searching for his fellow nightwatchman, Walter Bagshot, as a possible suspect. It then goes on to mention that we've been called in by Tussauds to help in the investigation.'

'That doesn't sound like Joe Dalton's style,' murmured Daniel.

'It isn't,' said Abigail. 'It's by someone called Robert Peake. Your friend Joe has got the lead article, on the bank raids that John told us about.'

'Ah,' said Daniel. 'What does he say?'

'Pretty much what John told us. That there have been three such bank robberies, each one carried out at night by the thieves breaking into the empty shop next door, making a large hole in the wall of the shop's cellar and gaining access to the bank vault. The three robberies all took place in London; one in Mayfair, one in Kensington, and one in Fitzrovia.'

'All expensive areas where one imagines the money and valuables lodged in those vaults would add up to a pretty penny.'

'Indeed, although Joe doesn't say how much was taken.'

'I doubt if the banks would be keen to let the amounts be known. As it is, there'll be panic among some very wealthy bank customers. Does he give any details about the actual robberies?'

Abigail passed the newspaper to him. 'Take a look. The thieves obviously select their targets carefully. The rooms above both the shop and the bank are empty, used for storage. The robberies are discovered the following morning when the bank staff arrive.' As Daniel read the article, she added, 'The robbers didn't appear to try and disguise their method of entry. They didn't try and repair the wall afterwards.'

'Waste of time,' said Daniel. 'They'd only be able to make the wall in the cellar of the shop look good; the side in the bank vault would still show what they'd done. No, this was all about doing a job at speed. Each one must have taken some planning. They'd have to know that the shop had a cellar, and that no one lived above the premises. They'd also have to know where the bank vault was in relation to the cellar in the shop.'

'Inside information?' asked Abigail.

'Somehow I doubt it. The more people in the know, the greater the risk of people talking. My guess is good observation. Delivering something to the shop which needs to be taken down to the cellar. Asking for documents to be put in store in the bank vault, and being shown them put in safe storage.' He gave a thoughtful frown.

'You've just thought of something?' asked Abigail.

'The newspaper report only mentions money and valuables, which suggests jewellery. I wonder if the thieves also took documents with them. A lot of the documents stored in bank vaults contain private and important information that the people who lodged them don't wish to be made public.'

'Opportunities for blackmail?' asked Abigail.

'It's certainly something to consider. If it was me I'd be asking the people who lost things from their bank storage if they'd been contacted to offer their valuables or documents back.'

'But it isn't you,' pointed out Abigail. 'It's Inspector Jarrett. Our case is the murder of Eric Dudgeon at Madame Tussauds.'

'True, but I can't help but wonder if they might be connected.'

'How?'

'It's the breaking through into the cellar wall, and the previous nightwatchmen at Tussauds leaving so conveniently and two men, former members of the Royal Engineers, taking a job there.'

'Is Tussauds next to a bank?' asked Abigail.

'No,' admitted Daniel.

'Then I can't see a connection.'

'No, but the business of Dudgeon and Bagshot being on hand to take up the posts worries me. There's something going on there.'

'That I agree with,' said Abigail. 'But I don't think it's anything to do with robbing a bank.'

Superintendent Armstrong banged his fist hard on his desk in annoyance, causing everything on the surface of the desk to shake. The superintendent was a big man in every way: tall, broad, muscular, with powerful and big fists. He was also a man with a bad temper.

'Have you seen these?' he demanded of Inspector Jarrett,

who stood almost to attention on the opposite side of the superintendent's desk.

'These' were the day's newspapers.

'Yes, sir,' said Jarrett. He was in his forties, a short man in stature, with many other things about him also short. His hair was cropped close to his scalp. His moustache was a short bristle of black, resembling a toothbrush. He also had a short temper, and was a man of very few words, most of them sour and delivered curtly with a suspicious look. He invariably wore black, his clothes having a crumpled look, as if he'd slept in them. And, to complete the short theme, his trousers were also a little short, revealing a pair of crumpled grey socks rising up from his heavy boots. 'Rubbish and tittle-tattle,' he added.

Armstrong pushed the newspapers aside with an angry grunt. 'Any word on this Bagshot character?'

'No, sir,' said Jarrett. 'I called at his lodgings, and by all accounts he never went back there. Everything in his room's the same as when he left to go to work.'

'Don't you think that's strange?' mused the superintendent. 'You'd think, if he was going to do a runner, he'd grab his stuff.'

'Maybe he didn't want his landlady to see him. If he was the one who cut off Dudgeon's head, he'd be covered in blood.' He regarded Armstrong warily. 'You still think he's the one who did it, sir?'

'Has to be,' said Armstrong. 'Otherwise, where is he? Was the landlady any help as to where he might have gone?'

'No, sir. But she did say that Wilson had called on her.'

'Wilson!' Again, Armstrong's fist thudded onto his desk

in anger. Then he glared at Jarrett. 'How come he was there before you?'

'I can only guess because he's not tied up with paperwork,' grunted Jarrett. 'We have to make sure everything's done proper. We're answerable. Wilson's answerable to no one.'

'Yes, I suppose so.' Armstrong scowled.

'I also found out from the landlady where their local was, the Railway Tavern. So I went round there.'

'And?'

Jarrett shook his head. 'Nothing useful. There was a prostitute there who it seems was walking out with Dudgeon. She got all teary-eyed and upset when I started asking her questions.'

Armstrong nodded. 'It's never easy breaking bad news to someone.'

Jarrett hesitated, then said awkwardly, 'Actually, she already knew.'

'Oh? Who told her?'

'Wilson, sir.'

'Wilson again!'

For a moment, Jarrett thought the superintendent was going to get up out of his chair and hit something, possibly him. But instead Armstrong settled down and sat, quietly seething, before he said, 'Get out there and find Bagshot. And bring him in before Wilson can get his teeth into it! Him and that woman, Fenton.'

'Yes, sir.'

Jarrett headed for the door, and Armstrong shouted after him, 'And tell Inspector Feather I want to see him.'

'Yes, sir.'

Jarrett left the office, feeling relieved. When the

superintendent was in a bad mood, like now, the best thing to do was stay out of his way, something that Jarrett fully intended to do. He'd go out and try and see if the uniforms had managed to track down Walter Bagshot. But first he had to tell John Feather he was next in the firing line. Which wouldn't be pleasant, especially after one of the sergeants had told Armstrong he'd spotted Feather sitting in Freddy's with Wilson and the Fenton woman. *Rather him than me*, he thought.

He knocked at Feather's door and poked his head in. Feather was sitting at his desk, making notes. His sergeant, Cribbens, sat at a separate desk, smoking the foul-smelling shag he filled his pipe with.

'Super wants you,' said Jarrett.

'Both of us?' asked Feather, gesturing towards Cribbens.

'No, he just mentioned you,' said Jarrett, and went.

What now? thought Feather, getting up. There was nothing new to report on the bank robberies. The only good thing there was that there hadn't been another lately. The bad thing was the story on the front page of *The Telegraph* about the bank raids.

Feather strode along to the superintendent's office, and at the command 'Enter!', walked in. Armstrong looked up at him, sourly.

'Any news on the robberies?' he demanded.

'Nothing, sir. I've been going through Inspector Calley's notes to see if he's got anything for me worth following up. I've also sent notices to all the banks next to shops to put nightwatchmen in, but there's no word on who's been doing them. I've got everyone asking their informants, but so far with no luck.'

Armstrong nodded, then said, 'A little bird told me you were seen in Freddy's, having coffee with Wilson and Fenton.'

'Yes, sir,' said Feather. He'd been expecting this. 'I'm afraid it was unavoidable. They came in while I was having a coffee.'

'You should have walked out!'

'My coffee had only just arrived, sir. But as soon as I finished it, I left.'

'I don't want you talking to them, Inspector.'

'No, sir. And I told them so. And also that they are not to come to Scotland Yard under any circumstances.'

'Good.'

'However . . .' said Feather hesitantly.

'What?' demanded Armstrong.

'Well, sir, it occurred to me that sometimes contact might be useful to find out what they're up to. You know, what they're looking into.'

'Because then we can look into it and pip them?' said Armstrong, his face suddenly showing interest.

'Yes, sir. That sort of thing. However, you know best, sir, and I'll make sure that if they do try and get in touch with me, I tell them firmly not to do so again.'

'No, wait,' said Armstrong, his expression thoughtful. 'There might be something in what you say. We're hampered because we have to work through official channels, but that pair don't have to follow any rules. That's what gives them the advantage.'

'That's possible, sir,' agreed Feather.

'More than possible, it's a damn certainty!' Armstrong fell

silent, thinking it over. 'We have to be clever about how we handle this, Inspector. We can't be seen to be working with them, otherwise they'll get the credit for whatever we do. We have to keep them at a distance. At least, officially.'

'Yes, sir.'

'That means they're barred from coming into this building, or any of our officers talking to them.'

Feather frowned, puzzled. 'In that case, sir, how do we find out what they're up to?'

'We pull them in for questioning,' said Armstrong. 'Not here, of course, but the local station in Baker Street. Jarrett can do it. He and Wilson don't like one another, so there's no chance of anyone thinking we've helped them, but we have the threat of charging them with obstructing the path of justice if they refuse to tell us what they know.'

Feather hesitated before saying warily, 'With respect, sir, neither Daniel nor Abigail—'

'Daniel and Abigail?' barked Armstrong, angrily.

'Begging your pardon, sir, Mr Wilson and Miss Fenton. They're both clever and they'll find a way to avoid giving Inspector Jarrett what they know if they feel he's threatening them.'

'Then we'll charge them!'

'But what with, sir? If we don't know what it is they're keeping to themselves, we can't prove they're obstructing the police investigation.'

Armstrong grimaced and smashed his fist down on his desk, with a snarl of 'Damn!' He sat there, fuming, and Feather could almost see the superintendent's brain working as he tried to come up with a way out of this dilemma. Finally, he said, 'All right, Inspector. You do it.'

'Me?'

Armstrong nodded, still glowering venomously. 'He likes you. She likes you. They talk to you.'

'But I'm not on the Tussaud murder case, sir.'

'No, you're not, and that's the point. But what you do is pass anything they give you, any hints or suspicions about any avenue they're looking into, on to Inspector Jarrett. But you do it away from here. And not at Freddy's, either.'

'Where can I see them, sir?'

'You know where they live.'

'I do, sir.'

'Drop in on them, one friend to another.' He smiled. 'The good thing about this is that you're not involved in the Tussauds murder, so you can't pass anything on to them about the investigation. But you can pick up what they're up to.'

'Yes, sir,' said Feather, and Armstrong frowned at the uncertainty of his tone.

'What's the matter?' he growled.

'Well, if I can't tell them what's happening with the Tussauds murder . . .'

'Because you don't know,' grunted Armstrong.

'Agreed, sir.' Feather nodded. 'What can I talk to them about? Apart from social chat. Usually when we talk it's about police business.'

Armstrong thought, then said, 'These bank raids. That's what your job is right now. And there's no chance of them getting any credit for that because they're not looking into that. You talk to them about the bank raids, and probe discreetly

59

what they're up to with this Tussauds murder. Then pass on anything you pick up to Inspector Jarrett.'

'Right, sir. Will you tell Inspector Jarrett what the plan is, or shall I?'

'I will, thank you, Inspector,' responded Armstrong rather primly. 'I'm in charge here.'

'Yes, sir.'

After Feather had left, the superintendent sat scowling at the newspapers. Things had been bad enough with these bank robberies, but now the murder at Tussauds had been added to the mix, everything had got even worse. It was especially bad with those bastards in the press lauding that bloody pair of so-called Museum Detectives to the heavens, making damning comparisons between them and Scotland Yard, and always naming him, Superintendent Armstrong, when they did so. Bastards! He was sure it was these newspaper stories that had led to him being summoned before the Metropolitan Police commissioner on his arrival to Scotland Yard that morning. He'd guessed that the summons presaged bad news, and he was right.

'The bank robberies are bad enough,' the commissioner had intoned gravely, 'but this murder at Tussauds is even worse. We're being made to look fools.'

'I hardly think that's fair, sir,' said Armstrong. 'I've put our best man, Inspector Feather, on the bank robberies, and the murder at Tussauds only happened yesterday.'

'I'm talking about how they depict us in the newspapers,' snapped the commissioner. 'Comparing us unfavourably to these Museum Detectives.'

'To be fair, sir, they don't have the same restrictions that we have to operate under.'

'But we have far greater manpower than they do!' barked the commissioner. 'There are only two of them! Are you telling me that we, the Metropolitan Police, with hundreds of uniformed officers and a highly experienced detective division, cannot compete with them when it comes to solving crimes?'

'The fact is, sir, that the newspapers have completely exaggerated the accomplishments of Wilson and Fenton. They have been associated with just two investigations of deaths at museums in London, one at the British Museum and the other at the Natural History Museum.'

'And now a third at Madame Tussauds,' retorted the commissioner.

'And quite unnecessarily,' defended Armstrong. 'The murders at the British Museum and at the Natural History were solved by Inspector Feather and myself, with perhaps some assistance from Wilson and Fenton. But to say that Wilson and Fenton solved them and Scotland Yard were baffled is an absolute lie, a complete distortion.'

'Perhaps you can explain that to the prime minister and the home secretary when you meet them later today.'

Armstrong stared at the commissioner, his mind racing. The prime minister and the home secretary?

'I'm sorry, sir, I don't understand,' he said.

'I was contacted by the prime minister's office. The government is seriously concerned about these bank robberies. These are obviously not just ordinary robberies. There have been three so far, and each one has happened in a very expensive part of London. Some very important people have lost large sums of money, and important personal documents as well. The government are concerned there might be a political motive involved.'

'If it's political, sir, then surely that comes under Special Branch.'

'It could well do. That's why you and the head of Special Branch will attend a meeting with the prime minister and the home secretary at 10 Downing Street at two o'clock this afternoon.'

CHAPTER SIX

The office of the railway maintenance supervisor at King's Cross station was a wooden hut at the far end of platform one, backing on to a large brick barn-like structure. It looked like the storehouse for the maintenance work, containing all manner of tools, some light, some heavy. A man wearing a tweed jacket and a tie sat at a desk studying what looked to be workers' time sheets.

'Mr Edward Hurst?' asked Daniel. When the man nodded, he added, 'My name is Daniel Wilson and this is my partner, Abigail Fenton. We are private enquiry agents hired by Madame Tussauds to look into the tragic death of a Mr Eric Dudgeon.'

Hurst nodded again. 'I saw it in the papers. Had his

head cut off by the guillotine there.'

'Possibly,' said Daniel, 'although that is still being looked into. We understand that he worked for you, along with Walter Bagshot.'

'That's right,' said Hurst. He gestured to a chair next to his desk. 'If you've got questions, perhaps the lady would like to take a seat.'

'Thank you,' said Abigail, sitting down.

'We've been told they worked on the Gasworks Tunnel.'

'They did indeed.'

'What exactly is the Gasworks Tunnel?' asked Daniel.

'It's actually three parallel tunnels that carry the East Coast Main Line from King's Cross terminus north under the Regent's Canal,' said Hurst. 'The first one was built in 1852 as part of the Great Northern. That's now in the middle, the later two being built either side of it. The second tunnel to the west of it was built in 1878. The third one, to the east, was built in 1892. That's the one Eric and Walter worked on.'

'What did they actually do?'

'Well, like the name says, they were part of the team that dug the tunnel. It's what they were used to in the army. You know, being in the Engineers.'

'And they carried on tunnelling?'

'Not once the Gasworks Tunnel was finished.'

'Which was when?'

'Three years ago. Since then they'd been working on general maintenance. Track-laying, keeping the embankments safe.'

'Good workers?'

'Very good,' said Hurst. 'Reliable. Honest. Solid.'

'We heard stories that they were caught in a cave-in while

they were tunnelling,' said Daniel.

Hurst looked at them, frowning. 'A cave-in? Here?' He shook his head. 'There was the occasional fall of earth from the top or the sides, but you get that when you're tunnelling. Nothing as serious as a cave-in.'

'No workers injured?'

Again, Hurst shook his head. 'No, and I'd know if there was. I was a gang foreman at that time when the Gasworks Tunnel was being dug, before I got made up to maintenance manager.'

'Why did Eric and Walter leave?' asked Abigail.

'I don't know. They came and said they'd had an offer and that they were going to work at Tussauds waxworks, and they asked for a reference. Which I was glad to give them, they were both good workers.' He gave a sad shake of his head. 'Terrible what happened. The papers say the police are looking for Walter for it. You know, for killing Eric. Is that right?'

'There's some doubt about that,' said Daniel carefully. 'That's why we've been asked to look into it.'

'Personally, I don't believe it,' said Hurst. 'Them two were as close as any people I've ever known. I can't believe either would hurt the other. Not like that.'

Daniel and Abigail elected to walk to Madame Tussauds after leaving King's Cross, aware that the route along Euston Road, then passing Great Portland Street and coming into Marylebone Road, was quicker on foot rather than by horse-drawn bus.

'Fortunately the fog seems to have vanished today,' said Abigail.

'So far,' said Daniel, doubtfully. 'We'll see how long that lasts.'

'Mr Hurst was another with nothing bad to say about Eric and Walter,' observed Abigail.

'It's interesting that we have two different versions of why Dudgeon and Bagshot left the railway and came to work at the museum,' mused Daniel. 'Tussaud said they told him there'd been a cave-in at a tunnel, but Hurst says there was no such cave-in, and they hadn't worked in a tunnel for the last three years.'

'Hurst also said that Dudgeon and Bagshot had asked him for references because they were going to work at Tussauds, but it appears that was before they actually went to ask at the museum if there were any jobs available.'

'In other words, they knew there would be because they knew that Bruin and Patterson were leaving at short notice.'

Daniel nodded.

'So we are talking about a conspiracy,' said Abigail.

'But to what end?' asked Daniel. 'And why did it end in Dudgeon's murder and Bagshot vanishing?'

'You still don't think that Bagshot killed Dudgeon?'

'No, I don't,' said Daniel. 'But whatever's going on, the museum is at the heart of it.'

They were now near to the museum's main Marylebone Road entrance, and Daniel stopped. 'Look,' he said. 'A bank.'

There was indeed a bank, not next door to the museum, but separated from it by a newsagent's and a chemist's.

'Two former Royal Engineers, both experienced tunnellers, arrive to take up the job of nightwatchmen at a place just three doors away from a bank,' said Daniel.

'John Feather said the banks that were robbed were next door to a place, and they had adjoining cellars,' Abigail pointed out.

'If you can break into one cellar, you can break through to the next one further on,' said Daniel.

He made for the newsagent's, where he bought a copy of *The Times*, and then asked the man behind the counter, 'Do you have a cellar here?'

The newsagent looked at him suspiciously, then with equal suspicion at Abigail. 'Who wants to know?' he demanded.

Daniel explained who they were, and that they'd been hired by the museum to look into the recent death of the nightwatchman.

'What's that got to do with if I've got a cellar?' asked the man, still suspicious. Then he said, 'This is about that other story in the paper. Them bank robberies. Because of the bank two doors away.'

'We're wondering if they might be connected,' said Daniel.

'No, not in any way,' said the man. 'For a start, there's no cellar here. Nothing but solid earth under this shop. And I know, because I watched it being built after they'd finished the museum. There was just a flat area of solid earth and rock from all the soil they dumped after doing the foundations for the museum. The bank was there already, but there was nothing between that and the museum until the chemist's and this shop were put up.'

'When was that?' asked Abigail.

'Ten years ago,' replied the man.

'And you never thought of having a cellar put in?' asked Daniel.

'No,' said the man. 'More trouble than they're worth. When it rains a cellar fills up with water, and what's the point of that if your stock is newspapers? They'd all be ruined. No, I keep my stock in the shop.'

Enquiries at the chemist's next door elicited the same response: there was no cellar beneath the chemist's, just solid earth and rocks, the spoil from digging the museum's foundations.

'So that rules that out as a possible motive,' said Abigail as they left the chemist's and made for the museum entrance.

'Not necessarily,' said Daniel. 'They were tunnellers, remember.'

'And how long would it take them to tunnel under two shops?' asked Abigail. 'Only working at night? Months. Possibly a year. No, Daniel, I agree the museum's at the heart of it, but no one's going to spend a year doing something like that, not when they can break through a cellar wall in one night, the way that John described.'

They entered the museum and stopped when they saw that John Tussaud was engaged in conversation with a tall, portly, well-dressed man in his late thirties, bespectacled and sporting a luxuriant moustache.

'It's Arthur Conan Doyle,' whispered Daniel, awed.

'I know,' Abigail whispered back.

Tussaud spotted them and hailed for them to join him and Doyle.

'Allow me to introduce Mr Arthur Conan Doyle,' said Tussaud.

'Who is immediately recognisable.' Daniel smiled, shaking Doyle's hand. 'This is a great pleasure, sir.'

'Tussauds have the honour of making a wax image of Mr Doyle and he is here today for me to take his measurements.' To Doyle, he said, 'These are Mr Daniel Wilson and Miss Abigail Fenton. We've brought them in to look into the recent tragic murder here.'

'The nightwatchman.' Doyle nodded. 'Dreadful! I read about it in the newspapers.' He smiled at Daniel and Abigail. 'The Museum Detectives! Your fame goes ahead of you!' And he offered Abigail his hand.

'Hardly on a par with yours, Mr Doyle,' murmured Abigail, shaking it.

'Tush!' Doyle beamed. 'Miss Fenton, I have to tell you that I've not long returned from a trip to Egypt, where your name is still revered. My wife, Louise, and I spent ten months there. We went out in autumn, last year, and have only returned last month.'

'I assume you visited the pyramids.'

'How could anyone go to Egypt and not have that experience?' boomed Doyle heartily. 'I climbed the Great Pyramid, and my Lou and I went camel-trekking to many other famous sites, but I still felt we were only touching the surface, so to speak. You have been there and entered inside the Great Pyramid, and others.'

'Alas, it's been a long time since I was actually on an expedition,' said Abigail. 'At least three years. Certainly since I joined Mr Wilson in his detective work.'

'So it's your fault, Wilson!' chuckled Doyle. 'Of course, I knew of your work before this Museum Detectives business. You were part of Abberline's team investigating the Jack the Ripper killings.'

'Indeed, sir,' said Wilson.

'I'd have liked to have been a detective,' said Doyle with a tinge of regret.

'Surely you've already done that through your creation, Sherlock Holmes,' suggested Abigail.

'Yes and no,' grumbled Doyle. 'At first it was a way to earn a crust and support my family. Being a general practitioner wasn't paying, but in the end Holmes dominated! Even in Egypt, all anyone wanted to ask me about was blasted Holmes!'

'I recall an interview you gave to a magazine in which you said there would be no more Holmes stories,' said Daniel.

'And there won't be! I did what I said I'd do and laid him to rest three years ago.'

'"The Final Problem",' said Daniel. 'The Reichenbach Falls and Professor Moriarty.'

'You've read it?' asked Doyle.

'I've read every Holmes and Watson story,' said Daniel.

'And how did you find them? As a professional detective, I mean.'

'Fascinating, and very well reasoned.'

'Did you work out the answers to the mysteries before the denouement?'

When he saw Daniel hesitate before replying, he barked out in triumph, 'Of course you did! I expected nothing less. In fact that was one of the things that had begun to irk me, the depiction of Scotland Yard detectives, particularly Lestrade, as fools. That was my editor, you know. He kept insisting on it. Said the public liked it. Well, I didn't. It was fun at first, giving someone in authority for Holmes to challenge. I've never been a fan of authority figures. But the more Scotland Yard detectives I came into contact with, the more I realised I was doing a disservice to some highly intelligent men. Do you know Inspector John Feather?'

'I do indeed,' said Daniel.

'A very clever man. He should have been a superintendent by now. But he's been held back, in my opinion, because the oafs above him need him in place to preserve their inflated positions.' He glowered slightly as he added, 'As you will see, I have not gone over completely to the view that the detective squad at Scotland Yard is full of creative intelligences. Have you ever met Inspector Jarrett?'

'Yes,' said Daniel.

'He makes my Lestrade look like an intellectual giant. And as for his boss, Superintendent Armstrong . . .' He stopped, then gave them an apologetic smile. 'Forgive me. I'm getting on my high horse again. One of the reasons I turned to history and the esoteric for my writing. Have you read my Brigadier Gerard stories?'

'Er . . . no,' admitted Daniel.

'You should,' said Doyle. 'That's where my future lies as a writer. Far better than anything I wrote featuring Holmes.' He turned to Abigail. 'And you, Miss Fenton? As an Egyptologist, have you, perchance, read my stories "The Ring of Thoth" and "Lot No. 249"?'

'I have, and I enjoyed them both enormously.'

'I envy you, Miss Fenton.'

'Envy me?' asked Abigail, puzzled.

'As I said, you have been inside the pyramids. You were one of the first to see, and actually touch, the ancient artefacts before they were put on public display. Believe me, they still talk of you and your exploits out there. You made an impact!'

Daniel was amused to see the flush of red rising up Abigail's neck, coupled with her awkward smile of gratitude. It was rare to see her discomfited this way.

71

'Actually, Mr Doyle,' interrupted Tussaud tentatively, 'we really ought to get on. I've got the studio set up to measure your head and do the preparatory clay work, but I wondered how you felt about doing a life mask?'

'A life mask?'

'The same as a death mask, but we put straws up your nostrils so that you can breathe, and then we encase your face in plaster. It makes sure we have an exact impression of your features.'

'Sounds fascinating!' Doyle beamed. 'Indeed! Lead on, Mr Tussaud, and let's prepare the plaster!' He turned to Daniel and Abigail. 'And I look forward to further conversations with both of you – with you, Mr Wilson, to talk about detection, and you, Miss Fenton, to explore the topic of ancient Egypt.' He gave a wistful sigh as he added, 'It has often struck me—'

'The studio, Mr Doyle?' urged Tussaud politely, but obviously worried that once Doyle began talking about Egypt again it would be hard to remove him from Abigail and Daniel's company.

'Of course!' Doyle nodded with a smile, and he followed Tussaud out of the room as they made for Tussaud's studio.

'What a fascinating man!' exclaimed Abigail. 'An absolute life force!'

'He is indeed!' agreed Daniel. 'And not just as a writer. He's also a top-class sportsman. Cricket. Boxing. Football. He played in goal for Southsea Football Club. A man of boundless energy.'

'I pity his poor wife,' chuckled Abigail. 'He must be a nightmare to live with.'

'By all accounts they're a very happy and devoted couple,' said Daniel. 'I have that on the authority of Joe Dalton, who met them both when he interviewed Doyle for *The Telegraph*.'

He gave her a gentle smile as he added, 'By the way, I recall you telling me you thought that story about the reanimated mummy, "Lot No. 249", was tosh. But you told him you enjoyed it enormously.'

'It would hardly be intelligent to insult someone who our client, Mr Tussaud, esteems so highly,' countered Abigail. 'Mr Doyle obviously feels very proud of that story. And "The Ring of Thoth".'

'I don't know that one. What's it about?'

'It's another reanimation from the dead involving ancient Egyptian artefacts in a museum.'

'Tosh?'

Abigail hesitated. 'I'm not a literary critic so I'm not qualified to say.'

Daniel smiled.

'So, as Mr Tussaud is busy, where shall we start today?' asked Abigail.

'I'd like to look at the cellar,' said Daniel.

'You're not still harping on about the bank?' queried Abigail.

'Two tunnellers?' said Daniel.

'It's a coincidence,' said Abigail.

'Humour me.'

He approached one of the attendants, who had been informed of their investigation, and who took them down to the cellar. Inside were a series of large wooden crates, standing on end.

'Waxworks waiting their turn to go on display,' explained the attendant. 'We change the models now and then so that visitors have something different to look at, although it's the old favourites that keep 'em coming back. The Chamber of

Horrors. Nelson. The queen and her family.' He gestured at the crates. 'We keep them in boxes to stop the rats getting at them.'

'You have rats?' asked Abigail.

'Every cellar's got rats,' said the attendant. 'Anyway, I'd better get back to work. If you need me, just ask for Denis. I'm here all day.'

Denis left, and Abigail looked carefully around the cellar.

'You don't like rats?' asked Daniel.

'I can take them or leave them,' said Abigail. 'When I was in Egypt they were everywhere. I was thinking that if rats get in, where is their point of entry?'

'You're coming round to my way of thinking about the tunnelling?' asked Daniel.

'No, but I've learnt never to dismiss your ideas. I suggest we examine the wall.'

They began at the doorway, then worked their separate ways around the cellar wall as well as they could without disturbing the crates that were stacked against it, to avoid the risk of accidentally damaging the precious waxworks inside. They met up at the wall opposite the doorway.

'Well?' asked Abigail.

'The part I looked at appears intact, the lime between the layers of bricks looks undisturbed and is covered with dirt and grime.'

'Same here,' said Abigail. 'So how are the rats getting in?'

'Possibly there's a gap behind one of the crates. Rats only need the slimmest of spaces to squeeze through. Without a proper investigation, moving the boxes and taking some of the bricks out . . .'

'No,' said Abigail sharply. 'We've just established there's no sign of this wall being interfered with, and there's no bank vault next door to this cellar, just solid earth and rocks beneath two shops. This is not connected to the bank robberies.'

'Then what is it connected to?' asked Daniel.

'I don't know,' admitted Abigail. 'I suggest we talk to Denis and the rest of the staff and see what they can tell us about Eric and Walter.'

Thomas looked uncertainly at the dead body of the man laid out on the table, naked except for a pair of drawers.

'He's dead,' he said.

'Yes, he is,' said the Lady. 'This is an unusual commission. Someone wants him preserved in wax.'

'What, all of him?'

She nodded. 'It's a big job. As you know, usually we only do the heads and arms of a wax model and the body is made of wood, or sometimes a metal frame. Unless there's a chest that needs to be exposed. But the client wants this man preserved completely in wax.'

'It'll go off,' said Thomas doubtfully. 'Bits of it will start falling off.'

'No. It's been embalmed using formaldehyde. It will keep the body intact for a good while.'

'But when that stuff wears off, it'll start to rot,' said Thomas.

'In time,' agreed the Lady. 'But this poor man was very highly thought of, and his friends want to remember him as he was for as long as possible. So, under my supervision, your job will be to encase him in wax, and make a mask for his face. Just a thin mask so it echoes his features.'

Thomas looked at the body.

'It'll take a lot of wax,' he said uncertainly.

'Fortunately, wax is something we have in good supply,' said the Lady. 'Shall we begin?'

CHAPTER SEVEN

Superintendent Armstrong looked at the three grim-faced men sitting around the table with him in the conference room at 10 Downing Street. There was also a fourth man at the table, but he wasn't grim-faced or worried in any way. This was the secretary taking notes of the meeting and his only determination was to record everything that was said as accurately as possible. Although, Armstrong was fairly sure that the minutes of the meeting would be heavily edited before they were entered into the official record, in order to show the prime minister and the home secretary in the best possible light.

Why me? thought Armstrong bitterly. *Why me and not the police commissioner? After all, the head of Special Branch is here.*

But he already knew the answer: the commissioner was looking for a scapegoat when things went wrong, if the bank robberies couldn't be stopped.

Directly opposite Armstrong across the table was the Oxford-educated home secretary, Sir Matthew White Ridley, a slight man in his mid-fifties, his thinning hair brushed back and his noticeable side whiskers growing down almost to his chin.

Next to him sat the sixty-six-year-old prime minister, the Marquess of Salisbury. The prime minister was a bulky man, bald and with an enormous beard, who peered closely at the men sitting opposite him, Superintendent Armstrong and William Melville, the head of Special Branch. It was known that Salisbury was very short-sighted, which Armstrong guessed was the reason he peered at them with an intense gaze, rather than from any prejudicial disapproval. This was Salisbury's third term as prime minister, having previously occupied the position from 1885 to 1886, then from 1886 to 1892 when he and his Conservative party lost the election and the victorious Liberals' William Gladstone returned to take the premiership for the fourth occasion. *The topsy-turvy world of politics*, thought Armstrong ruefully. At least there was some sort of job security at Scotland Yard, although right at this moment Armstrong felt his was hanging by a thread.

William Melville, sitting next to the superintendent, was an interesting choice to lead Special Branch, because its original name when it had been formed in 1882 was the 'Special Irish Branch', its remit to infiltrate and fight Irish republican terrorism in the form of the Irish Republican Brotherhood.

Forty-six-year-old Melville was an Irishman born in County Kerry, although he had moved to England in the 1860s when he was just a boy, joining the Metropolitan Police in 1872.

The superintendent had made a point of finding out as much as he could about the other three men who'd be at this meeting, because he needed to be on his guard to protect his position. He was determined that, whatever the commissioner's intention, he would not be made the scapegoat for the bank robberies.

'These bank robberies,' intoned Salisbury. 'I understand there have been three so far, all carried out the same way, by breaking into the vault from adjacent premises.'

Armstrong and Melville both nodded in agreement.

'And the branches targeted were in affluent areas,' continued the prime minister.

'That is our information, too, Prime Minister,' confirmed Melville.

'And to date there have been no arrests,' said Salisbury in a flat tone. It was a statement, not a question, but the superintendent knew Salisbury was looking directly at him because he demanded an answer, and a reason why no arrests had been made.

'No arrests yet, Prime Minister,' said Armstrong.

'Why not?' asked Salisbury.

'The inspector originally assigned to the case, Inspector Calley, unfortunately suffered a broken leg after the third robbery, which prevented him continuing his investigations. Inspector Feather has now taken over the case and I have high hopes that he will put a stop to these outrages and arrest those responsible.'

'And recover the money?'

'That is certainly our aim, Prime Minister,' said Armstrong.

Although he said this with conviction, he knew it sounded weak. *But what else can I say?* he thought miserably, but not allowing his negative thoughts to show. He was saved from further questions by the intervention of White Ridley.

'Do you think it could be terrorist related?' asked the home secretary. 'Irish Republicans?'

Armstrong turned and looked at Melville. This was his department.

'So far we haven't had any indication that could be the case, sir,' he said, the soft estiges of his original Kerry accent still there in his careful English.

'The home secretary's concern is related to the recent defeats of the Irish Home Rule Bill,' said Salisbury.

So that's why we've both been brought in, thought Armstrong. *It's Irish politics again.*

For years there had been moves within parliament to try and pass a bill to give home rule to Ireland. The most recent had been just three years earlier, in 1893, when William Gladstone was prime minister of a Liberal government intent on giving Ireland the right to govern itself. That bill from Gladstone – the Second Home Rule Bill – had been approved by the House of Commons, but then narrowly defeated in the House of Lords because of domination by the large Conservative majority in the upper house. The following year Gladstone stepped down as prime minister, the defeat of the Home Rule Bill weighing heavily upon him, and his place as prime minister had been taken by the Earl of Rosebery. The following year, 1895, Rosebery led the Liberals at the general election, once again with a policy of Irish Home Rule, but this time those Liberals who opposed the idea broke away from Gladstone and formed their own party, the Liberal Unionists. That election resulted in a coalition government, led by Salisbury's victorious Conservatives alongside Lord Hartington's Liberal Unionists. With Salisbury's victory, the hopes of those who wanted an independent and free Ireland were dashed, and ever since the politicians in England, along with Special Branch, had been watching and waiting for a reaction by Irish Republicans.

'These are very large sums being taken, millions of pounds,' said the Home Secretary. 'Losses of this size could seriously undermine Britain's financial position, which is why we believe that it could be a political move by those wishing to attack Britain. We also believe that some of the items stolen were documents containing personal details of important people in government. If these were exposed to the public they could do serious harm to the government's reputation.'

He looked directly at Melville and asked, 'Do you know of any of these documents surfacing?'

'No,' said Melville. 'We are not aware of any incriminating material being offered for publication.'

'They may be holding it back and biding their time,' said Salisbury.

'Rest assured, my people are keeping a very close watch on known Irish Republican sympathisers in this country,' said Melville. 'To date we have had no information that suggests the Irish are involved in these robberies.'

'So, simply criminals,' said Salisbury, turning his hard gaze on Armstrong.

'And, if they are, sir, we will find them and stop them,' said the superintendent, his voice filled with a grim determination he did not truly feel.

'There is one other thing, Superintendent,' said Salisbury. 'According to the newspapers there was a murder yesterday at Madame Tussauds waxwork museum.'

'Yes, sir,' confirmed Armstrong, thinking: *What the hell has that got to do with the bank robberies? Surely he doesn't think that's also down to Irish terrorism?*

'This is very concerning,' said Salisbury, his tone and his expression conveying his grave seriousness. 'As you know, Tussauds are the jewel in the crown of wax images of the great and the good. I am due to have an image of myself modelled in wax for their tableau of British prime ministers. As part of the process, I will be attending the studio at the museum. I would hate to think that the prime minister of this country would be placing himself at risk if there is danger in the museum.'

'No, sir,' said Armstrong. 'You can take my assurance that there will be no danger for you there. The victim as I understand it was one of the two nightwatchmen on duty there. The second nightwatchman is being hunted as the believed perpetrator of this heinous deed.'

'We see from the newspaper reports that Tussauds have also engaged the assistance of what are termed the "Museum Detectives". A Mr Daniel Wilson and Miss Abigail Fenton.'

'Er, yes, I believe that to be the case, sir,' admitted Armstrong uncomfortably, wondering: *Where is this leading?*

'I have heard good reports of Miss Fenton,' put in

White Ridley. 'I was at Oxford with Gladstone Marriott of the Ashmolean, and he told me of the success she and Mr Wilson had in solving the murder of one of their senior curators.'

'My question, Superintendent, is why Tussauds feel it necessary to bring in private investigators,' asked Salisbury. 'Do they not feel confidence in Scotland Yard's ability to solve this crime?'

'I cannot say why Mr Tussaud felt the need to engaged Mr Wilson and Miss Fenton,' said Armstrong. 'But I can assure you that, as with the bank robberies, one of our top inspectors, Inspector Jarrett, has been assigned to the case and I am very confident that in a short time he will have the murderer in custody.'

'This Daniel Wilson,' pressed White Ridley, 'he used to be a detective at Scotland Yard, I gather, before he left and became a private investigator.'

'Yes, sir. That is true.'

'As he seems to be very successful at what he does, I wondered why he left Scotland Yard?'

Damn, thought Armstrong angrily. *That damn Wilson!*

'I believe it may have been because he decided to follow the example of his mentor, Inspector Abberline, who Wilson served under as a sergeant. Abberline took retirement from the police force and set up as a private investigator.'

'So Wilson was still a detective sergeant when he left Scotland Yard?'

'Yes, sir.'

'Why did he never get promotion to inspector?'

Because he was too much of a maverick, a law unto himself, going his own way in disobedience of orders, was what Armstrong wanted to say. Instead he said, 'I really can't say, sir. Possibly he didn't want that position.'

And even if he had, he wouldn't have got it on my watch, thought the superintendent vengefully. *Even now, after all this time, that damn Wilson still haunts me!*

CHAPTER EIGHT

It was ten to nine in the evening, just ten minutes before Madame Tussauds museum shut. Inside the museum, sixteen-year-old Joe Hobbs led Dolly Watts by the hand away from the crowd of visitors and down some stone steps to a door in a narrow passageway. Dolly was seventeen and had been walking out with Joe for the last two weeks, which had been two weeks of sexual frustration for Joe. She'd allowed him to kiss her, and even put his hand on her breast through her clothes, but nothing more. It had been his pal, Midge, who suggested sneaking into Madame Tussauds Chamber of Horrors after they'd shut for the day. 'There's nothing like a bit of horror and thrill to make 'em want to drop their drawers and let a bloke have a go,'

Midge had told him. Joe had checked the museum out two days before, looking for a good place to hide while he and Dolly waited for everyone to go home. He'd found a small cupboard where brooms and other cleaning stuff were kept. He'd checked to make sure that the cleaners wouldn't be opening the door for materials once the museum had closed, and discovered the cleaning staff came first thing in the morning. The plan was set. Hide in the cupboard, wait till everyone had gone and the nightwatchmen had done their rounds, then make for the Chamber of Horrors, where Dolly would be so excited she'd let him do whatever he wanted. And he knew what he wanted to do. Then, next morning, hide near the entrance and sneak out once the cleaners had opened the door and come in.

'You sure we won't get caught?' whispered Dolly nervously as Joe pulled the door shut once they'd sat down on some boxes.

'Sure,' said Joe confidently. 'I checked.' He put his hand on her thigh. 'No one's going to trouble us.'

He noticed that she didn't remove his hand. *This is going to be great*, he thought excitedly.

Daniel and Abigail were in their scullery, Daniel washing the dishes and Abigail wiping following their evening meal, when there was a loud knocking at their front door. Daniel looked enquiringly at Abigail. 'Are we expecting anyone?'

'Not to my knowledge,' said Abigail.

'I wonder who it can be?' Daniel frowned.

'There's one sure way to find out,' Abigail pointed out.

Daniel nodded, wiped his hands, and headed along the passageway, opening the front door to find John Feather standing there.

'John? Are you sure you should be here?' he said in surprise. 'Say the local bobby sees you calling at our house and it gets back to Armstrong?'

Feather grinned. 'It's all right, it's been sanctioned by the super himself.'

'Who is it?' called Abigail.

'It's John Feather!' Daniel ushered him in. 'We're in the kitchen.'

Feather followed Daniel through to the kitchen, where Abigail regarded him, concerned.

'Isn't this risky for you?' she asked. 'It's always a pleasure, but after what you told us . . .'

'That's what I said.' Daniel nodded. 'But according to John it's officially fine.'

'Not officially, *unofficially*.' Feather smiled.

He sat down at the table and outlined his conversation with Armstrong. Daniel and Abigail listened, at first bewildered, and then, as they realised how Armstrong had reached his decision, they both grinned and chuckled.

'You manipulated him!' laughed Abigail.

'I just pointed out the reality of the situation,' said Feather. 'That it will be to his advantage.'

'If we share whatever we find with you,' said Abigail.

'That's up to you,' said Feather. 'The question will be if Jarrett acts on whatever I pass to him, or if he dismisses it.'

'Which he's quite likely to do, knowing Jarrett,' said Daniel. 'Here's one for you to keep up your sleeve. I don't think Walter Bagshot killed Eric Dudgeon. All the evidence points to Bagshot having been abducted or killed.' And he told him what he'd found at the men's lodgings, and the universal view of the men.

'I'll bear that in mind,' said Feather. 'Maybe I'll pass that on when I think the time's right and more is known. At the moment, I feel Armstrong's backing Jarrett. But that's up to him. I'll have done what I was asked to do. And we can carry on meeting up.' He gave a slight scowl. 'I don't like being told who I can and can't socialise with.'

'Only not at Scotland Yard, and not at Freddy's,' noted Daniel.

'There's here, and you know where I live. Or, if I'm checking out a bank that's next door to a shop with a cellar and you might be accidentally walking past . . .' He grinned. 'I'm just obeying orders from the boss.'

'How's that going?' asked Daniel. 'The bank raids?'

'It's almost impossible,' sighed Feather. 'The powers-that-be want us to prevent any further raids, but we have no way of knowing where the crooks are going to strike next. I've sent out a message to all stations asking for their beat coppers to report where they know of a bank that's next to a shop that has a cellar, and where there's no one living at either premises. Do you know how many bank branches fit that description in London alone?'

'Quite a few, I'd imagine,' said Daniel.

'I've had reports of at least a hundred so far. We've recommended all those banks we've identified to hire nightwatchmen to stay in the vault overnight. Some have said they will, but others have said they can't afford the extra cost.'

'It will cost them a lot more if they're robbed,' said Abigail.

'That's what we've told them,' agreed Feather. 'The problem is that there's no need for the crooks to limit their

88

activities to London. When they realise that security is being tightened up in the capital I expect them to move elsewhere. Birmingham, Bristol, anywhere.'

Daniel gave a sympathetic sigh. 'I don't envy you this case, John. Somehow, murders seem less of a puzzle.'

Inside Tussauds museum, the two temporary nightwatchmen, Paul Dobbley and Gabriel Moth, sat in the watchmen's room. The rest of the museum was in semi-darkness, the only light that which filtered through from the street lamps outside, and the gas light in their room.

'What's the time?' asked Gabriel Moth nervously.

Paul Dobbley took out his watch and held it close to the gas mantle's flickering flame. 'Quarter to midnight.'

Moth gave a shudder. 'Horrible, innit.'

'What is?'

'Being here. In this place at night.'

Dobbley had worked for two years at the museum as a daytime attendant, and after the killing of Dudgeon and the disappearance of Bagshot, Tussaud had asked him if he would consider taking over night watch duties on a temporary basis.

'Just until I can find regular people to do the job.' And he'd offered Dobbley an increase in wages to compensate for the unsocial hours he'd be working. But there was a proviso. 'If you can find someone you can trust to work with you on the night shift. But you have to tell him it's only a temporary arrangement. Of course, if he turns out to be a good man at the job, I'd be happy to consider him for the job permanently.'

And Dobbley's thoughts had immediately turned to his brother-in-law, Gabriel Moth. Moth was the laziest person that Dobbley had ever known, shiftless and workshy, with the result that time after time Dobbley's sister, Evie, kept coming to him begging for a loan so they could pay their back rent, or buy food. Every time, Dobbley wanted to say no, tell her to kick Moth out into the street and tell him to get a job; but he couldn't. Evie was his little sister, now saddled with four kids, which made her situation even worse. Evie had turned up on the same day that the dead body of Eric Dudgeon had been found, shortly after John Tussaud had asked him to take on the temporary role of nightwatchman, and begged him for the loan of ten shillings. Dobbley knew he'd never see it paid back – but went straight to see his brother-in-law and told him: 'Gabriel, I'll lend Evie the ten shillings you're so desperate for, but on one condition. You come and work with me as nightwatchman at Madame Tussauds for a couple of days until Mr Tussaud finds men for the job permanent.'

'I can't!' bleated Moth. 'I've hurt my back.'

'You can sit in a chair, can't you,' snapped Dobbley. 'You're sitting on one now. Well, that's all you have to do. You sit. If there's any walking around the museum to do, I'll do it.'

'I don't know,' whined Moth. 'I'm not good with responsibility. I get the shakes.'

'In that case, Evie won't get the ten shillings she needs for the rent.'

'But if she don't pay the rent we'll be turned out!'

'Serves you right,' snapped Dobbley. 'If you can't pay your

way, being turned out's what you deserve.'

'But what about Evie. And the kids!'

'They can go to the workhouse,' said Dobbley. 'And so can you.'

'The workhouse?' repeated Moth, shocked. 'You don't mean that, Paul!'

'I do,' said Dobbley firmly. 'I've been supporting you and your lot for long enough. I can't afford to keep doing it. So, that's your choice. Join me at the museum or go to the workhouse.'

'They'll make me work at the workhouse!' moaned Moth. 'It'll kill me!'

'It's that, or sit in a chair at the museum. It's up to you.'

And so Moth had reluctantly joined him at the museum, and shown himself even more reluctant once he discovered about the murder.

'I can't be in a place where a murder's been done!' he said, aghast, when he was told about it on his first shift at nine o'clock at night.

'I thought you might say something like that,' Dobbley told him grimly. 'That's why I haven't given Evie that ten shillings yet.'

'You haven't?'

'No. The rent's due the day after tomorrow, that's what she told me. So that's when I hand over the ten shillings, *if* you've been here every night, and only if you have.'

'You're a cruel man, Paul Dobbley!' burst out Moth.

'No, I'm a near bankrupt, thanks to you,' snorted Dobbley.

In the basement, Joe Hobbs quietly pushed the door of the cupboard slightly open to listen for any sounds from elsewhere inside the museum. Everything was quiet. He pushed the door open wider and led Dolly out of the cupboard into the passageway, putting his finger to his lips to signify they had to keep quiet. Although dark, there was just enough ambient light filtering through from the windows of the upper floors for them to find their way up the stone steps. On the ground floor they saw the light beneath the door from the room where the nightwatchmen were ensconced, and crept soundlessly past it.

The carpeting to the ground floor and the stairs to the first floor hid their footsteps as they made for the Chamber of Horrors. Joe, holding Dolly's hand, could feel it trembling as they neared the infamous chamber, and he smiled to himself. *Yes*! he thought. *This is definitely going to be my night!*

Inside the chamber were the ranks of the evil, the murderers, some armed with the weapons with which they'd carried out their crimes: knives, swords, pistols, axes, and bottles of poison. In the shadows of the half-light of the street lamps peering through the windows, they looked even more menacing. The dramatic centrepiece that took up a large part of the room was the fearful wooden structure of the guillotine. The blade was down, and heads with bloodied stumps of neck were piled around the basket at the foot of the guillotine. A separate head was in the basket, as bloody as those that lay beside the wicker receptacle.

'That's where he was found,' whispered Joe. 'The nightwatchman. His head cut off, just like them.'

Dolly gave a shudder and swayed slightly, and Joe put his arm around her to keep her up. *I'll hold her up just for the moment*, he thought. *Then I'll let her lie down.* His throat tightened in excitement at the thought of what was about to happen between them. It just needed one more thing to push her, make her fanny twitch with excitement.

'Look at that one,' he whispered, and he nudged her towards the wax figure of one of the guillotine's onlookers, a man with a hideous leer on his face. 'Look at that face.' He pushed Dolly's hand towards the wax mask and stroked the grotesque features with her hand, then pushed her fingers into the open drooling mouth. Dolly gave a fearful whimper and recoiled from the figure, and as she did so her fingers caught the wax and a large part of the face fell away, then more crumbled, revealing the head of a man. However, this man was not a wax model, but very real, and very dead: the mouth hanging slackly open, the eyes dead and sightless, the skin a ghastly white.

'AAAAAAAARGH!!!!!' screamed Dolly, stumbling back from the awful image.

There was a strangled sound beside her, then Joe fainted and hit the floor with a thud.

CHAPTER NINE

The loud banging on their front door dragged Daniel and Abigail out of sleep.

'Who the hell's that?' slurred Daniel as he pushed himself out of bed and stumbled to the window, pulling back the curtains. A hansom cab was parked at the kerb.

'Who's there?' he called as he opened the window.

The figure of a coachman, dressed in a long cape and wearing a bowler hat, stepped back from their door and looked up, the gas light from the nearest street lamp showing his face.

'Sorry to trouble you, Mr Wilson, but it's an urgent message from Mr Tussaud at the waxwork museum. He asks if you and Miss Fenton can come urgently. He said to tell you another body has been discovered.'

'Very well. We'll be down as soon as we've dressed.'

Daniel shut the window and used the outside light to put a match to the gas mantle before pulling the curtains shut. Abigail was already getting out of bed. She shot a look at the clock.

'It's two o'clock,' she said.

'Murder doesn't keep to office hours,' commented Daniel as he pulled on his clothes.

Abigail pulled her dress over her head. 'I'm going to look as if I've just been dragged out of bed,' she complained.

'You have been,' said Daniel.

'Yes, but I don't have to like it.'

'I'm sure you had worse experiences when you were in a tent in Egypt,' said Daniel. He lit a candle. Abigail turned off the gaslight and followed him downstairs.

'I wonder who's been killed?' she said.

John Tussaud was waiting for them just inside the entrance to the waxworks museum.

'I'm terribly sorry to drag you out at this unearthly hour, but I didn't know what else to do,' he apologised.

'That's all right,' said Daniel. 'Who's been killed?'

'Walter Bagshot.'

'Bagshot?' repeated Abigail in surprise.

'He was found in the Chamber of Horrors.'

'The guillotine again?' asked Daniel.

Tussaud shook his head. 'Standing up, encased in wax like our models.'

'Where's the body?' asked Daniel.

'Where it was found.' He set off up the stairs towards the Chamber of Horrors, Daniel and Abigail following.

'Have the police been alerted?' asked Daniel.

'I informed a local constable who was walking his beat, and he said he'd get a message to Scotland Yard.'

'When was this?'

'The same time as I sent the cab for you.'

'I assume your nightwatchmen discovered the body?' said Abigail.

'Actually, it was a couple of intruders,' said Tussaud. 'A young man and a young woman. Their screams brought the nightwatchmen to the Chamber.'

'Where are these intruders now?'

'The watchmen locked them in a storeroom. They'll stay there until the police arrive.'

They entered the Chamber of Horrors and saw the body, naked except for a pair of drawers, encased in broken wax, lying on the floor. Abigail and John Tussaud stayed back as Daniel approached the body, careful not to disturb the large fragments of wax scattered around the dead man. He knelt down and studied the body, touching the dead man's face and the back of his head, before returning to join Abigail and Tussaud.

'I'd like to examine the body in detail, but that wouldn't be fair to the police inspector who arrives to examine the scene. When I was with Scotland Yard I often arrived at a murder scene to find there had been efforts by well-meaning people to clean up, or make their own clumsy examinations, which ruined any clues that might be found. One thing I'm sure of is that this man's been dead for at least two days, though that will need to be verified by the pathologist.'

'So he was killed about the same time as Eric Dudgeon,' said Abigail.

Daniel nodded. 'It looks as if he was killed with a blow to the back of his head by some heavy weapon. And iron bar or a hammer.'

'The same as with Eric Dudgeon.'

Again, Daniel nodded. 'And, for some reason, they left Dudgeon's body here, after decapitating him, but took Bagshot's body with them.'

'But why?' asked Tussaud, bewildered.

'I suspect so they could do this a few days later, to reinforce whatever message they're trying to send.' He turned to Tussaud. 'As I said, I don't want to disturb any evidence that may be found, so perhaps we can talk to the nightwatchmen.'

'Certainly,' said Tussaud. 'They're in their room.'

He led them along a corridor, then down a flight of stairs to a room near the entrance. Inside, the two nightwatchmen, Paul Dobbley and Gabriel Moth, were sitting on wooden chairs. Dobbley sprang smartly to his feet as the visitors entered, but Moth remained hunched on his chair, his face and posture a picture of misery.

Tussaud introduced Daniel and Abigail to the two men, then sat himself down while Daniel gestured for Dobbley to resume his seat.

'I shouldn't be here,' moaned Gabriel Moth. 'I need to go home. I'm in shock.'

'I sympathise, Mr Moth,' said Daniel, 'but the police will need to talk to you before you can leave.'

At the mention of the police, Moth gave groan and sank further down on the chair he was sitting on. Daniel turned his attention to the other watchman, Paul Dobbley, who seemed the more resolute.

'Which of you actually found the body?' he asked.

'Me,' said Dobbley. 'We heard this scream from upstairs, and I ran up there to see what was going on.'

'And you, Mr Moth?' asked Daniel. 'What did you do?'

'I stayed in our room.' Moth shuddered. 'I didn't know what was out there. Something terrifying, I knew that for sure.'

'What did you see?' Daniel asked Dobbley.

'This young woman, standing screaming, and this young bloke lying on the floor. At first I thought he must be dead, then I saw he'd just fainted. I saw what I thought was a waxwork figure, broken, lying on the floor. Then I realised the head poking through the wax was real. It was a dead body.'

'Did you recognise him?' asked Daniel.

Dobbley shook his head. 'It was Mr Tussaud who told me it was Walter Bagshot. I'd never seen him. I usually do days and Walter and Eric were on nights. And they'd only been here a couple of weeks.'

'Mr Dobbley and his brother-in-law are filling in while I find permanent replacements for Eric and Walter,' explained Tussaud.

'I won't be filling in any more!' groaned Moth. 'The next body found here could be mine!'

It was obvious after a few moments that there was very little to be learnt from the nightwatchmen that could throw any light on how the culprits had managed to smuggle Bagshot's wax-encased body into the Chamber of Horrors without being spotted. Dobbley admitted that they hadn't carried out any patrols of the museum, and his angry glance towards Moth told Daniel that the reason was Moth's refusal to walk around the museum at night, and a reluctance to be left alone while Dobbley carried out any patrols.

'We were planning to do a patrol when we heard the scream,' he told them defensively.

Daniel and Abigail left the room accompanied by Tussaud.

'What do you think?' asked Tussaud.

'I think that Mr Moth won't be much use to you as a nightwatchman,' said Daniel. 'But Mr Dobbley seems to be a good man.'

'Yes,' agreed Tussaud. 'I shall have to find a better companion for Mr Dobbley, I'm afraid.'

'I think now would be a good time to interview the intruders,' said Abigail.

'Do you have anywhere we can talk to them?' asked Daniel.

'You can use my office,' offered Tussaud.

'I suggest somewhere less comfortable,' said Daniel. 'The fact that the young woman screamed and the young man fainted means they'll be feeling on edge. I want to keep them that way. We're more likely to get the truth out of them before they start to recover their senses.'

'How about the chamber itself?' suggested Abigail. 'If it unnerved them before, it'll keep them fearful.'

'Possibly too fearful,' said Daniel thoughtfully. 'The body's still in there and the last thing we want is to set the woman off screaming again. How about putting some chairs in the passageway just outside it?'

'Yes, we can do that,' said Tussaud. 'I'll get the nightwatchmen to bring three chairs up.'

'And then can you have them bring the intruders up

separately. The woman first.'

Tussaud nodded and hurried off.

'Why the woman first?' asked Abigail.

'I'm guessing the man was the prime mover behind the intrusion. Let's find out what she says before we listen to him start lying.'

'Why would the man necessarily be behind it?' asked Abigail.

'We had situations like this when I was at Scotland Yard, and most times it was the men urging women to take risks in certain situations.'

'Ah! Excitement equals sexual gratification,' said Abigail in disapproval.

'Exactly,' said Daniel. 'Although there have been instances when the women have been the ones to take the initiative, but mostly it's the men. And if this woman is a screamer, my guess is she wasn't the one who instigated their visit. Screamers aren't usually the leaders in things like this.'

Paul Dobbley appeared, carrying three wooden chairs in a stack, which he proceeded to set out by the entrance to the Chamber of Horrors.

'Thank you,' said Abigail. 'Your colleague isn't helping you?'

'He's too afraid to leave our room!' Dobbley snorted. 'Mr Tussaud said you wanted the young woman first.'

'Yes please,' said Abigail. 'Can you extricate her from her companion?'

Dobbley gave a derisive grunt. 'Her companion's even more scared than my brother-in-law.' As they looked puzzled at this, he explained: 'Moth. He's married to my sister. Which is why I suggested him for this job, thought it might help him out.' He scowled. 'It's the last time I try and do him a favour.'

Dobbley stomped off, and reappeared a few moments later with a hand firmly on Dolly's shoulder, steering her along the corridor, and then pushing her down onto one of the chairs, before striding away again.

Dolly looked fearfully towards the Chamber of Horrors, then nervously up at Abigail and Daniel. 'We didn't do nothing,' she whispered.

Daniel remained standing while Abigail sat down next to the young woman.

'What's your name?' she asked.

'Dolly. Dolly Watts.'

'How old are you?'

'Seventeen.'

'Whose idea was it to sneak into the Chamber of Horrors after the museum had closed?' asked Abigail.

'Joe's.'

'Why?'

'He said . . . he said we'd get a thrill out of it. It'd be a laugh.'

'How did you get in?'

Dolly told them about hiding in the broom cupboard in the basement, then coming up the stairs when they thought it was all quiet.

'And how did you discover the body?'

Dolly shuddered at the awful memory. 'Joe said to touch one of the figures next to where the guillotine was. Its face. I did, and the wax came off, and I realised . . .'

Suddenly she dropped her face into her hands and began to sob and shake. Abigail looked questioningly at Daniel, who nodded. 'Thank you for that, Dolly. I'll have to take you back to the room for the moment, while we talk to Joe.'

'When can I go home?' she asked plaintively.

'I'm afraid you'll have to talk to the police first, so it won't be until they get here.'

'When will that be?'

'That depends on them, I'm afraid.'

'But you've already asked me questions,' she said, pleadingly.

'But we're not the police,' said Daniel.

'Who are you?'

'We're private investigators hired by the museum.' He held out his hand to her. 'Can you walk?'

Dolly pushed herself up from the chair and stood, wobbling slightly. Abigail took her arm. 'Hopefully it won't be too long before the police arrive,' she said. 'Now, where's the room they put you in?'

Daniel followed Abigail and Dolly until they came to a door with a key in the lock. Daniel turned the key and pushed the door open. A young man immediately leapt up from the chair he'd been sitting in. Joe Hobbs.

'You can't keep me here!' he blustered.

'Yes we can,' said Daniel. 'You'll stay here until the police arrive to question you. But right now, we need to talk to you.'

'Why?' demanded Joe. 'Who are you?'

'The museum has hired us to investigate the recent murders here.'

'M . . . murders?' bleated Joe. 'I ain't got nothing to do with no murders!'

'That's what we're here to find out,' said Daniel. He turned to Dolly. 'You stay here, Dolly, while we take this young man away and talk to him.'

'You ain't taking me anywhere!' said Joe, sitting down on the chair.

Daniel turned to Abigail. 'Would you go and tell the nightwatchmen we need their assistance. And tell them to bring a cosh and a length of strong rope.'

'No!' burst out Joe, and he sprang to his feet again.

Daniel stepped forward, took Joe by the arm and led him out of the room. Abigail followed them, locking the door behind her. They led Joe back to the three chairs outside the Chamber of Horrors, and sat him down. This time, Daniel took the chair next to the nervous Joe, who kept shooting glances towards the entrance to the chamber.

'So, it was your idea to sneak into the Chamber of Horrors tonight.'

'Others have done it!' bleated Joe. 'It's a laugh!'

'Did you know the dead man was in there, covered in wax? Was that part of your plan, to get Dolly excited, to show her a real dead man.'

'No!' shouted Joe, and he jumped to his feet, but at a warning glare from Daniel he sat down again.

'Your idea was to get her excited so she'd have sex with you,' said Daniel.

Joe swallowed. 'Only if she wanted to,' he said hoarsely.

'So was the dead man part of the plan? You chose which figure you wanted her to touch.'

'It was the face!' protested Joe. 'It was 'orrible! Really scary! Worse than any of the others!'

'Do you know who the dead man is?'

Joe shook his head violently. 'No.'

'You didn't recognise him?'

'I didn't even look at his face!'

'Then how do you know you don't know him?'

Joe looked from Daniel to Abigail, the back to Daniel again, helpless. 'You're trying to trick me!'

'Did you know his dead body was going to be here?'

'No! I didn't know anything like that was going to be here! I thought they'd all be like – you know – waxwork models.'

There were the sounds of footsteps, and then John Tussaud appeared. Behind him was the glowering figure of Inspector Jarrett, accompanied by two uniformed constables.

'Mr Wilson—' began Tussaud, but he was interrupted by Jarrett, who demanded angrily, 'What are you doing here, Wilson?'

'Our job,' said Daniel, getting to his feet. 'I'm sure Mr Tussaud has told you the museum have engaged us to look into the murders here. Tonight we have a second, discovered by this young man and his companion.'

The inspector's eyes switched to Abigail.

'I assume you must be Miss Fenton,' he said.

'I am. And you must be Inspector Jarrett.'

'I sent for them, at the same time I sent for Scotland Yard,' Tussaud explained to Jarrett.

Daniel and Abigail let Tussaud tell the inspector what had occurred.

'Walter Bagshot?' said Jarret when Tussaud had finished.

'So, not the murderer but another victim,' commented Daniel.

'Yes, well, you can never tell,' said Jarrett defensively. 'This is the young man who found the body, you say?'

'It is. His name's Joe Hobbs and his companion's name is Dolly Watts. She's currently locked in a room here.'

'Well, she's about to be locked in another,' snapped Jarrett.

He turned to the uniformed constables. 'Take him down to the van and put him in it, then put her it as well. If they resist, handcuff them.'

'You can't arrest me!' protested Joe. 'I ain't done nothing!'

'I'll be the judge of that,' barked Jarrett.

The constables took Joe by the arms and marched him away.

'What will happen to them?' asked Tussaud.

'I'll take them with me to Scotland Yard, after I've looked at the body and questioned the nightwatchmen.'

'What will you do with the body?' asked Tussaud.

'Take it in the van to the Yard as well,' said Jarrett. 'Our medics will give it a proper examination.'

'I don't think the intruders will react well to travelling in the van with the dead body,' commented Abigail. 'They might get upset.'

'They can get upset all they want,' snorted Jarret. 'If they don't like it they should have thought of the consequences before they broke in.' He turned to Daniel and Abigail and told them curtly, 'And I'll examine the body on my own. There's no need for you two to be here any more.'

'I think there is,' said Daniel. 'There are still things to look into. And that's what Tussauds have employed us to do.'

Jarrett scowled. 'So long as you don't get in my way.'

He stomped into the Chamber of Horrors.

'What should we do?' Tussaud asked Daniel and Abigail.

'My advice is to stay out of his way,' said Daniel. 'But when he brings his men to remove the body, can you make sure that some of the wax that encased it remains.'

'You think it might be important?'

'It might tell us something about whoever did the encasing. And now, while Inspector Jarrett goes about his business, I wonder whether we could trouble you for a cup of coffee? It will help to keep us awake.'

CHAPTER TEN

Daniel and Abigail settled themselves in Tussaud's office with two very welcome cups of coffee, while the museum manager busied himself hovering around Inspector Jarrett as he carried out his examination of the dead body, the Chamber of Horrors itself, the front and rear doors, and then went to interview the two nightwatchmen.

'A bizarre turn of events,' commented Abigail as she sipped at her coffee. 'Bringing Bagshot's body in and displaying it like that.'

'It's sending some kind of message,' said Daniel. 'But what message, and who's it aimed at?'

'What did you think of Inspector Jarrett taking Joe and Dolly in?'

'The same as I've always thought about him: he's a man who follows the rule book, and if the rule book says anyone found at the scene of a homicide is a possible suspect and should be taken into custody for close questioning, then that's what he'll do – even though it's patently obvious to anyone with half a brain that they're nothing to do with the body except discovering it.'

'What will he do with them?'

'Let them go, eventually. Once he gets approval for that from Superintendent Armstrong.'

'You don't like him' said Abigail.

'Did you?' asked Daniel.

'No,' she admitted.

John Tussaud entered, wiping his brow. 'The inspector's gone,' he announced.

'Good,' said Daniel. 'Then if you don't mind, I'd like to look at the scene in the Chamber of Horrors with you, especially the remains of the wax that encased Walter Bagshot.'

'The inspector took quite a bit of it with him,' said Tussaud. 'For examination.'

'But he left some behind?'

'Oh yes.'

Daniel and Abigail followed Tussaud to the Chamber of Horrors and the melee of broken pieces of wax on the floor.

'What do you think?' asked Daniel as Tussaud picked up one of the larger pieces of wax and studied it.

'Well, someone who knows about using wax – at least to a certain degree – was involved.'

'What's your opinion of the work, the use of wax?' asked Daniel.

'Crude, but effective,' replied Tussaud. 'It's been done by someone with a certain amount of experience, although it's a far lower standard than we have here at Tussauds.' He frowned. 'What puzzles me is how they managed to get it in without anyone seeing them.'

'I think that's simple enough,' said Daniel. 'Remember, the key to the back door was missing, and everyone assumed that Walter Bagshot had taken it. This says that whoever killed the two men had it. I'd strongly advise you to change the locks on the museum's doors.'

'Yes, of course. I'll do that first thing.' He frowned again. 'Do you think Walter was killed at the same time they killed Eric?'

'I do,' said Daniel. 'From what I saw of the body. Although the police surgeon will be able to tell us for certain.'

'In that case, why take him away, only to bring his body back a few days later?'

'Maximum publicity,' said Daniel.

'Bad publicity for the museum,' said Tussaud with a shudder.

'I believe the murders were a way of sending a message to someone,' said Daniel. 'Returning Walter two days later, sure his body would be discovered soon after, ensures that message is widely known.'

'But what's the message?' asked Tussaud. 'And who's it aimed at?'

'At the moment, that's a mystery to which we don't have the answer,' admitted Daniel.

'How long would Walter's body have stayed upright before collapsing?' asked Abigail.

'Not very long,' said Tussaud. 'All our waxworks have a metal armature inside them as a support. There was no armature here; it was just the shell of wax holding his body up. A day at most.'

'Do you have any enemies in the wax business?' asked Abigail.

'Enemies?'

'The fact that Walter Bagshot's body was encased in wax suggests someone with a knowledge of the wax modelling process,' enlarged Abigail. 'I was wondering about rival establishments. Other wax museums who might want to disrupt your business.'

'By killing someone?' said Tussaud, horrified.

'It's extreme, I agree,' said Daniel. 'But when I was with Scotland Yard we had quite a few murders where the motive would have seemed trivial. Two people arguing about ownership of a fence dividing their properties, and one killed the other. A shopkeeper who was angry because another shopkeeper copied his window display, so he set light to his rival's shop, killing the shop owner and his family.'

Tussaud shuddered. 'I can't imagine anything like that happening in the wax museum business.'

'I'm sure the shop owner who was burnt to death by his rival didn't think such a thing was possible,' persisted Daniel. 'You must have rivals, every business does.'

'There are other wax museums, but we don't consider them to be rivals; their workmanship is of a far lower standard than here at Tussauds. Wax museums and travelling exhibitions of wax figures have been around for a long time. When my great-grandmother first came to England in 1802, there was already a well-known wax museum in Fleet Street. Mrs Salmon's Waxworks. In fact it lasted through a change of names as different people bought it until 1831, when it closed for good.'

'Do you know when it was first established?'

'I believe it was set up as a travelling exhibition some time during the early 1700s. Mrs Salmon died in 1760, and it was sold to a man named Clark. I heard all this from my father, who was passionate about the history of waxworks.'

'What about less well-known wax museums? More recent ones who might be jealous of Tussauds?'

'Frankly, we don't have much to do with the lesser wax museums. As I said, the quality of their work is generally not up to our standard, so we don't see them as a threat. An irritant, perhaps, when they advertise themselves as "the original wax museum", which is a blatant lie, and one even puts out handbills saying "the museum where Madame Tussaud learnt her trade", which is preposterous! We've had to threaten Maurice Greville with legal action, but it doesn't seem to stop him and his absurd claims.'

'Maurice Greville?' asked Abigail.

'The owner of Greville's wax museum in Piccadilly Circus,' said Tussaud. 'A charlatan. The reputable exhibitions we are very happy to co-exist with. Westminster Abbey, for example, with their wax figures of kings and queens throughout history. Outstanding quality. Not as good as ours, obviously, but close.'

Having had their night's sleep interrupted, Daniel and Abigail returned home where they managed to refresh themselves by catching a few hours' sleep, until the noises from the street outside; the rumbling metal wheels of heavy wagons on the cobbles of the road, shouts of hawkers and newspaper sellers, children playing noisily, a mender of pots and pans plying his trade with a plaintive cry of 'Pots and pans mended!', made further sleep impossible.

While Abigail took a bath in the tin tub brought in from the scullery and placed before the coal range for warmth, Daniel cooked them a late breakfast of eggs and sausages and fried bread.

'Do you really think it could be a rival to Tussauds behind this, trying to damage their business?' Daniel asked as they sat down to their meal.

'Not really,' admitted Abigail. 'I just thought I'd mention it as a possibility. But, on reflection, a man murdered by a guillotine in the Chamber of Horrors, followed by a dead body of another murdered man encased in wax, would most likely have the opposite effect and draw in greater crowds.'

'Yes, that was my thinking as well,' said Daniel. 'With both Dudgeon and Bagshot dead, the key now lies with the previous watchmen, Bruin and Patterson.'

'You still think it was set up that they left at short notice to make sure that Dudgeon and Bagshot took the nightwatchmen jobs?' asked Abigail.

'I do,' said Daniel. 'The question is, did the four men arrange it between them, or was there an intermediary?'

'Someone pulling the strings.'

'Exactly. And I'm convinced that it revolves around the fact that Dudgeon and Bagshot were engineers.'

'With tunnelling experience?'

'Yes,' said Daniel. 'I'm sure that's in the picture somewhere. But what was the plan? If we know that, we'll know why they were killed.'

'Patterson and Bruin,' said Abigail thoughtfully. 'We need to find them. They'll know.'

CHAPTER ELEVEN

Donald Bruin and Steven Patterson sat on the barge tied to a metal ring set in the concrete wall of the Lee Navigation, the canal to the west of Hackney Marsh, and looked along the towpath towards the footbridge. Thin wisps of silvery mist rose from the waters of the canal and drifted along the towpath and around the moored barges. There were seven barges moored here, end to end along this part of the canal. When a barge being hauled by a horse arrived at this stretch, the horse was de-reined and walked along the towpath, while one of the bargees used a pole to punt their craft past the line of tied-up barges. He then re-attached the horse at the far end of the line.

Beyond the hedge that fringed the towpath, Hackney Marsh

stretched for about a mile of flat open land to where the River Lea snaked southwards, to join the Thames.

'No sign of him,' said Bruin, unable to keep the disappointment out of his voice. They'd been disappointed for two days now. Harry Michaels had been due to turn up and pay them, just as he'd paid them the last two Tuesdays, but it was now Thursday and there'd been no sign or word from him.

It had all seemed so straightforward. They'd been in the Parr's Head, their local in Somers Town, stretching their money out to buy a couple of pints, when a cheerful-looking chubby man in his late twenties, dressed in a suit of brown check material, had come to their table.

'Mind if I join you, gents?' he'd asked.

'Help yourself,' said Bruin, and the man had sat down, pointing at their half-empty glasses.

'Can I treat you to a pint?' he'd asked.

Bruin and Patterson exchanged wary glances, then Bruin shrugged. What the hell, there were two of them and the man in the suit didn't look like he could take them on. And if he was after something from them that they didn't want to do, all they had to do was say no.

'That'd be very amicable,' said Patterson.

With that, the man got up and walked to the bar, returning almost immediately with three full pint glasses held between his large hands. Again, Bruin and Patterson exchanged glances: the drinks must have been already poured. What was going on? What was the man's game? Whatever it was, he was providing beer, which was always welcome, especially when – like now – they'd spent their last pennies.

'My name's Harry Michaels.' The man beamed. 'I believe I'm addressing Mr Bruin and Mr Patterson.'

'You might be,' said Bruin carefully. 'But we'd be interested to know how you came to know our names.'

'A friend of mine,' said Michaels. 'Gerald Carr.'

At this, Bruin's face tightened and he got to his feet, glaring at Michaels. 'If you've come to threaten us . . .' he growled.

'No no, nothing of that sort, I assure you!' protested Michaels. 'The very opposite. I've come to offer you a job opportunity which will solve quite a few of your problems, including Mr Carr.'

Bruin sat down again and he and Patterson regarded Michaels suspiciously. Gerald Carr had recently bought their debt from a moneylender called Nat Jackley. In fact, Carr had bought quite a few debts from Jackley. Not that Jackley had wanted to sell them, not for the price that Carr was paying, but when Gerald Carr wanted something, he usually got it. Gerald Carr was not a nice man. He was possibly the nastiest and hardest man in Somers Town, and so far Bruin and Patterson had managed to avoid having anything to do with him. Until now. Now, as a result of Carr buying their debt, they faced a very harsh future. It was said that Carr cut the fingers off people who owed him money – one finger a week until the debt was paid. Carr's collectors were due to call at their house in two days' time, and Carr had informed the pair that his people would be armed with a sharp handaxe. Bruin and Patterson had considered leaving London, but they knew that Carr would find them. Carr had contacts everywhere.

Bruin and Patterson's problems were that they were soft

touches, especially when they'd had a bit too much to drink. Sob stories from women tugged at their heartstrings, and their pockets. Both men fell in love too easily and usually with 'inappropriate women', the sort that Bruin's mother had warned him against. And so their money vanished, and so did the women.

'We never learn,' Patterson had sighed one time.

'We'll be stronger next time,' said Bruin firmly. 'Next time we'll say no. There's no money to be had from us.'

But next time, too much drink and too many tearful kisses had led them once again to Nat Jackley, only to be told the bad news that their debt was no longer Jackley's, but Gerald Carr's.

'I've got a barge moored over at Hackney Marsh on the Lee Navigation canal,' said Michaels. 'It's empty at the moment but in a month's time I'll be getting a cargo delivered to be taken to Birmingham. I'm looking for two men to sit on the barge for the next month until the cargo arrives, take delivery of it, and then transport it to Birmingham. There's good accommodation on the barge, very comfortable. And I'm offering the following: if you take the job, I'll clear your debts with Gerald Carr, and pay you each week in cash while you're moored at Hackney Marsh, with a cash payment when the cargo arrives, and the balance when you arrive in Birmingham.'

He then named a sum of money as the final payment that almost made Patterson choke on his beer.

'I'll also give you the money for your rent that's due on your house here in Somers Town.'

Patterson and Bruin looked at one another, eager but at the

same time wary. They'd learnt years ago that when an offer was made that was too good to be true, it usually was too good to be true – there was always a catch. But they couldn't see the catch here. Michaels would pay Carr their debt, getting him off their back. Then he'd pay them a regular sum each week while they minded the barge, then a big payment when the cargo arrived and an even bigger payment when they delivered it to Birmingham.

'What d'you say?' asked Michaels. 'Are you interested?'

'We are, but with an offer as good as this, what's the catch?' asked Bruin.

'It's not really a catch,' said Michaels. 'But I need you on the barge tomorrow.'

'Tomorrow?' echoed Patterson.

'It's short notice, I know, but that's why I'm prepared to pay good money,' said Michaels. 'If you say yes, I'll go and see Carr today and clear your debt. And tomorrow I'll take you out to the barge and pay you your first lot of wages.'

'Tomorrow?' repeated Patterson, his tone unhappy. 'That'll leave our current employer in a bit of a spot.'

'Where do you work?' asked Michaels.

'Madame Tussauds,' said Bruin. 'We're the nightwatchmen.'

'When are you due there next?'

'Tonight.'

Michaels shrugged. 'It's up to you,' he said. 'That's my offer, but I need someone on that barge tomorrow.' He gave them a rueful look. 'However, if you can't do it . . .'

'No, no!' said Bruin quickly. 'We can. It's just that we're not used to leaving anyone in the lurch. And Mr Tussaud has been very good to us.'

Michaels said nothing, just sipped his beer as he watched Bruin and Patterson frown as they struggled with their decision.

'It's up to you,' he said again. 'But I need to have your answer now. If it's a no, then I need to find a couple of other fellows today.'

Bruin and Patterson looked at one another unhappily, then Bruin nodded. 'Yes,' he said. 'We'll do it.' But suspicion entered his voice as he added, 'But we need to make sure you've paid Carr off.'

'No problem,' said Michaels. 'You can come along with me to his place and see me do it.'

Bruin and Patterson looked questioningly at one another again, and then Patterson nodded.

'We'll do it,' said Bruin.

And short time later, they looked on as Michaels handed over a bundle of notes to Gerald Carr.

'Done.' Michaels beamed at them. 'We have a deal. Tomorrow make your way to the River Lee Navigation canal by Hackney Marsh. I'll meet you there by the bridge at noon and take you to the barge.'

A handshake had followed, and then Michaels had left them. Bruin and Patterson then made their way to Madame Tussauds where they told John Tussaud that they had to leave at short notice, and that their work that night would be their last. He tried to get them to change their mind by offering them an increase in their wages, but they were only too aware that they'd made a deal with Michaels which involved getting Gerald Carr off their backs. So they apologised for the short notice but said they had to leave in the morning. They then went to see their landlord and gave him notice, saying they'd be leaving immediately, and paid their back rent with the money Michaels had just given them.

The next day they were lodged on the empty barge, with Michaels giving them their wages, at this early stage enough to survive a week on. The next week he was back with more wages, and the same the following week. They'd been expecting him to repeat this process again two days ago, but this week, for some reason, he hadn't turned up, and now they were running out of money, just a few pennies left.

'Here's someone!' said Bruin, seeing a man walking along the towpath towards them.

'It's not Michaels,' said Patterson.

'Maybe he's sent someone else,' suggested Bruin.

The man arrived by the barge and studied them. He was tall and muscular, wearing overalls beneath a jacket, dark-haired and with a full beard. He also wore a pair of heavy boots.

'Have you come from Mr Michaels?' asked Bruin.

'Who?' The man frowned. He shook his head. 'No, I've come for my rent. For this barge.'

'We don't pay rent,' said Bruin. 'We work for Mr Michaels. This is his barge.'

The man shook his head again.

'Wrong. It's my barge. Mr Michaels – if that's what you call him, though he told me his name was Stafford – asked to rent the boat from me for a month. He said he needed somewhere for a couple of men to stay.'

'Yes, that's us,' said Bruin. 'He told us he wanted us to keep an eye on the barge until his cargo arrives.'

The man frowned. 'It's not his cargo, it's mine. I told him I'd be needing to move it in six weeks.'

Bruin and Patterson exchanged looks of bewilderment.

'I don't understand,' said Bruin. 'He said we could stay here rent-free if we looked after the boat for him. And he paid us.'

'Every week.' Patterson nodded. 'That's why we took the job.'

'He was due to pay us again on Tuesday gone,' added Bruin. 'But we haven't seen him.'

'He was due to pay me my rent yesterday, but he never turned up,' said the man. 'I always get suspicious when people don't pay me when they say they will. It suggests they're not going to.'

Patterson and Bruin looked at him, helplessly.

'We don't know anything about that,' said Bruin. 'All we've told you is true. Mr Michaels – that's what he said his name was – came and offered us a good deal to come and look after this barge, exactly as we said. For the last two weeks he's turned up every Tuesday, asked us if everything's been all right, paid us and gone.'

'Well, the rent's overdue now,' said the man. 'So pay me the rent that's due and you can stay, but you can only stay for another three weeks, and then I've got to move it. We're off to Birmingham when my cargo arrives.'

'We'll move it for you,' offered Bruin.

The man shook his head. 'I've got my own crew. They're going to move it.' He held out his hand. 'But pay me my rent and you can stay on it till it goes.'

'We haven't got any money,' said Patterson. 'We were expecting Mr Michaels to pay us.'

'You and me both,' grunted the man. 'But it looks like he ain't going to.' He thought it over, then asked, 'Where does he live?'

'We don't know,' said Bruin. 'He never told us. Just paid us the money.'

'We can look after the boat until you go!' offered Patterson. 'We'll do it in lieu of rent!'

The man shook his head firmly. 'If you can't pay the rent, then you're off. I don't want people I don't know living on my barge rent-free.'

'But Mr Michaels said . . . !' appealed Bruin.

'Mr Michaels has gone. If you ask me, there's no such person. Like I said, he told me his name was Stafford. You've been done and I've been done, but I'm cutting my losses. I'll be back with my crew, and I want you out.'

CHAPTER TWELVE

Inspector Jarrett scowled at the backs of Joe Hobbs and Dolly Watts as they were led out of his office by Sergeant Ted Pick, on their way down to the reception area at Scotland Yard to be released. There was no doubt in Jarrett's mind that the pair, whatever they may have been going to get up to in the Chamber of Horrors, had nothing to do with the body of Walter Bagshot being left there, encased in wax, and that annoyed him. It was always so much easier when the culprit was caught red-handed at the scene of the crime. The two nightwatchmen, Dobbley and Moth, could also be disregarded. Moth, particularly, who seemed terrified of his own shadow. Unless he was a very clever actor. But if Moth had been involved, it would have had to be in conspiracy with Dobbley, and Dobbley had an impeccable reputation as straight and honest, according to John Tussaud. No, he'd have to look elsewhere for the murderer, or murderers. Getting Bagshot's body into the museum and placing it where it had been found was the work of two, maybe three, people. The one thing he was sure of was that whoever they were, at least one of them knew about this wax modelling business; Tussaud had admitted as such.

This thought reminded him of something he'd seen in the notes he'd made after Dudgeon's body had been found at the museum, and he'd got his sergeant to look into the Tussaud family. He began to sort through the notes on his desk, and as Sergeant Pick re-entered, found what he was looking for and smiled, such a rarity that it took his sergeant by surprise.

'Is everything all right, sir?' asked Pick.

'Everything is very all right, Sergeant.' Jarrett beamed, and he brandished a sheet of paper. 'Do you remember I asked you to look into the Tussaud family?'

'I do, sir,' said Pick.

'Well according to your notes, there used to be two Tussaud brothers at the museum.'

'That's right, sir. John, the elder, and Louis, the younger.'

'And after the firm got taken over and the elder brother was put in charge, the younger one went off and set up on his own, with his own museum in Regent Street, but inside of a year it burnt down and everything was destroyed.'

'That's right, sir.' Pick nodded.

'The question is: who burnt it down, Sergeant?'

'From what I can gather, it was an accident, sir.'

Jarrett gave a wicked smile. 'There are no accidents, sergeant. Every event has a cause.' He tapped the sheet of paper. 'Two brothers against one another. Family rivalries. It's one of the oldest stories in history. Look at all the kings who bump off their brothers.'

Pick looked at him, puzzled. 'I'm not sure what you're saying, sir. Do you think that Louis Tussaud was responsible for the murders at the museum?'

'It fits, Sergeant. One brother gets the plum job and the other is given the boot.'

'With respect, sir, Louis Tussaud left of his own volition. And on good terms with his brother.'

'On the surface, Sergeant! On the surface! But what's beneath? I'll tell you. Resentment. Are you seriously telling me Louis Tussaud's museum burnt down by accident?'

'Yes, sir.'

'You don't think that big brother John saw it as a threat and had it burnt? And, in turn, that Louis decided to have his revenge?'

'Louis Tussaud's museum burnt down in 1891, sir. That's five years ago.'

'Plenty of time for him to build up this feeling of anger and resentment. I've got a feeling about this, Sergeant. I think it's time to have a word with Mr Louis Tussaud. Go and pick him up and bring him in.'

'Shall I tell him why, sir?'

'Tell him we're investigating the recent tragic events at the Marylebone Road Tussauds, and we'd like to talk to him to get his professional advice. That should do the trick. We'll see how he reacts. If he's innocent, he'll come in very happily. If he gets stroppy and refuses, that'll be a sign of guilt, and then we put the squeeze on him.'

'Right, sir.' He held out his hand. 'Can I have that piece of paper, sir. I wrote Louis Tussaud's address on it.'

Jarrett handed the sheet of paper to Pick.

'There you are, Sergeant. Go out and bring him in.'

'I'm still not convinced this visit is worth our time,' observed Abigail doubtfully. She and Daniel were standing outside the garish purple and yellow entrance to Greville's Famous Waxworks in Piccadilly Circus. 'We've already dismissed the idea of a rival waxwork killing the nightwatchmen in an attempt to discredit Tussauds. We both agreed it's more likely to attract the sort of ghoulish people who haunt the Chamber of Horrors.'

'The person who did the murders, certainly the person who encased Bagshot, has experience of working in wax,' explained Daniel.

'So we visit every wax museum in London?' asked Abigail.

'If necessary,' said Daniel. 'That's what much police work is about, walking miles and asking questions. That's why policemen have flat feet.'

They entered the museum, passing three waxworks of soldiers from history who seemed to be on guard just inside the main doors – a Roman, a Viking, and a British redcoat – and came upon a stout, florid-faced man wearing a light brown suit with a pattern of large, checked squares, along with a large purple bow tie, engaged in conversation with a blonde woman in her fifties sitting in a booth marked 'Box Office'. The pair looked up as Daniel and Abigail walked towards them.

'We're not yet officially open,' explained the man, coming towards them. 'Half an hour and the cleaners will be gone.'

'I'm afraid we're not here to see the exhibition,' said Daniel. 'I'm Daniel Wilson and this is my partner, Abigail Fenton.'

'The Museum Detectives!' exclaimed the man delightedly. 'Allow me to introduce myself. Maurice Greville, proprietor and artist-in-chief at Greville's Famous Waxworks. I read in the newspapers that Tussauds had hired you.' His smile vanished to be replaced by a look of mourning and sympathy. 'What a tragedy! That could have been us!'

'Why?' asked Abigail.

'We have a Chamber of Horrors here, too. Certainly the equal of Tussauds. With a guillotine.'

'Do you have nightwatchmen?' asked Daniel.

'Well, no,' admitted Greville. 'But if we did, it could have been one of them found with his head in a basket.'

'You don't feel the need of having nightwatchmen?' enquired Abigail.

'The expense is not one we feel is justified,' said Greville. 'We are a small museum. And being in a prominent position here in Piccadilly Circus, which has a lot of activity at night, affords us a good measure of security.'

Daniel gave Abigail an amused look, aware that 'night activity' in Piccadilly Circus meant the bustling trade in prostitutes of both sexes, along with their clients.

'Perhaps it would be better to continue this conversation in my office?' suggested Greville with a smile. He turned to the blonde woman. 'If anyone wants me, Doris, tell them I'm engaged temporarily.'

Daniel and Abigail followed Greville down a corridor to a door with the words 'Manager, Strictly Private', and led them in. It was a small room, dominated by a large desk with three chairs ornately decorated with red cushions and gilt woodwork. The walls were crammed with framed photographs of famous figures in wax, with Maurice Greville standing proudly beside each. Greville gestured for them to sit, then asked, 'How may I help you?'

'It would appear that the person who committed the atrocities at Tussauds has a talent for wax sculpture.'

'Oh?' Greville frowned. 'What makes you think that?'

'A second body has been found there, encased in wax.'

'A second body?'

'The other nightwatchman. His body was discovered in the Chamber of Horrors. The head, in particular, had been sculpted in wax.'

'That doesn't necessarily mean the deed was done by a wax artist,' said Greville defensively.

'No, it doesn't,' agreed Daniel. 'But it is a skill that has to be learnt. Someone just couldn't do that kind of work without training and knowledge.'

'Yes, that's true,' said Greville uncomfortably. 'But if you're suggesting that myself or any of my team of artists . . .'

'Not at all,' said Daniel quickly. 'We've come to you because you know the trade.'

'The *art*,' Greville corrected him.

'The art.' Daniel nodded. 'And, therefore, the artists. Can you think of anyone who might have a grudge against Tussauds? Anyone, for example, who might have left them, possibly under a cloud, who then came to work for you?'

'Absolutely not,' said Greville firmly. 'Most of my artists I've trained up myself. There has been only one who joined us from Tussauds, and she certainly didn't leave under a cloud; she was one of their better people and only moved on to improve her prospects.'

'Who was this?'

'Caroline Duckworth. A true artist!' He gave a sigh. 'Sadly, we lost her.'

'She died?' said Abigail, shocked.

'No. She got married. Gave up the wax business completely.' He sighed again. 'A great loss to the profession!'

'Being in the business, as it were, I wonder what you can tell us about Louis Tussaud?'

'Louis?' Greville frowned. 'What about him?'

'Do you know why he left Tussauds to set up on his own?'

'I assume because his nose had been put out of joint after the old man sold the place and John was given the job of manager and chief model artist by the new owners.'

'His own wax museum burnt down, I understand.'

'Yes. A tragedy. But these things happen.'

'We'd quite like to talk to him. Do you have an address for him?"

'About his brother?'

'Not necessarily. In the same way we're hoping you might be able to shed light on things in the wax business.'

'The *art* of wax,' Greville corrected him primly.

'Yes, of course,' said Daniel. 'My apologies. You see, we're both very much newcomers to the world of wax.'

'You really think these murders were committed by someone from our world?' asked Greville.

'We don't know, but there's certainly a connection.'

'Well, if you think that Louis might have had anything to do with what happened at Tussauds, you're very wrong,' said Greville. 'For one thing, he'd never do anything to hurt his brother, or his family. In the second, I happen to know he's been out of London for the past month.'

'Oh? Do you know where?'

'Yes. Blackpool. I believe he's considering opening his next venture there and he wants to explore what possibilities the town may hold.' He leant forward, an attempt at an ingratiating smile on his face as he said to Daniel, 'Actually, Mr Wilson, as you're here, there's something I'd like to ask you.'

'Yes?'

'I've decided that our own Chamber of Horrors could do with something a bit special, something that Madame Tussauds seem to have overlooked, for some bizarre reason.'

'Oh?' asked Daniel, intrigued.

'Who is the most notorious murderer, the most bloodthirsty, that this city has seen this century?'

Daniel looked at Abigail, his face clouding with a hint of annoyance. He knew where this was leading. As if to prove him correct, Greville announced in ringing tones: 'Jack the Ripper! And you, Mr Wilson, are the one man with intimate knowledge of him.'

'He was never caught,' pointed out Daniel.

'But not for want of your trying, I'm sure,' enthused Greville. 'I want to design a tableau depicting Jack the Ripper in all his horror, which will send shivers down the spines of everyone who sees it. It will be the talk of the town. Nay, of the nation! And as you and Inspector Abberline were such crucial figures in the investigations, we'd like you to be represented. Effigies of yourself and Mr Abberline.

'I've written to him asking if he would agree for his representation to be exhibited, but so far we've not had a reply from him. We wonder if you would approach him about it.'

CHAPTER THIRTEEN

Bruin and Patterson trudged along the towpath away from the barge, watched by the barge's owner and the four men he'd brought with him in case they resisted their eviction.

'I thought it was too good to be true,' sighed Bruin. 'Better money than we were getting at Tussauds and a big cash payout at the end.'

'Michaels conned us.'

'But why?'

Bruin shrugged. 'No idea. But whatever plans he had are out of the window now. He's done a runner.'

'What are we going to do?'

'We could try going back to the museum. We left on good terms. And Mr Tussaud complimented us on what good workers we'd been and said there'd always be an opportunity there for us again.'

'Yes, but we left him at short notice. He may not forgive us for that.'

'Only because we had short notice ourselves,' pointed out Bruin. 'What else were we to do? Mr Michaels turns up with a wad of banknotes and saves us and our fingers from that Carr bloke, but he needs us to start the very next day. We didn't know it would turn out this way. We both thought he was genuine.' He nodded determinedly. 'That's what we do. We go and see Mr Tussaud.'

Abigail had to hurry to keep up with Daniel as he stomped away from Greville's wax museum, his face like thunder.

'You're angry,' she said.

'Angry doesn't cover it,' snapped back Daniel.

'He's a businessman,' pointed out Abigail. 'He's talking about a business opportunity. After all, he made a good point: Tussauds haven't featured Jack the Ripper in their Chamber of Horrors. There is a gap in the market.'

'I will not allow myself to be portrayed in wax by that oaf,' snorted Daniel. 'Did you see those wax models of his on display? They were appalling. Second-rate.'

'You're comparing them to Tussauds,' said Abigail.

'Yes I am.'

'I admit that some of them didn't look much like the person they were depicting . . .'

'Didn't look like them?' echoed Daniel indignantly. 'His Queen Victoria looked more like the Duke of Wellington! I dread to think what I'd end up looking like. And I certainly wouldn't dream of contacting my old guv'nor and try and persuade him to be part of this appalling charade.'

'Abberline might be flattered at the idea.'

'If he was he'd have written back to indicate his agreement. His silence speaks volumes.'

'Very well,' said Abigail. 'If that's how you feel. Where are we going now?'

'Morton's of London Wax Museum,' said Daniel. 'They're the next on the list.'

'Let's hope they, and the rest of them, don't ask you to get measured for a wax effigy for a Jack the Ripper tableau.' Abigail smiled. 'Otherwise you'll be in the foulest possible mood by the time we get home.'

Inspector Jarrett looked up from his desk at his sergeant, as Pick returned from his assignment. Jarrett frowned as he saw the sergeant was on his own.

'Where is he?' he asked. 'In the cells?'

'Blackpool,' said Pick.

'Blackpool?'

Pick nodded.

'You mean he's done a runner?'

Pick looked doubtful. 'I don't think you can describe it like that, sir. I went to the address we had for him, and was told that he went to Blackpool about a month ago. So he was in Blackpool when the first watchman was killed, and when the body of Walter Bagshot was sneaked into the wax museum, so he can't have done it.'

'Accomplices, Sergeant!' said Jarrett. 'Send a telegraph to the Blackpool police. I want Louis Tussaud apprehended and taken into custody pending you bringing him back to London.'

'Me, sir?'

'As soon as we get word that Tussaud is in custody there, you head north and bring him in. And take a constable with you, in case he's difficult. These arty types have sometimes got the strength of ten men.'

It was nearly six o'clock by the time Daniel and Abigail finished visiting the other four wax museums in London, and it was Abigail who remarked that the standard of work seemed to deteriorate more with each one. Two of the museums employed people who'd both worked at Tussauds: Ernest Maxim at Worple's Waxworks and Deirdre le Faux at the London Wax Museum. Both were in their twenties, and although they proudly showed off their work to Daniel and Abigail, afterwards both Daniel and Abigail agreed that the reason both had left Tussauds was because neither could actually be described as a top-notch wax artist.

'But we're not looking for a top-notch artist,' pointed out Abigail. 'We're looking for someone who knows how to use wax.'

'In that case we'll bear them in mind,' said Daniel. 'But, in my opinion, neither of them would have the stomach for what was done to Dudgeon and Bagshot. But we'll see what John Tussaud has to say about them.' He frowned and added, 'The one intriguing thing we turned up was the boy who's disappeared.'

'From Morton's,' said Abigail. 'Their thirteen-year-old apprentice.'

'Yes,' said Daniel. 'Thomas Tandry. According to Morton's he just didn't turn up for work a few days ago.'

'Perhaps he got fed up with it,' said Abigail. 'Apprentices don't exactly earn a great deal, and they usually get given the worst jobs to do.'

'But he'd not given any indication he didn't want to work there any longer. And what's more mysterious is him vanishing from his lodgings the way he did, according to Mrs Morton.'

'You think something's happened to him?'

'I do,' said Daniel.

'Connected with the case?'

'I don't know,' Daniel admitted. 'I agree that thirteen-year-old boys can suddenly vanish for all manner of reasons. It could all be just a coincidence. Maybe I'm so wrapped up in this I'm seeing everything we come across as forming part of this whole case, whether it is or not. But I'd like to find out what's happened to him.'

'Perhaps John Feather might be able to help,' suggested Abigail.

'He might, although I can see him saying that with all that's going on, searching for a runaway thirteen-year-old boy is pretty low down on Scotland Yard's list of priorities.'

On their arrival at Tussauds they were met by one of the attendants, who told them, 'Mr Tussaud told me to watch out for you. He's in his office and asked that you go straight up as soon as you arrived.'

Abigail gave Daniel a puzzled frown as they walked up the stairs to Tussaud's office. 'Did you know he was expecting us to call?' she asked.

'No,' admitted Daniel. 'Which suggests something else has happened.'

Tussaud leapt to his feet from behind his desk, a look of relief on his face, as Daniel and Abigail entered his office.

'Thank heavens you got my message!' he said.

'Message?' queried Daniel. 'No.'

'I sent a messenger to your home.'

'We've been out all day talking to people at the other wax museums,' explained Abigail. 'What's happened?'

'Daniel Bruin and Steven Patterson arrived here a few hours ago, asking if they could have their old jobs back. Apparently their new job opportunity didn't work out. After what happened last night I'm delighted to have them back. I told them what happened to Dudgeon and Bagshot, and they were shocked. I think they feel it could have been them as the victims. I've asked them to wait here because I was sure you'd want to talk to them, which was why I sent a message to your home to tell you about them.'

'We'll definitely talk to them,' said Daniel. 'Where are they?'

'In the watchmen's room,' said Tussaud. 'The same place you saw Dobbley and Moth.'

There was a knock at the door, which then opened to admit the familiar figure of Arthur Conan Doyle.

'John!' Doyle beamed. 'Here I am for my next round of measurements.' His smile became broader as he caught sight of Abigail and Daniel. 'Miss Fenton! This is most opportune; I was hoping I'd run into you. Could we have a word?' Turning to Tussaud, he said, 'I'm sure you can forgive a few minutes' delay before we start, but there is something quite important that I want to talk to Miss Fenton about.'

Tussaud looked at Daniel and Abigail, and then at

Doyle, showing his discomfort.

'Actually, Mr Doyle, something has just occurred about the tragic events here; two men have arrived that Mr Wilson and Miss Fenton are eager to interview . . .'

'That's all right.' Daniel smiled. 'I can talk to them while Miss Fenton talks to Mr Doyle.' He looked at Abigail. 'Would that be all right with you?'

'Excellent.' She nodded.

'Capital!' Doyle beamed. 'In that case, may we use your office, Mr Tussaud? Possibly while you prepare things in your studio?'

Tussaud nodded. 'I'll take Mr Wilson to meet the two men and then – as you suggest – do some preparations, and I'll see you in my studio when you're ready.'

Daniel and Tussaud left, and Doyle and Abigail settled themselves on two chairs.

'Capital man, Tussaud.' Doyle smiled. 'I like him immensely.'

'I agree,' said Abigail. She looked at him enquiringly. 'My interest is piqued, Mr Doyle. What is the important thing you wish to talk to me about?'

'I'm planning to sponsor a dig,' said Doyle.

'A dig?'

'An archaeological exploration in Egypt. You remember I told you I recently spent a lot of time there and how intrigued I was, and still am, by the culture of ancient Egypt. I'm planning to undertake an exploration of the Sun Temple of Niuserre. Do you know it?'

'Yes, it's at Abu Ghurob, part of the area known as the Pyramids of Abusir, although it's separate from the main pyramids there.'

Doyle nodded. 'I shall be accompanying it, but I want you to be the leader of the expedition.'

She stared at him, stunned. 'Me?'

'I can think of no one better. It won't happen until next year, there are lots of things to put in place, but what do you say?'

She continued to stare at him as her mind tried to cope with the enormity of what he was offering her. 'I can only say, this is an opportunity I never ever thought would be avilable to me. Are you sure you mean *me* to lead the expedition?'

'Absolutely. Are you in agreement?'

'Well . . . yes, in principle. It's the most incredible offer I've ever had.'

'Excellent! Who do you think should accompany us?'

Abigail looked at him, her mind in a whirl. 'To be honest, Mr Doyle, I need time to consider this.'

'Of course,' said Doyle. 'We'd need a good team. They don't all have to be British, but it would be good if that could be the case. Most of the site seem to be overrun with Germans, French and Belgians. That's why I thought of the Sun Temple of Niuserre. It's less well known than, say, the Great Pyramid. You were at Hawara with Petrie, weren't you?'

'Yes,' said Abigail.

'Well if you can cope with Flinders Petrie you can certainly cope with leading an expedition to Abu Ghurob,' chuckled Doyle.

CHAPTER FOURTEEN

Daniel sat in the watchmen's room with Bruin and Patterson. The more he listened to their story, the more convinced he became that they were not part of any conspiracy, at least, not as active participants. Their return to Tussauds had been prompted by the disappearance of the mysterious Mr Harry Michaels they talked about.

'Why did you leave Tussauds?' asked Daniel.

'Like we told Mr Tussaud, we got offered this job. A good one, too.' And they outlined the generous terms they'd been offered by Michaels to look after an empty barge, and then take a cargo to Birmingham.

'But he never turned up this week to pay us. And it turned out it wasn't his barge, he was renting it from this other bloke, and he hadn't paid the last lot of rent on it. So the owner turfed us off.'

'Just to make sure I've got this clear, Michaels was paying you your wages, and also this man the rent for the boat, up to this week, when he suddenly disappears.'

'That's the size of it,' said Bruin.

'Was this Michaels local?'

'He sounded it, but we hadn't seen him around before.'

'Why the urgency?' asked Daniel. 'Why did you hand in such a short notice to Mr Tussaud? Just one day. Less than that, really, one night before.'

Bruin and Patterson looked uncomfortable. 'Yeh, well, that's the way this bloke Michaels said he wanted it. We'd have preferred to give Mr Tussaud proper notice.'

'So why didn't you?' pressed Daniel.

Bruin and Patterson looked even more uncomfortable. Finally, Patterson said, 'You were a detective with the police, weren't you. At Scotland Yard. That's what the papers say.'

'I was,' said Daniel.

'Did you ever hear of a bloke called Gerald Carr?'

Did I, thought Daniel angrily. One of the nastiest pieces of work he'd ever encountered, but the police had been unable to nail him for anything because of the climate of fear around him.

'I know of Carr,' said Daniel. 'How does he fit into this?'

'Me and Steven owed him money,' said Bruin. 'Michaels said he'd pay our debt if we went with him straight away. If we didn't, he wouldn't pay Carr for us.'

Daniel stared at them. 'How on earth did two intelligent men like you allow yourselves to get in hock to Gerald Carr? You lived in Somers Town; you must have known his reputation.'

'We didn't borrow the money from him, we borrowed it from a bloke called Nat Jackley,' said Patterson.

'Carr bought our debt off Jackley,' added Bruin.

Or took it from him with the threat of violence, more likely, thought Daniel bitterly. He knew Jackley, a moneylender, but with no history of violence. Easy prey for someone like Carr.

'I need to know the name of the barge Michaels had rented, and where it's moored,' said Daniel.

'We're telling the truth,' insisted Bruin.

'I'm sure you are, but I need to try and trace this Michaels character.'

'You think he was behind what happened to the other two blokes who replaced us?' asked Bruin.

'At this stage I don't know,' said Daniel. 'But the only way to find out is by talking to him.'

'The barge is called *Mary-Jane*,' said Bruin. 'It's on the River Lee Navigation canal by Hackney Marsh, on the towpath side. About a hundred yards downstream from the footbridge.'

'The bloke who said it's his barge also said that Michaels gave him a different name. Stafford, I think.'

'In which case I need a description of Michaels, in case that isn't his real name.'

'I guess he was in his twenties. Shortish – shorter than us – about five foot six. He looked smart. Wore a suit of brown check material. Chubby sort of bloke, but with a long thin face and a long thin nose. Short brown hair.'

'Beard or moustache?'

Bruin and Patterson shook their heads.

'Scars or any identifying marks?'

Again, they responded in the negative. Daniel made notes of all this in his notebook, then asked, 'One last question: have either of you ever worked as tunnellers?'

'Tunnellers?' repeated Bruin, puzzled.

'Yes, digging tunnels. For railways, canals, that sort of thing.'

Both men shook their heads.

'Strictly open air for both of us,' said Bruin. 'We were working on farms before we came to work here as nightwatchmen.'

Daniel stood up.

'Thank you, gentlemen,' he said. 'I think you've told me everything I need to know. Where can I get hold of you if I need to get in touch with you again?'

'Here, I suppose,' said Patterson.

'We ain't had time to sort out any lodgings yet,' said Bruin, 'having just been turfed off the boat this morning. We wanted to see if Mr Tussaud would take us back first, and then when he said he would, he told us he wanted us to stay here and wait for you.'

'We thought of asking our old landlord in Somers Town if he had anything,' said Patterson. 'But we don't fancy being too close to Gerald Carr. I know our debt's paid off, but you never know what he's going to do.'

Daniel wrote down the address in Marylebone where Dudgeon and Bagshot had been staying. 'This is where Eric Dudgeon and Walter Bagshot were staying,' he told them. 'The landlady's name is Mrs Pershore. She might have let the room already, but as this has all happened so recently there's a chance it might still be available. She's looking for respectable men as tenants. Tell her you're going to be working at Tussauds, that might help. Tell her Mr Tussaud will give you references if she wants one.'

Bruin put the piece of paper in his pocket. 'Thanks,' he said. Then he looked inquisitively at Daniel. 'Was it anything to do with us?' he asked. 'What happened here?'

'Only the business of Michaels wanting you out so he could put the other two men in,' said Daniel. He shook hands with both men. 'I'm glad the job was still open for you.'

'Do you think we'll be safe here, though?' asked Patterson apprehensively, looking around the room.

Now that is a different question, thought Daniel, *and one to which I don't have the answer*. However, aloud he said, 'I'm sure you will,' putting as much sincerity into his voice as he could permit himself, and hoping he wasn't wrong.

He made his way back to Tussaud's office and knocked at the door, entering when he heard Abigail's voice calling. She was on her own.

'Where's Mr Doyle?' asked Daniel.

'He's with John Tussaud in his studio. He left some time ago.'

'You should have come and joined me in the watchmen's room.'

'I didn't want to interrupt,' said Abigail. 'You might have been in a crucial piece of questioning. How did you get on?'

'More importantly, what did Mr Doyle want to talk to you about?' asked Daniel.

'He's planning a dig at the Sun Temple of Niuserre at Abu Ghurob in Egypt.'

'And he wanted your advice?'

'No, he wants me to lead the expedition.'

Daniel stared at her, astonished, then sat down.

'Lead it?' he repeated, awed.

'Yes,' she said.

'Isn't that a particular honour?' he asked. 'That's the impression I got from your previous involvements in expeditions.'

'Yes,' she said. 'The convention is that an expedition is named after its leader. A Flinders Petrie, for example. Or Gautier and Jéquier. As far as I know, no woman has ever had that honour.'

'So you'll be the first.'

She looked at him, uncertain.

'I'm not sure,' she said doubtfully.

'Why on earth not?' he asked. 'This is the opportunity of a lifetime.'

'I'm not sure if I'm up to it.'

'You've been on expeditions before,' said Daniel. 'Plenty of them.'

'Yes, but as one of a team. And it's a long time since I've been in the field.'

'Abigail, you can do this. It's an incredible opportunity, one which you may never get the chance of again. Alternatively, it could be the start of a whole new branch of your career, as a *leading* archaeologist.'

'But these things aren't over in a matter of weeks,' protested Abigail. 'Some take years.' She reached out to take his hands in hers and gripped them tightly, passionately. 'I don't want to be away from you for that length of time, Daniel.'

'I could visit,' Daniel told her. 'If Conan Doyle is able to pop out to Egypt, so can I.'

'The sea journey takes weeks.'

'It'll be worth it to be with you.' He returned her squeeze. 'This is what you do. Who you are. It's who you were when I met you and I know how important it is to you. You've forsaken it because of what we've been doing together, the investigating. But you'd regret it for ever if you turned this down.'

The door opening interrupted them, and they separated their hands and got to their feet as John Tussaud entered.

'Ah, here you are,' he said. 'I saw Bruin and Patterson and they said you'd finished with them, so they were off to arrange lodgings. They said you'd given them an address.'

'Yes,' said Daniel. 'The house in Marylebone where Eric Dudgeon and Walter Bagshot were lodging. The room might be available. I assume you've finished with Mr Doyle?'

'For today,' said Tussaud. 'What did you make of Bruin and Patterson?'

'I think they were just innocent dupes who got caught up in someone else's scheme,' said Daniel.

'So it would be safe to take them back?'

'I believe so.'

'You said you'd been talking to the other wax museums in London today,' said Tussaud. 'Did you get any information that might point to who did this terrible thing?'

'We're not sure,' replied Daniel. 'We wondered if someone involved in making wax models might be involved, especially after what was done to Walter Bagshot's body. Just in case there might be some connection, we asked at each one if they had wax artists who'd previously worked for you.'

'In case they left under a cloud, you mean?' asked Tussaud. He shook his head. 'There are none that I can recall. All our previous artists left on what I'd describe as good terms. No animosity. Who did you turn up?'

Daniel took out his notebook.

'Deirdre le Faux at the London Wax Museum, Ernest Maxim at Worple's Waxworks, and Caroline Duckworth at Greville's.'

Tussaud gave a sigh. 'Sadly, they all departed because they felt that I wasn't giving them the really important figures to depict, the famous, especially those from modern times. The truth is, they were adequate at the art, but nothing more than that. Of the three, Caroline Duckworth was better than either Ernest or Deirdre, but she had a very high opinion of her talents that I didn't share. I believe that's why she left us. She was ambitious and she realised she wouldn't achieve what she wanted here. She thought Greville's would give her the recognition she felt she deserved.'

'He said that she left to get married and gave up the wax business.'

'Really? Who did she marry?'

'I don't know,' said Daniel. 'I didn't ask.'

'I imagine it would have to be someone who was successful and rich. As I say, she was very ambitious and wanted to make a name for herself.'

'Socially?'

Tussaud smiled. 'Socially and financially, in my opinion. Wax was a means to an end for her. For the true artist in wax, it's not about financial rewards, it's the satisfaction of a representation one is proud of.' He looked enquiringly at them. 'Is there anything else? It's been a long and emotional day, with Bruin and Patterson returning, and then the session with Mr Doyle. A wonderful man, but he can be exhausting!'

'Actually, Mr Tussaud, there is one other question,' said Abigail. 'Nothing to do with the case, but it intrigued me. When we met with Maurice Greville he was keen to involve Daniel in a Jack the Ripper display for his Chamber of Horrors.'

'Which I declined, very firmly,' said Daniel, his face showing his distaste for the proposition.

'The thing is, he made the point that the Ripper is the most infamous murderer of recent times and said that audiences would clamour to such a display. Yet I notice that you don't feature him in your own chamber.'

'There is a very simple reason for that,' said Tussaud. 'We keep strictly to the policy of our founder, Madame Tussaud, that there should be no models of persons whose likeness is not absolutely known, unlike unscrupulous people like Greville. There were suspects in the case of Jack the Ripper, but no one was positively identified.'

'That is true,' said Daniel. 'And can I say, Mr Tussaud, that I absolutely support your policy. There has been far too much unpleasant speculation about the identity of the Ripper, with certain people's names being dragged through the mud unnecessarily.'

'You must have had your own particular suspect, as one of the chief investigators in the case,' said Tussaud.

'I did.' Daniel nodded. 'My chief, Inspector Abberline, shared the same view, but we lacked the necessary proof due to the reluctance of key witnesses to come forward and give testimony. And the person we viewed as the culprit is now long dead.'

'And you will not reveal their name?' asked Tussaud.

'No,' said Daniel. 'Without the vital proof I spoke of, it would be just sensationalism that could cause great upset to people close to them. Perhaps one day the truth will be made public, but not in my lifetime, I believe.'

CHAPTER FIFTEEN

As Daniel and Abigail walked away from the museum he told her about his conversation with Bruin and Patterson. 'I'm sure they weren't part of the plot, they were unwittingly part of a con by this Harry Michaels. Although we don't know why, as yet. Tomorrow I suggest we go to Hackney Marsh and see if we can find the barge's owner. He might be able to throw some light on this mysterious Mr Michaels.'

'Should we tell Inspector Jarrett that Bruin and Patterson have returned?' Abigail asked.

'No, we'll tell John Feather and let him do it,' said Daniel with a smile. 'He can say he wormed the information out of us, and that'll make Superintendent Armstrong think his plan is working, and he'll encourage John to keep in with us.' He looked at his watch. 'It's half past eight. John should be at home now, and finished his supper.'

John Feather's house was in Frederick Street, just off Gray's Inn Road and not far from King's Cross Station, a double-fronted redbrick terraced building with ornamental window boxes packed with colourful blooms on the two ground floor windows that were either side of the front door.

'It's a decent-sized house,' commented Abigail, who was visiting Feather's home for the first time.

'It needs to be,' said Daniel. 'He and Vera have got four growing children, as well as Vera's mother living with them. And Vera's so soft-hearted she invariably has her children's friends staying over for a night.'

He knocked at the door and it was Feather himself who opened it. His face lit up at the sight of them.

'Daniel! Abigail! This is a surprise! What news?'

Daniel smiled. 'Our biggest news is that Abigail's off to Egypt.'

'What?' said Feather, startled.

'She's going to be leading an expedition, so it will be in her name. The Abigail Fenton expedition.'

Feather stared at Abigail, who looked embarrassed. 'When do you go?' he asked.

'Nothing's been decided yet,' she said.

'Arthur Conan Doyle is sponsoring it, and he's chosen Abigail to be the leader,' continued Daniel.

'I still haven't definitely said I will,' said Abigail. 'So far I've said yes in principle, but there's still a lot to think about. I may not go at all.'

'You should,' said Daniel. 'It's the chance of a lifetime.'

'If you do, when will you go?' asked Feather.

'Next year some time.'

'How long will you be away?'

'That depends. Usually the first visit to a dig takes about four months while it's explored, and if there's anything to find then you go back for a second time to finish. And that can be anything up to six months.'

'So you'd be away for a whole year!'

'Yes, and that's what's giving me second thoughts,' said Abigail. 'I really don't want to be separated from Daniel for that long.'

'Plenty of married couples are apart for much longer,' pointed out Feather. 'Army and navy people, for example. Scientists exploring for new plants.'

'That's what I told her,' said Daniel. 'And I could go out there to visit.'

'Out where?' asked a girl's voice.

They looked and saw they'd been joined by a girl of about sixteen.

'Egypt,' said Feather. 'Miss Fenton is considering going out on an archaeological expedition there . . .'

'*Leading* it,' corrected Daniel with a smile.

'You're an archaeologist?' asked the girl.

'I am,' said Abigail.

'Sorry, I haven't introduced you,' said Feather. 'This is my niece, Marion Budd. She's come to stay with us for a while. These are Mr Daniel Wilson and Miss Abigail Fenton. They're friends of mine. Mr Wilson and I worked together when he was at Scotland Yard.'

'I remember you,' Marion said to Daniel. 'I was only very small, but I met you with Uncle John and Aunt Vera. It was in Hyde Park.'

'Yes,' said Daniel. 'I was on a case there, and your uncle and aunt happened to be out enjoying the sunshine. How incredible you should remember. That must have been about ten years ago. You'd only have been six.'

She smiled. 'Yes, but the memory stayed with me. I remember thinking you looked like one of the gods in my book about the ancient Greeks, tall and so handsome. And you haven't changed.'

Feather's wife, Vera, appeared from inside the house, wiping her hands on a tea towel.

'I heard voices.' Her face brightened when she saw who was at the door. 'Daniel! Abigail! How wonderful. I keep hearing about you from John, and reading your exploits in the newspapers . . .'

'Oh please!' begged Abigail. 'All that is none of our doing.'

'And not only do we both find all that stuff in the newspapers embarrassing, it also stops us doing our job properly,' said Daniel ruefully. 'It means that certain important people are upset by it, and as a result we're both barred from Scotland Yard.'

Vera shot a concerned look at Feather, who shook his head. 'Don't worry,' he said reassuringly. 'Daniel and Abigail calling here is permissible, indeed, sanctioned by that certain important person, providing it's done discreetly and without anyone knowing about it.'

'In that case, you'd better come in,' said Vera. 'You never know who might be passing.'

'She's going to Egypt,' said Marion as they entered the house.

Vera gave Abigail an inquisitive look, prompting Abigail to say, 'I may be, but that's not why we're here.'

'Somehow I didn't think it was,' said Feather. 'Shall we go into the parlour?' As Marion pushed open the door of the parlour and walked in, Feather added, 'Actually, Marion, this is business. So perhaps you'd go with your Aunt Vera.'

'Oh!' said Marion, her face screwing up with disappointment.

'Come on,' said Vera. 'You can help me with this stew I'm making.'

'But . . .' said Marion, with a hopeful look towards Daniel.

'It is business, and as such we need to keep it within ourselves,' said Daniel.

'But I'm family!' protested Marion.

'Yes, you are, but this is not family business,' said Feather. 'It's business business. Now off you go.'

Marion gave a pout, and reluctantly went off with Vera.

'How long's she been here?' asked Abigail as the three sat down.

'A week,' said Feather, lowering his voice and adding with a sigh, 'It feels longer. Now, what have you got for me to pass on to Armstrong?'

'Bruin and Patterson, the previous watchmen at Tussauds, have turned up,' said Daniel.

Feather looked at them, stunned. 'Dead?'

'No, very much alive. It appears they've been staying on a barge on the Lee Navigation canal by Hackney Marsh. They were hired by a man called Michaels to go and live on board and keep an eye on the cargo, and all at short notice. But now this man Michaels seems to have vanished, so they went back to ask John Tussaud if their old jobs were still open, and it was then they learnt about the murders of Dudgeon and Bagshot.'

'So they say,' commented Feather suspiciously.

'If they already knew, I can't see them returning to the museum, can you?'

'No,' agreed Feather reluctantly. 'All right, let's say they didn't know that murder was in mind, but they surely must have got suspicious about being asked to leave at such short notice.'

'Money, John. And a really good business opportunity. That's what they were sold.'

'So this Michaels character conned them into leaving so he could put Dudgeon and Bagshot in.'

Daniel and Abigail nodded.

'That's the way it looks to us,' said Abigail.

'But why?'

'Daniel has a theory,' said Abigail.

Feather looked enquiringly at Daniel, who outlined his thoughts: 'Two men, former engineers with the army, who worked as tunnellers digging the Gasworks Tunnel out of King's Cross station, but for the last three years they've been working as general navvies. Which is heavy work. They take a job as nightwatchmen at a museum that's just two doors away from a bank. Doesn't that strike you as suspicious in view of what you said about the series of bank robberies?'

'Those robberies were the result of the crooks breaking through from the cellar next door, not two doors away,' countered Feather. Then he looked thoughtful. 'However, if the place between the bank and the museum has got a cellar . . .'

'It hasn't,' said Daniel. 'I checked. It's solid earth.'

'In that case they couldn't do it,' said Feather.

'They're engineers and one of them was recently a tunneller,' insisted Daniel.

'Is there any sign of the wall of the cellar in the museum having been broken in any way? Any signs of tunnelling?' asked Feather.

'No,' admitted Daniel. 'But that doesn't mean they weren't intending to. And so far we've only been able to make a surface examination of the cellar walls.'

Feather shook his head. 'You're clutching at straws, Daniel.'

'That's what I said,' put in Abigail.

'And if that was the case, why would someone want to kill them?' asked Feather. 'And in such weird ways?'

'I don't know,' sighed Daniel. 'But I said before, the way they died suggests whoever did it was sending a message to someone.'

'What message? And to who?'

'I don't know,' admitted Daniel again. 'It could be a warning.'

'A warning about what?'

'Say Dudgeon and Bagshot were demanding a bigger share of the money from the man behind the job? This man, Michaels. So he kills them, or has them killed.'

'But why in this bizarre fashion?'

'Say this Michaels uses different people each time for the bank robberies.'

'But the museum isn't next door to a bank, it's two doors away, through solid earth.'

'That's right, and because Michaels knows that the police will be on to their way of working, breaking in from a cellar next

156

door, he decides to hire some tunnellers who can tunnel their way through from further away. When they start demanding a bigger share he has them killed to send a message to the other crews he's got working for him that that's what will happen to them if they get difficult.'

Feather shook his head. 'I can see where you're coming from, but there's no evidence to back any of this up. If there was any evidence of tunnelling in the museum, I'd take this to Armstrong. But there isn't. You said so yourself. The best thing we can do is find this bloke, Michaels. He's the only one who knows what the game's about now Dudgeon and Bagshot are dead.

'What I'll do is pass on to Armstrong about Bruin and Patterson turning up, and the fact they were hired by this character Michaels to leave the museum and go and live on the barge. With Jarrett looking for Michaels, he might even find him. If he does, I'll let you know.'

'Thanks, John. Oh, and there's one other thing. A thirteen-year-old apprentice from Morton's of London Wax Museum has disappeared. His name's Thomas Tandry. I think there could be a connection with the body of Walter Bagshot mysteriously turning up at Tussauds encased in wax.'

Feather stared at him, bewildered. 'A thirteen-year-old boy? What on earth makes you think he could be involved?'

'The fact that he's vanished.'

'Thirteen-year-old boys vanish all the time. And thirteen-year-old girls. You know that, Daniel.'

'Yes, but it's the wax connection that gets to me.'

Feather shook his head. 'Just like the tunnellers, I think

in this case you're letting your imagination run away with you.'

'I'd still like to find him.'

'I'd like to find everyone who gets reported missing, but it's all about resources. You know that. At the moment our priority is these bank robberies, and for Jarrett it's the murders at Tussauds.' He gave a heavy sigh. 'I'll mention about this missing boy to Inspector Jarrett and maybe he'll look into it.'

'He won't,' said Daniel.

'All I can do is tell him about it,' said Feather. 'What's the boy's name again?'

'Thomas Tandry. Thirteen years old. An apprentice wax modeller at Morton's of London Wax Museum.' He gave Feather the boy's address at the lodging house. 'He disappeared from there the same day he vanished from Morton's.'

'I'll pass that on,' said Feather, folding the piece of paper and putting it in his pocket.

'Thanks, John,' said Daniel. 'Oh, and there's one more thing.'

'More?' echoed Feather, in mock indignation.

'When Bruin and Patterson told me about Michaels, the name Gerald Carr was mentioned,' said Daniel.

'In what way?' Feather frowned, suddenly alert.

'It seems that Bruin and Patterson owed Carr money. Michaels said he'd pay Carr what they owed if they left Tussauds for his job at short notice. So they did.'

'Very wise,' said Feather. He frowned. 'But it doesn't sound like Carr to let them off so easily. Once he's got his hooks into someone he squeezes them. A nasty piece of work.'

'I know, and the same thought struck me. Could Carr be in it with this Michaels?'

'It's possible, but why would Michaels disappear?'

'Maybe Carr had a hand in that,' suggested Daniel. 'Say he found out that Michaels was double-crossing him in some way.'

'If he did, he'd be signing his death sentence,' said Feather. He lapsed into thought, then said, 'It would be wonderful if Carr was involved in some way. We've been after him for years and never managed to put him away.'

'Maybe. If there is something, Inspector Jarrett will uncover it and collar Carr,' said Daniel with a smile.

Feather laughed. 'And pigs might fly! Still, it's worth mentioning Carr's name just to have someone poking around in his business.'

'I'm thinking of doing that myself,' said Daniel. 'Just in case he's the power behind Michaels in whatever their game is.'

'Be careful, Daniel,' warned Feather. 'You're not in the police now, you don't have the backing of a uniformed squad. Gerald Carr is ruthless and if he feels you're a threat to him, he'll have no compunction about killing you.'

As Daniel and Abigail walked away from Feather's house, Abigail, concerned, asked, 'Is this man Carr really that dangerous?'

'Very,' said Daniel.

'Then I think you ought to be very careful in the way you approach him, from what John just said about him killing you.'

'Don't worry, I know Gerald Carr of old. I'll certainly be careful.'

'I'd also be careful of young Marion,' commented Abigail. 'That girl has her eyes on you.'

'Nonsense! She's just a child.'

'I saw the way she looked at you. And she's a child with a very developing woman's body,' said Abigail.

CHAPTER SIXTEEN

Septimus Morris, manager of the Belgravia branch of Billings Bank, checked the time by his watch as he neared the doors of his bank – 8.30 a.m. – and nodded with satisfaction as he saw the three members of his counter staff, Derek Wilson, Arthur Crum and Margaret Bannister, standing waiting. Good staff. Punctual. Courteous to the customers, well-turned out, a credit to the bank, and to himself.

'Good morning,' he greeted them.

'Good morning, Mr Morris,' they chorused in return.

He took out his keys and used the two largest to open the security locks in the thick, strong front door, then walked in, his staff following. Wilson, Crum and Margaret immediately went to their stations behind the counter. Morris, for his part, first went into his office to hang up his overcoat before heading for the discreet door at the back of the bank that led down to the vault. He pressed the switch, and smiled proudly at the fact that his branch was one of the first to have the new form of lighting – electricity – as opposed to the old-fashioned gas mantles. He walked down the stone steps to the basement room and approached the wall of iron bars that led to the safes and cupboards with private materials stored on behalf of the bank's important clients.

He stopped in his tracks as shock washed over him. Through the bars he could see that the cupboards had been forced open; the drawers and compartments inside just splintered wood. The shelves where the metal boxes containing the precious bank notes had been stacked were now empty. Morris stumbled to the iron bars and could feel himself choking with rising panic. The brick wall at the back of the inner vault had been partly demolished, piles of broken bricks lying around, and a gaping hole revealed the dark cellar beneath the premises next door.

Daniel and Abigail crossed the footbridge over the canal and walked along the towpath, checking the names of the barges moored along it.

'I'm puzzled,' said Abigail. 'Are there two River Lees here? I ask because I've seen a sign for the one we've just crossed and one for another River Lea, but spelt differently. L-E-A.'

'Yes, that's always caused confusion to people who don't know the area,' said Daniel. 'It's actually the same river. Its source is in Luton, which is how that town got its name. It was originally called Lea Town, and the river that began there was the River Lea. But where it had to be made navigable for boats, sections were turned into canals, and in those sections it was called the River Lee. This section, for example, is called Lee Navigation because it was built as a canal off the original river to flow down the west side of Hackney Marsh to the Thames. The original River Lea continued on its original course and flows down the east side of the marsh.'

'I still think it's very confusing,' said Abigail.

'The people who work on the river understand it,' said Daniel. 'Ah,' he said as he spotted the *Mary-Jane*. 'We're here.' Loudly, he shouted, 'Ahoy, *Mary-Jane*!'

'Ahoy?' said Abigail, with a quizzical look at him.

A stocky bearded man appeared from the door of the barge's cabin and regarded them warily.

'Good morning,' said Daniel. 'My name is Daniel Wilson and this is my partner, Miss Abigail Fenton. We're private enquiry agents who've been hired by Madame Tussauds waxwork museum to look into some recent events there.'

'What events?' asked the man suspiciously.

'Two murders, and we believe they may be connected to the man who recently rented your barge and called himself either Michaels or Stafford.'

The man regarded them with even greater suspicion and shook his head. 'I don't know nothing about any murders and I ain't getting involved. So you can sling your hook.'

Daniel nodded. 'I understand. In that case we'll tell Scotland Yard that you have no wish to talk to us, and they'll take over, which will mean you being taken in for questioning and your barge impounded.'

The man stared at him. 'Scotland Yard?'

'For some years I was a detective at Scotland Yard, and we're working with them on this case. Inspector Jarrett and Superintendent Armstrong. They'll confirm who we are when they come to take you in for questioning and remove your barge for examination.' He paused. 'Or we can talk now, informally, and leave it at that.'

'No police?'

'There'll be no need as far as we're concerned,' said Daniel.

The man scowled. 'All right. You'd better come aboard.'

Daniel and Abigail walked up the narrow gangplank and joined the man on the deck of the barge, following him through the door and down a short flight of stairs to the cabin below. It was small but neat and tidy with two bunks, one on each side of the cabin with a table in between, fixed to the floor. There was a small, pot-bellied stove with a flue that went up and through the roof of the cabin. The man gestured for them to sit on one of the bunks, then took the other opposite.

'Wilson and Fenton?' he grunted.

'That's us,' said Daniel.

'Both of you are detectives?'

'We are,' said Abigail. 'Have you heard about the murders at Tussauds?'

The man shook his head. 'Who got done?'

'Two nightwatchmen,' said Daniel. 'You know our names. May we have yours?'

'Marshall,' said the man. 'Herbert Marshall.'

'Thank you, Mr Marshall. We're interested in the man

who rented the barge from you.'

'He said his name was Stafford.'

'Did he say why he wanted to rent it, and for how long?'

'He just said he needed somewhere to put a couple of his blokes up for a few weeks and he'd heard that I wouldn't be moving it for a month.'

'Where did he hear that from, did he say?'

Marshall shook his head. 'No, but he could have picked it up from asking around. Everyone knows everyone else's business on the canals. It's how we keep in touch if needed.'

'Can you describe Mr Stafford?' asked Abigail.

The word picture Marshall painted of Stafford was the same as that Bruin and Patterson had given for Michaels, right down to his suit of brown check material.

'Did he give any address where you could get hold of him, if you needed to?' asked Daniel.

'No,' said Marshall.

'You say that everyone knows everyone else's business in the canals,' said Abigail. 'I'm guessing that when he didn't turn up to pay you the money he owed you, you asked around about him?'

'I did,' said Marshall. 'No one knew who he was. But it was how I found out how he knew about my barge. He'd been asking around if anyone had a boat that might be available for rent, but staying moored here.'

'So, in short, you'd never seen him before, and you have no idea where he could be got hold of.'

'That's right,' said Marshall. 'As long as he paid up, I wasn't interested in what he was up to.'

'He might have been planning something criminal with

your barge,' said Abigail. 'Or even planning to steal it.'

Marshall chuckled. 'You don't know canal people. The only way to move this barge is by hitching a horse to it. If that had happened, word would have got to me. Or if something suspicious was going on. Us on the canal, we watch out for one another. But here was nothing, just those two blokes living here, causing no bother. Until Stafford didn't arrive with the money.'

'At which point you turfed them off.'

'I did.'

John Feather stood in Superintendent Armstrong's office and gave his report on that morning's discovery of the bank robbery at Billings Bank in Belgravia. 'Same method as the others. The bank vault broken into through the cellar in the next-door property, a chemist's shop.'

'No one saw or heard anything?' asked Armstrong.

'No,' said Feather. 'Apparently the chemist is closed for the morning every other day, only opens at noon. Today was one of those half-days.'

'Who knew he'd be closed this morning?' asked Armstrong.

'Anyone who can read,' said Feather. 'He's got a notice on his shop door with his opening hours.'

'Damn!' growled Armstrong. 'Why don't these people have nightwatchmen patrolling the premises?'

'We did send a letter out to every bank branch recommending them to do just that, sir, but it seems the attitude of so many of them is "It won't happen to us".'

'Anyone living nearby notice anything overnight? Unusual activity? Vehicles? They must have used a horse and carriage to transport the loot away.'

'I've got the local constables asking questions, but so far no one has reported seeing anything.'

'Do we know how much was taken?'

'The manager, a Mr Morris, is going through his ledgers to give me a final total. But he believes it could be as much as half a million pounds in cash.'

'Half a million!'

'It is Belgravia, sir. Apparently there was quite a bit lodged relating to some property transactions that were due to take place later today.'

'Inside information, do you think? One of the bank staff knowing there'd be a particular large amount of cash in the vault on that particular night?'

'It's always a possibility, sir, although Mr Morris swears to the loyalty and honesty of his staff.'

'He would, of course,' said Armstrong sourly. 'He's protecting himself. If it turned out that he'd employed someone who'd leaked bank details to the robbers, he'd be for the boot himself.'

'I've arranged to see the staff concerned later today, sir. If there is anything suspicious there, I'll find it.'

'I hope you do, Inspector. This is becoming a nightmare. God knows what the newspapers will make of it!'

'Yes, sir,' said Feather. He looked at his watch. 'I'd better get back there, sir, to talk to them. I just wanted to come and make my report to you first, in case questions are asked.'

'Of course bloody questions will be asked!' snarled Armstrong angrily. 'Those blood-suckers are on my back about it! Not just the press, the Bank of England, the government . . .' He subsided, then waved his hand at Feather. 'Off you go, Inspector. Let's hope that one of them turns out to be the rotten apple in the barrel.'

'Yes, sir,' said Feather. 'There's one more thing, before I go.'

'Yes?' asked Armstrong suspiciously.

'You remember your proposal for me to keep contact with Wilson and Fenton and winkle out if they get any leads about the Tussauds murders.'

'And?' asked Armstrong warily.

'They have, sir. They've located the two nightwatchmen who left at short notice, that led to the two dead watchmen taking the job. Donald Bruin and Steven Patterson.'

'So?'

'Wilson and Fenton believe the two men left at short notice as part of a conspiracy to get Dudgeon and Bagshot in.'

'What makes them think that?'

'Because Bagshot and Dudgeon lied about their reasons for leaving their previous jobs on the railway. Wilson believes they had been lined up to take the jobs at Tussauds.'

'For what reason?'

'Wilson isn't sure but he thinks it's to do with both Dudgeon and Bagshot having been in the army, in the Royal Engineers. Wilson was trying to find the watchmen they replaced because he thought they might throw light on the issue: namely, who persuaded them to quit so abruptly so that he could get Bagshot and Dudgeon in. It appears it was a man called Michaels.'

Armstrong frowned. 'It all sounds a bit complicated.'

'I agree, sir, but I thought I'd pass on what I heard, as you asked. You pointed out yourself, sir, that sometimes Wilson comes up with the goods with no apparent reason.'

Armstrong nodded thoughtfully. 'So in this case he thinks these two previous watchmen were involved?'

'Only incidentally, not as part of the conspiracy itself. At least, that's his opinion. He discovered that Bruin and Patterson were paid to leave at short notice and live on a barge on the Lee Navigation canal, ostensibly to take care of the barge's cargo by this man, Michaels. Michaels seems to be the man behind it. Currently, Bruin and Patterson are back at Madame Tussauds.'

Armstrong looked bewildered by this. 'What? Guilty men returning to the scene of the crime, do you think?'

'As I said, sir, Wilson doesn't seem to think Bruin and Patterson are guilty of anything except leaving at short notice. It seems they've returned to Tussauds and asked for their old jobs back. Do you want me to pass this on to Inspector Jarrett, or will you?'

'I will, Inspector,' said Armstrong firmly. 'We don't want too many people knowing how we're handling this. I'll get Jarrett to bring this Bruin and Patterson in and question them. Well done, Inspector. But remember, we'll keep this just between us.'

'Yes, sir. Wilson also seems to think that the murders – especially the sudden and mysterious reappearance of the dead body of Walter Bagshot – might be connected to the disappearance of a thirteen-year-old boy called Thomas Tandry.'

'What makes him think that?'

'Tandry was an apprentice wax worker at Morton's of London Wax Museum.'

'So? there must be loads of wax workers.'

'But this one's disappeared.' He gave the piece of paper with the boy's details to the Superintendent.

Armstrong looked at it, then said, 'I'll mention it to Jarrett. I'm sure it means nothing, but you never know when it comes to Wilson.'

'Thank you, sir. Do you still want me to keep in touch with him and Fenton?'

'Yes, I do! We're going to get the credit for this one, Inspector, not them.'

'Oh, there's another thing that Wilson mentioned. He thinks there might be a tie-up between this bloke Michaels and Gerald Carr.'

'Carr? That vicious snake! What evidence has Wilson got?'

'None, as far as I know. I think it's one of his intuitions. I just thought I'd mention it. If Carr was involved in these murders and he was done for it . . .'

'That would be a feather in our cap!' Armstrong beamed. 'I'll tell Jarrett to bring Carr in and grill him. See what he coughs up.'

CHAPTER SEVENTEEN

Daniel and Abigail crossed the busy thoroughfare that was Fleet Street, the home of London's newspapers, doing their best to avoid stepping in the piles of horse droppings that dotted the roadway.

'One of the problems with trying to cross any of the major roads in London on foot,' complained Abigail, 'is that you invariably end up with your shoes and the bottom of your dress caked in horse manure.'

'There used to be crossing sweepers,' said Daniel. 'Usually children, often orphans and waifs and strays who'd managed to make a broom by tying twigs to a stick and who'd clear the horse dung for you for a penny when crossing the road.'

'Why did they stop?' asked Abigail. 'I would have thought there was a fortune to be made at that job.'

'Because the amount of traffic increased to such a degree that it was deemed dangerous. Carriages, cabs, omnibuses, heavy wagons, all in a hurry. Some of the children got run over. Now sweepers go out at night and collect up the manure in carts, which they sell to people for growing their vegetables.' He looked up at the building in front of them, which bore a proud sign of metal letters announcing that this was the home of *The Telegraph*. They entered and at reception asked if Joe Dalton was available. Fortunately, he was, and a few moments later they were sitting at his desk in the main room, a large open hall with a high ceiling where the overriding smell was that of ink.

Dalton was a portly, jovial figure who'd grown a big, bushy beard since the last time Daniel and Abigail had seen him.

'What's with the beard?' asked Daniel. 'If it's a disguise to avoid being spotted by people who might be upset by what you write about them, it's a waste of time. The rest of you is very distinctive.'

Dalton chuckled. 'I'd always wanted to be a pirate,' he told them. 'This is my respectable version of that dream. Although it started when I realised how much time I spent shaving every morning, valuable time when I could be chasing stories. In this business the first one there gets the inside track.'

'The bank robberies,' said Abigail.

'At the moment,' said Dalton. 'But I can't imagine you're here about that. But the murders at Tussauds aren't my brief; that's Robert Peake's.'

'Yes, so we saw,' said Daniel. 'But we don't know Mr Peake.'

'I can introduce you,' offered Dalton. He looked around the large, bustling room, where everyone seemed to be engaged in different sorts of feverish activity. 'Though it looks like he's out at the moment.'

'Actually, it's more information about high society we're after,' said Daniel. 'You move in those circles.'

Dalton laughed. 'Hardly move in them. I'm tolerated because they can get their names in the paper.'

'We're trying to find a Caroline Duckworth.'

'Why?'

'We' want to talk to as many people as we can who are insiders in the wax business,' said Abigail. 'She used to work at Tussauds, and then at Greville's wax museum, and she's said to be quite good.'

'We believe she may have married someone with money,' added Daniel.

Dalton chuckled. 'You can say that again!'

'You know her?'

'She became Mrs Dixon. She married Charles Dixon, a very rich cove who had a big house in Lowndes Square in Belgravia. He died about three months ago. Heart attack. So Mrs Dixon is now a very rich widow.'

'Where did his money come from?'

'I'm guessing it must have been inherited. He didn't appear to work.' He looked at them quizzically. 'Is she a "person of interest", as Scotland Yard are fond of saying?'

'We're not considering her as a suspect, more as someone who might be able to suggest anyone she knows who might have a reason for what happened. Some kind of anti-Tussaud motive. Do you have her address?'

'Of course,' said Dalton, pulling a small box towards him. He flipped the top of the box open to reveal a load of cards. 'My contacts list,' he explained. 'Addresses of the rich and powerful.'

'Some burglar would pay a fortune for that box,' observed Daniel.

'Not really. Any reporter worth their salt has the same information.' He rifled through the cards until the found the one he wanted. 'Here we are. Mrs Caroline Dixon.' He wrote the address on a piece of paper and passed it to them. 'She's also well known for her charitable work. Organising social evenings to raise money for good causes.'

'What sort of good causes?' asked Abigail.

'Her main one is raising funds for the Nightingale Fund to train nurses.' He gave a smile of admiration. 'Wonderful woman.'

'Which one?' asked Abigail. 'Caroline Dixon or Florence Nightingale?'

'Both,' said Dalton. 'Nightingale is that very rare creature, a totally honest and good person. Did you know she was called Florence because she was born in Florence in Tuscany?'

'No,' said Daniel. 'So she's really Italian?'

'No, her parents are English, very well-connected with their own estate here, which is where she was brought up.'

'And Caroline Dixon?'

'The fact that she puts so much energy into raising funds for Nightingale says all there is to know about her character. Another excellent woman.'

'Interesting,' mused Daniel. 'We were told that she's money-grabbing.'

'If she is, she's doing it for a good cause,' said Dalton.

'Have you met her?' asked Abigail.

'I have,' said Dalton. 'I was invited to a soiree she was giving. Again, it was to raise funds for Nightingale's nurses. I think she hoped the publicity would lead to more of the upper classes opening their wallets and purses.'

'Did it?'

Dalton gave a smile of satisfaction. 'I believe it did. At least, I had a note of thanks from Mrs Dixon afterwards. As I say, a lovely and gracious lady.' He looked at the clock. 'Ah, a deadline approaches. I'm afraid I have to get back to the grindstone of wordery.'

Daniel and Abigail smiled and stood.

'Thank you, Joe, you've been very helpful,' said Daniel.

'Always happy to be of assistance,' said Dalton. 'And if you do get any information on the Tussaud murders, I'd be happy to pass it on to Robert.' He smiled. 'It would mean he'd owe me one.'

As Daniel and Abigail walked away from the *Telegraph* offices, Daniel observed thoughtfully, 'It's interesting that we have two very different opinions of Caroline Dixon. Both John Tussaud and Greville described her as money-grabbing and fiercely ambitious to be rich. But according to Joe, she's the exact opposite, a veritable philanthropist, giving it away.'

'Possibly that's because she was left a rich widow,' said Abigail. 'She achieved her ambition and now she's in a position to do something positive with that money.'

'Having money doesn't necessarily change people's characters,' said Daniel. 'Grabbing, acquisitive people often continue to be grabbing and acquisitive however much money they have.'

'But not always,' countered Abigail. 'There are many instances of people who've been poor and received a sudden windfall which they've shared with others who are less fortunate.'

'But those sort of people are often generous-natured to start with,' said Daniel.

'People can change,' insisted Abigail.

'I agree,' said Daniel. 'But this is such a massive about-turn. I think I'd like to meet with Mrs Dixon and see for myself.'

'*We'll* meet with her,' Abigail corrected him. 'I can see that you're already prejudiced against her. At least one of us will need to have an open mind.'

Superintendent Armstrong looked up from his desk as Inspector Jarrett entered and snapped smartly to attention.

'I'm here to report developments, sir,' he said crisply. 'I believe we may have a suspect in the Tussaud killings.'

'Good news, Inspector. Who is it?'

'Mr Louis Tussaud, sir. Younger brother of John Tussaud. My reasoning is that whoever did that with Bagshot's body, putting it in wax, has got to be practised at the wax business.'

'There's more than one wax museum in London other than Tussauds,' pointed out Armstrong. 'Lots of people working in wax.'

'Yes, sir. But why pick on Tussauds? Louis Tussaud was part of the family business at the Marylebone Road museum, before he got edged out by his brother. Reason for resentment there I feel, sir.'

'Possibly, but murder's a severe reaction if it's just resentment about being pushed out.'

'True, but after he left he set up his own waxworks, which shortly after was burnt to the ground. Although there was no evidence to suggest that John Tussaud, or anyone at Tussauds, was responsible for the fire, Louis Tussaud must have suspected it and let that suspicion fester, gradually building up to a desire for revenge, hence the murders.'

Armstrong looked doubtful. 'It's possible, Inspector,' he said carefully.

'It's the only one that fits, sir,' said Jarrett. 'I've discovered that he fled to Blackpool, so I've telegraphed to there for him to be apprehended and brought back to Scotland Yard to be questioned. I've detailed Sergeant Pick to bring him back.'

Armstrong nodded thoughtfully.

'Good work, Inspector,' he said. 'But there's another line of enquiry it might be worth you looking into. It appears that the two men who worked at Tussauds as watchmen before Dudgeon and Bagshot, a Donald Bruin and a Steven Patterson, have turned up at Marylebone Road. There's a suggestion that they might have been part of a conspiracy to get Dudgeon and Bagshot in as watchmen, a conspiracy that involved a man called Harry Michaels, and also Gerald Carr, someone – as you know – we've never been able to nail for anything.'

'Where did that suggestion come from, sir? About the conspiracy?' asked Jarrett.

'One of the informers out on the street heard it and passed it to the local beat constable in Somers Town,' lied Armstrong.

'Right, sir,' said Jarrett. 'I'll bring Bruin and Patterson in and talk to them while I'm waiting for Louis Tussaud to arrive.'

'And Carr,' said Armstrong firmly. 'If we can put him

inside that will be a big feather in our cap. If he's involved, let's nail him. Oh, and someone mentioned something that might be associated with the Tussaud murders.' He handed the piece of paper with Thomas's details on it to Jarrett. 'Apparently some boy who was an apprentice at Morton's of London Wax Museum has disappeared. There was talk that he might have been involved in encasing the dead body of Bagshot in wax.'

'Talk from who, sir?' asked Jarrett, looking at the details on the piece of paper.

'Some un-named source.' Armstrong shrugged. 'Someone with an axe to grind, I suspect, who just wants to stir up trouble. I leave it to you to look into, Inspector.'

John Feather sat in the bank manager's office chair that was usually occupied by Septimus Morris and regarded Arthur Crum as the bank clerk entered and sat in the chair on the other side of the desk. Crum was nervous and edgy, Feather noticed. Derek Wilson and Margaret Bannister had been upset at what had happened, Bannister to the point of tears at what would happen to them as a result of the bank robbery, but there was something about Crum that was different to the other two clerks. He was on the defensive even as he sat down.

'I've got just a few questions for you, to make sure I've covered everything,' said Feather, adopting a sympathetic tone to see if it would make Crum feel at ease. It didn't.

'I don't know anything,' Crum blurted out. 'Just what Mr Morris told us.'

'You didn't go down and look at the vault?'

Crum swallowed, then nodded. 'Yes. We all went because Mr Morris shouted and called for us to come and look. It was terrible.'

'Indeed,' said Feather sympathetically. 'You must have been quite shaken up by it.'

'More than just a bit,' said Crum defensively. 'It could have happened when we were here! At work during the day!'

'What makes you say that, Mr Crum?' asked Feather.

'Well, isn't that when most bank robberies happen? When banks are open?'

'Not this kind of robbery,' said Feather. 'Haven't you seen about the recent spate of bank robberies carried out this way?'

'No,' said Crum.

'It was in the newspapers.'

'I don't read the newspapers,' said Crum.

'But your colleagues do,' said Feather. 'Both Mr Wilson and Miss Bannister said they'd read about the recent bank robberies being carried out this way, at night, through the next-door cellar. Didn't they mention it to you?'

'Not that I can recall.'

'That seems strange. After all, you all work at one of the most prestigious branches of this bank, here in Belgravia, I would have thought it would have entered the conversation at some point.'

'We don't have time for casual conversation,' said Crum primly. 'We're too busy.'

'I understand.' Feather nodded. 'It was just I was sure that Miss Bannister and Mr Wilson said they'd mentioned it to you because they were quite nervous about the prospect of it happening here.'

Crum hesitated, then said nervously, 'Perhaps they did, but – as I said – I can't recall it. To be honest, I don't have a lot to do with my colleagues. We discuss work, and that's about it.'

'I would have thought discussion of these bank robberies would have constituted talk about work. After all, you all knew that the shop next door has a cellar adjacent to your bank's vault . . .'

'I didn't know that!' said Crum quickly. Too quickly, thought Feather.

'So you don't have much to do with your colleagues outside of work?' asked Feather.

'No,' said Crum.

'What do you do?' asked Feather. 'Outside of work?'

'I don't understand the question,' said Crum, bewildered.

'Who are your friends and acquaintances? Family? Are you married?'

'I don't see what enquiring about my private life has to do with this robbery,' Crum rebuked Feather sternly.

'I'm just trying to get the whole picture, Mr Crum,' said Feather. 'I'm asking the same questions of everyone.'

'Well, I'm afraid I shan't be answering those sorts of questions,' said Crum stiffly. 'My personal life is my affair and has nothing to do with what happened here. Now, I would like to leave. I have work to do.' And he rose to his feet.

'Yes, of course,' said Feather politely. 'But I hope you'll reconsider when we talk again.'

'Talk again?' asked Crum, and now his concern was apparent. 'Why would we talk again?'

'Because we have not yet apprehended the people who committed this crime,' said Feather. 'Someone knows something, and it's my job to identify who, and what they know.' He gave Crum a smile. 'And who they might have talked to.'

CHAPTER EIGHTEEN

Lowndes Square consisted of a large central garden, planted with a variety of exotic blooms, bounded by a terrace of grand houses in stucco and white, fronted with Romanesque pillars, along with another imposing series of buildings, equally grand, that had been built as apartment blocks.

'It looks as if Mrs Dixon has definitely achieved her ambition,' said Daniel as they approached the address they'd been given by Joe Dalton.

He tugged at the bell pull and they heard the sonorous chimes from inside the house. The door was opened by a butler formally dressed in a long frock coat over a striped waistcoat. The butler peered at them, an imperious, almost disdainful look on his face.

'Good day,' said Daniel. 'My name is Daniel Wilson and this is my partner, Miss Abigail Fenton. We wonder if it would possible to see Mrs Caroline Dixon.'

'Mrs Dixon does not see anyone without an appointment,' said the butler coldly. He then added, equally coldly, 'And she does not make appointments with people she does not know except in exceptional circumstances.'

'I understand,' said Daniel politely. 'We would like to make an appointment, and these are exceptional circumstances. Perhaps you'd inform Mrs Dixon that we are not just casual callers – we are admirers of her work on behalf of the Nightingale Fund and were given her address by Mr Joe Dalton from *The Telegraph*.'

The butler hesitated, then said, 'If you'd wait, I'll see what Mrs Dixon's instructions are.'

With that he closed the door on them.

'Well, her money hasn't made her a more welcoming person,' said Daniel sourly.

'Don't be judgemental,' said Abigail. 'The butler's job is to protect his mistress from unsolicited callers. He may not be representing her attitude, just his own.'

'I've usually found that servants reflect the characteristics of their employers,' said Daniel.

They waited, and a short while later the door opened again and the butler looked out at them.

'Mrs Dixon will see you,' he said, though his manner towards them was no less hostile.

'See?' whispered Abigail as they followed the butler along a luxuriously decorated corridor, hung with paintings by French masters.

'I reserve judgement,' Daniel whispered back.

The butler led them into a large drawing room, decorated in the French style with ornate plasterwork adorning the walls and ceiling and heroic statues placed around the room. Daniel was reminded more of a gallery in a museum than a place to live. Caroline Dixon was in her early fifties, a handsome woman dressed in clothes that stressed her wealth: a voluminous purple dress finished with white lace, and enough gold jewellery on her fingers and around her neck to feed a small nation for a year. She gestured at an Imperial-style chaise longue near to the gilt and floral armchair where she sat.

'Please, sit,' she said. Her tone, though polite, was reserved. As they sat she said, 'I understand you are here about the Nightingale Fund?'

'Er, not exactly, Mrs Dixon,' said Daniel. 'My name is Daniel Wilson and this is Miss Abigail Fenton. We've been hired by John Tussaud at Tussauds wax museum to investigate two tragic deaths that occurred there recently.'

She looked at them, a puzzled expression on her face. 'But you told my butler that Mr Dalton from the *Telegraph* had sent you.'

'Forgive my contradicting your butler, Mrs Dixon, my actual words were that we had been given your address by Mr Dalton. I quoted him, with his approval, to show that we are great admirers of you and your work. I have known Joe Dalton for many years, and I'm sure he would verify our good characters to you.'

She stood, studying them. 'I'm still not sure what the purpose of your visit is? Who exactly are you?'

Once again, Daniel gave her their names. 'For many years I was a detective at Scotland Yard working with Inspector Abberline. Miss Fenton is the renowned archaeologist and Egyptologist, known particularly for her work on the great pyramids of Egypt with Flinders Petrie.'

She gave a vague smile. 'I'm sorry, these names are unfamiliar to me. But do please tell me how I can help you?'

Briefly, Daniel related the circumstances of the two murders at the museum.

'How ghastly!' She shuddered. 'But, and I repeat again, I'm still not sure what I can contribute.'

'The second body was found encased in wax, which suggests that the person who did it may have had some experience working with wax. We understand that you once worked at Tussauds, and also at Greville's.'

'I beg your pardon!' Her sharp tone showed her anger. 'If you are daring to suggest that I—'

'No, no,' said Abigail hastily. 'Not at all. We have come for your advice as an expert. We are also talking to everyone we meet who works with wax or has worked with wax, to see if they can think of why anyone would want to carry out this campaign against Tussauds. To be honest, we're clutching at straws here.'

Dixon looked at her, then at Daniel, her expression cold as she told them, 'I've had nothing to do with the world of wax since I married my late husband. I'm glad to say that it is well behind me now and I can concentrate on my dedicated aim, which is to raise funds for the wonderful work that dear Miss Nightingale is doing to train nurses. And not just for this country, but for the world.' She picked up a small, golden bell from the small table beside her and rang it. 'And now, my butler will show you out. I would appreciate it if you do not trouble me again. If you do, you will not be received.'

As they walked away from the house, Daniel said, 'She's lying.'

'What makes you say that?' asked Abigail.

'I saw some copies of *The Telegraph* neatly bundled up awaiting disposal just inside a cupboard. She must have read about the murders, and about our role as the Museum Detectives.'

'Not necessarily,' said Abigail. 'Not everyone knows of us, Daniel.'

'A woman who used to be a sculptor in wax at Tussauds and who takes *The Telegraph*?' said Daniel. 'The headline of the story would be enough to make sure she reads it. In which case, she would be aware of who we are.' He frowned thoughtfully. 'Why would she lie?'

'There are plenty of people who take the newspapers but deliberately avoid the sensational stories,' insisted Abigail.

'I agree,' said Daniel. 'But there's still something there that doesn't ring true.'

'Look at it from her point of view,' continued Abigail. 'Previously she struggled to make a good living as an artist in wax. Her ambition was to make money. She achieved that by marrying a very rich man, and when he died she became a very rich widow. I doubt if she wants to be reminded of her previous life, so us coming to talk to her about her time working at Tussauds would be very uncomfortable for her. Something she doesn't want or need to be confronted with. Her image of herself is of a woman being a philanthropist,

186

providing financial help to the very admirable work that Florence Nightingale is doing.'

'You may be right,' admitted Daniel. 'But I still feel there's something not right here.'

'Your copper's nose?' Abigail smiled.

He gave a rueful grin. 'Old habits die hard.'

Jarrett scowled as he read the telegram from the Blackpool police informing him that *Tussaud gone abroad. Said to be on Continent.*

'Doesn't that strike you as even more suspicious, Sergeant?' said Jarrett, passing the telegram to Sergeant Pick.

'I suppose it does, sir,' said Pick. 'But these arty types are always going off to the Continent.'

'I don't believe in coincidences,' grunted Jarrett. 'In the meantime, let's go and bring in these two watchmen from Tussauds, Bruin and Stevenson, and see what they've got to say. And at the same time we'll have Gerald Carr brought in.'

'Gerald Carr?' said Pick warily. 'He's a nasty character, sir. I doubt he'll come easy.'

'Then we'll bring him in wearing shackles,' growled Jarrett. 'And, if he resists, we'll bounce a truncheon or two off him.'

'He's got a gang who protect him,' said Pick, still cautious.

'We've got a gang as well, Sergeant. It's called the police force. If they put up a fight they'll get one, as well as finding themselves charged with resisting arrest.' He smiled. 'We'll see how Mr Gerald Carr likes that. But first, let's go and bring in these watchmen.'

Gerald Carr sat in the first-floor room that doubled as his living space and the office he ran his business from. Or, as he viewed it, his empire. He was a short, stocky man with a round, almost babyish face, accentuated by the fact he was virtually bald, just a few long strands of hair going from side to side on the top of his scalp. The baby-face image vanished as soon as one saw his eyes. The eyelids were hooded and the eyes beneath were black and malevolent, reminiscent of a cobra's and just as menacingly calculating.

The room was spartan, with very little in the way of decoration. A desk, a few wooden chairs, wooden filing cabinets and a long couch that doubled as a bed. The only adornment was a bust of Napoleon on Carr's desk. The Emperor Napoleon was Carr's hero, the figure he'd decided to model himself on when he set out to rule. This yard in Somers Town was his base, his headquarters, his fortress. From his quarters on the first floor he looked out on the yard, with various buildings forming three sides of a square and two tall wooden gates directly opposite his quarters in the fourth wall, which were locked and barred at night, making his fortress impregnable. It needed to be. Like his hero, Gerald Carr had enemies who'd like nothing better than to see him dead. Fortunately, as a result of ruling his empire by fear and physical pain, very few dared to make attempts on him. And, in case anyone tried, he had his faithful bodyguards in the barn beneath his quarters keeping watch. He had thought of having dogs patrol the yard, but he'd heard incidents of some savage dogs turning on their masters. And what was the use in having a guard dog if it wasn't savage? So instead he had bodyguards, working on a rota in pairs from the moment the tall gates opened early in the morning to when they closed in the evening. Now and then, if Carr felt the need to entertain a female acquaintance, the bodyguards stayed until it was time for her to go.

It was a system that had kept him safe for years, strengthened every time someone tried to cheat him and received their due punishment as an example to others. Or if they refused a request or an offer of business. Like Nat Jackley, who'd initially rejected his offer of letting him buy his money-lending business. Jackley said the price offered was too low. Carr had Jackley brought into one of his barns and his bare feet placed on a coal brazier, the flames peeling off his skin as he howled and screamed. When Carr finally let his men haul Jackley's feet out of the burning coals, he told Jackley that the price of his refusal to cooperate, which had put Carr to unnecessary work in arranging the brazier, was that the price offered for his business would now be one penny. Any further refusals and the rest of his body would be subject to the hot coals; first his feet and legs, then his hands and arms.

Now Jackley hobbled around on two crutches on the rare occasions when he left home.

If you're going to build an empire, someone has to suffer: that was Carr's credo.

A movement in the yard below caught his eye. One of his minions, Foxy Wood, had come in through the gates and was making for the wooden stairs that led to Carr's quarters. One of Carr's bodyguards stepped forward, shotgun at the ready, and stopped Foxy. That was one of Carr's rules. Even if you know them, stop them and ask them what they want.

Otherwise, one day someone who might be thought of as a friend could well stroll in and attack him. Foxy opened his jacket at the bodyguard's orders and let himself be searched for weapons. When all was clear he was allowed to continue on his way.

Carr sat and waited for Foxy to appear. 'This is unexpected, Foxy. Do you have news of anything out there?'

'Out there' was everywhere beyond the yard in Somers Town and Carr had a network of people who kept their eyes and ears open with orders to report anything of interest to him. Power came from knowledge, especially knowledge about people.

'I do,' said Foxy. 'I saw something interesting today, Mr Carr.'

'Go on?'

'You know that Mrs Dixon? The one with the big house in Lowndes Square?'

Carr nodded.

'Well, I was watching it, like you told me, and you'll never guess who went in to see her.'

'Who?'

'Them couple they call the Museum Detectives. You know, that bloke who used to be on Abberline's squad, Daniel Wilson, before he went private. And that woman, Fenton.'

'Abigail Fenton,' said Carr.

'That's her.'

'And they were let in?'

Foxy nodded. 'And they were in there for a while. Long enough to chat, anyway.'

'What happened after?'

'I dunno, Mr Carr. They just left. I stayed where I was, watching the house.'

'Did the Dixon woman come out afterwards and go off anywhere?'

Foxy shook his head. 'No. No one come out.'

Carr looked thoughtful. 'That's not good,' he said at last.

'What do you want done, Mr Carr?'

'Let me think about it.' He produced a silver coin, which he slid across the desk towards Foxy, who picked it up with a grateful nod, and then left.

So, the Museum Detectives and Mrs Dixon. This needed to be dealt with before it became bigger than it should.

The Lady sat at her workbench, delicately applying paint to the wax head on its stand. This was the part she most enjoyed, adding the flesh tones that were so realistic the head seemed to come to life. This was what she had learnt at Tussauds, the technique handed down through generations: the tints on the cheekbones and the ears, the shadows beneath the eyebrows, the gradation of darkness into the nostrils so that they seemed be inhaling air. Lesser wax artists simply used a general dark brown inside the cavities, but the colouring techniques she'd learnt from her days at Tussauds made her work – like this head – live, the personality of the original shining through.

There was a gentle tap at the door of her studio, and at her call of 'Come!' Ralph, her prime henchman, entered.

'Pardon me for interrupting, my lady,' he said, 'but we've located Harry Michaels.'

'Where?' she asked.

'He's hiding out in Wembley.'

She stopped her work with the delicate paintbrush and nodded. 'Excellent,' she said. 'Bring him to me.'

John Feather's visit to the small terraced house in Camden Town where Fred Calley lived found the injured police inspector sitting on a wooden chair, his right leg in plaster from ankle to the knee, propped up on a wooden stool in his small backyard, which housed the handful of chickens that kept him and his family provided with eggs.

'John!' Calley beamed. 'Good to see you! Fancy a cup of tea? Or I've got a beer.'

'Tea would be nice,' said Feather.

'Betty!' called Calley. When his wife appeared from the scullery he said, 'Can you put the kettle on for a brew, please, dear?'

Betty nodded and disappeared back into the house.

'Poor Betty,' sighed Calley. 'She has to do everything since I've been laid up with me leg. Bring the coal in. Chop the wood for the fire. Look after the chickens. All the things I used to do, as well as her own.'

Feather looked at the four brown hens that scratched at a small patch of earth next to the small knocked-together hut where they roosted at night.

'How is the leg?' he asked.

'It itches,' said Calley. 'The doc says that shows it's getting better.' He indicated for Feather to sit on the upturned beer crate beside him, and asked, 'So, how are you getting on with the bank jobs? I hear there was another one last night.' He grinned. 'I keep up with what's happening. The local beat copper usually drops in late morning for a cuppa and to catch me up with what's going on. He told me about the Belgravia hit.'

'That's what I wanted to talk to you about. There were three you investigated before you broke your leg.'

'That's right.' Calley nodded.

'Did any of them involve the bank having especially large sums of money in the vault the night they were done? I'm asking because it seems the Belgravia one had a sizeable amount in, more than it usually might have had.'

Calley frowned thoughtfully. 'Actually, I asked that very question at the first one that got done, but after they said no, I didn't ask the next two. You're thinking that someone inside the bank knew there'd be extra cash?'

'It's just a thought,' said Feather. 'I've got some suspicions about one of the bank clerks. He was particularly nervous and edgy when I talked to him and started asking questions.'

'Seems like he might be worth hauling in, being given a proper going over. Questions only, of course. I didn't mean . . .'

'I know you didn't, Fred.' Feather smiled. 'Beating a confession out of someone has never been your style nor mine.'

'A pity the same can't be said of all of our colleagues.'

'Tea!' announced Betty, appearing with two mugs. She looked at Feather and grinned. 'I'm glad you're here, John. It's what he needs. Someone to talk to about policing.'

As she withdrew back to the house and Feather took a sip from his cup, he noticed that Calley seemed preoccupied.

'You've just thought of something, Fred?'

'I have,' said Calley. 'It was you saying about that edgy, nervous bank clerk. When I was talking to the clerks after the third robbery, at the Mayfair branch of Paget's Mercantile, there was one of them who struck me as being a bit edgy. If I hadn't

193

had the accident, I'd have gone back to have another word with him, but breaking my leg like I did put everything else out of my head.'

'Who was he?' asked Feather. 'This clerk?'

'Derek Parminter,' said Calley. 'The name still sticks because of that feeling I had that something wasn't right about him. He gave all the right answers to my questions, but there was something about his manner. Shifty.'

'Derek Parminter at Paget's Mercantile.' Feather nodded. 'Thanks, Fred. I'll have a word with him, along with the one I had my doubts about at Billings.'

Inspector Jarrett sat glowering at the two men sitting opposite his desk: Donald Bruin and Steven Patterson. Sergeant Pick sat at one side, his notebook open in front of him, pencil poised, although the inspector had told him not to bother with actually taking any notes. 'The sight of the notebook, knowing that everything they say will be taken down in writing, will be enough to intimidate them.'

'Say they notice I'm not writing?' asked Pick.

'Pretend,' said Jarrett. 'Just wiggle your pencil about.'

The two men looked intimidated enough, just by being dragged into Scotland Yard.

'Tell me why you came back to Tussauds museum,' said Jarrett.

'We already told that other bloke,' said Bruin. 'That other detective.'

'What other detective?' demanded Jarrett.

'Wilson something,' said Bruin.

'Daniel Wilson?'

Patterson nodded.

Damn Wilson! thought Jarrett irritably. Aloud, he said, 'Daniel Wilson is not a proper detective.'

'He said he was,' said Patterson.

'No, he said he was a private detective,' corrected Bruin. 'Hired by Mr Tussaud.'

'Oh yes, that's right,' said Patterson.

'Tell me why you came back to Tussauds,' repeated Jarrett.

'Because we got kicked off the boat,' said Bruin. 'We had nowhere to live, no work and no money. We thought that Mr Tussaud might take us back. And he did.'

'Why did you leave there in the first place?'

Once again, just as they'd done with Daniel, the two men told their tale: the offer of the job from Michaels, and Michaels paying the money they owed Gerald Carr.

'So was this bloke Michaels working for Carr?'

'I don't think so,' said Bruin. 'All we saw was him paying Carr the money we owed him.'

'Because he wanted you to look after his barge.'

'That's right,' said Bruin.

'Only it turned out it wasn't his barge,' said Patterson. 'He was only renting it from this other bloke, the one who really owned it. And Michaels had told this bloke his name was Stafford, not Michaels.'

'Didn't that strike you as suspicious?' asked Jarrett.

'Only once he'd told us about it, but that wasn't until after he told us to get off his boat.'

'And you'd never met the two blokes who took over from you as nightwatchmen at Tussauds? Eric Dudgeon and Walter Bagshot.'

Both men shook their heads.

'We didn't know anything about them, until Mr Tussaud told us they'd been murdered.'

'At the museum!' added Patterson, horrified. 'That could have been us!'

'Did you ever meet Louis Tussaud?'

The two men exchanged puzzled looks, then Patterson asked, 'Who?'

'Mr John Tussaud's younger brother.'

'No,' said Bruin. 'The only one of the family we met was Mr John. He was the boss.'

'Did John Tussaud ever mention his brother?'

'No,' said Bruin. 'At least, not to us. But then we never saw that much of him. He was there during the day, and we were there at night.'

'Tell me about this bloke Michaels,' said Jarrett. 'What did he look like?'

As they had done with Daniel, the two men gave the inspector a description of Michaels, and this time Jarrett gestured to Pick to make notes of what they said.

'And you'd never seen him before he approached you in the pub?'

'No.'

Finally, after going over the same topics two or three times, and receiving the same answers from the two men each time, Jarrett reluctantly admitted to himself that they were a dead end. They'd just been pawns in someone else's game, and that game seemed to have been played by Michaels – now disappeared – and Gerald Carr.

'All right, you may go,' he told them. 'But for the moment.

I may well want to talk to you again.'

He gestured for Pick to conduct them down to reception and out of the building, then sat in brooding silence, weighing up the facts as they were known so far. Two dead men and a man behind the plot gone missing. But what was the plot?

Sergeant Pick returned and looked at him questioningly.

'What do you think, sir?' he asked. 'Think they had anything to do with the murders?'

'No,' grunted Jarrett sourly.

Pick suddenly spotted the piece of paper with Thomas Tandry's details on it on the desk, and he picked it up.

'Is this something, guv?' he asked. 'I see it mentions wax.'

Jarrett looked at it, then shook his head. 'Some runaway kid. Whoever's reported him missing is using the Tussaud murders to try and get us looking for him by claiming he might be involved.'

'Involved in what way, sir?'

'He was an apprentice at one of the wax museums.'

'Tussauds?'

'No, not Tussauds, otherwise we'd obviously be looking into it,' snorted Jarrett irritably. 'One of the other backstreet places where the figures look nothing like who they're supposed to be. Like I say, it's someone using this wax business to get us looking for him. If we go down that road we'll be spending all our time looking for everyone who's vanished just because they once worked in the wax trade. Candlemakers, and Lord alone knows who else.'

On Daniel and Abigail's return to their home in Camden Town they found an envelope waiting on their doormat addressed to

Miss Abigail Fenton in an ornate script.

'An educated hand,' commented Daniel.

Abigail opened it. 'Well done, Detective,' she said. 'It's from Mr Conan Doyle.' She scanned it, then announced, 'He invites me to have lunch with him at the Langham Hotel tomorrow to discuss the expedition.' She shook her head. 'He's being pushy. I still haven't told him I'll definitely be going.'

'I get the impression that being pushy is a core part of his character,' commented Daniel. 'It's what makes him who he is, and why he's been so successful.'

She looked at him, concerned.

'Are you still of the same mind about me going?' she asked, worried.

'Yes,' said Daniel. 'I love you and will miss you, but I'll be coming out to see you. As I've said before, this is the opportunity of a lifetime. To lead an expedition of your own.'

'It'll be Conan Doyle's expedition,' she said. 'He's putting up the money for it.'

'But he won't be the leader,' said Daniel. 'The expeditions to Hawara you went on with Flinders Petrie were funded by Jesse Haworth, but they were known as the Petrie expeditions, not Haworth.' He took her in his arms and looked earnestly into her eyes. 'I know you love me, I never doubt that, but this is something that you have to do, for the other half of you that is Abigail Fenton. The world-renowned archaeologist.'

'I'm not world-renowned,' she corrected him.

'You will be after this,' said Daniel.

Police Constable Charlie Gordon strolled down Lower Regent Street towards Piccadilly Circus. It was one in the morning. Many of his colleagues didn't like walking the beat in the middle of the night, but for Charlie, this part of London was different from most other beats. For one thing there was far less traffic; you could cross the road far more safely than during the day, when the horse-drawn vehicles packed the streets and there was always the danger of a horse getting spooked and kicking out. And unlike other areas, here there were always people around in the early hours. Not as many as during the day, but still, they were around. Most of them he knew by sight. They were the Night People, prostitutes who served in the local brothels, of which there were many, or used a darkened alley for a quick service. Gamblers who frequented the late-night gambling clubs in Soho. Actors and theatre staff heading home after a stint at one of the many theatres in the area. Waifs and strays who took refuge in shop doorways. It was one of these waifs and strays, a small boy he only knew as Arch, who ran towards him as he neared the Circus.

'Mr Gordon!' shouted Arch. 'There's a bloke who looks dead down by Eros.'

'Dead? Don't you mean dead drunk?' asked Gordon.

The little boy shook his head. 'I know drunks. They stink of drink. This bloke don't.'

Gordon quickened his step and hurried towards the fountain and the statue of Eros, bow and arrow in the god's outstretched arms, that topped it. As Arch had reported, a man was sitting on the pavement at the base of the fountain, his eyes and mouth open, and he seemed to be staring fixedly at something on the other side of the road. Automatically, Gordon shot a look in that direction.

Greville's wax museum, now closed for the night, its windows and doorway dark. He turned his attention back to the man, checking for a pulse. None. The man was definitely dead, and looked as if he'd been dead for a while. Gordon saw that there was something white inside the man's open mouth. Puzzled, he tentatively pushed the tip of his finger into the man's mouth and his finger poked against some chalk-like powdery substance. He took his finger out examined the white powder now staining the end of his finger.

'What's that, Mr Gordon?' asked Arch.

'I'm not sure,' said Gordon. 'I'll need to get it checked. But it looks to me like this bloke's had plaster of Paris stuffed down his throat.'

CHAPTER NINETEEN

Inspector Jarrett and Sergeant Pick stood in the mortuary in the basement of Scotland Yard, watching as Donald Bruin and Steven Patterson studied the dead body of the man laid out on the mortuary table.

'Well?' demanded Jarrett.

Bruin turned to him and nodded. 'Yes, that's him,' he said. 'That's Mr Michaels, the bloke we told you about yesterday. What's happened to him?'

'We'll know when the medico has a chance to get to work on him,' said Jarrett. 'Is there any more you can tell me about him?'

'Nothing more than we told you yesterday,' said Bruin.

Jarrett nodded. 'Very well,' he said. 'You can go. We know where you are if we need you.' He turned to Pick.

'Sergeant, please escort them out.'

As Pick left the room with Bruin and Patterson, Jarrett turned back to look at the corpse. Plaster of Paris poured down the bloke's throat then left to harden, suffocating him, the medic reckoned, though he'd know more once he opened him up.

As soon as Jarrett had arrived for work that morning, he'd been told about the dead body that had been discovered by Eros in Piccadilly Circus. The sight of the dead man tallied with the description the two watchmen had given of Michaels when he'd brought them in for questioning the previous day. He'd sent Pick to bring them back in and now had confirmation. Michaels, the man who'd set up the scam in order to get Dudgeon and Bagshot into the wax museum, was also now dead. But why plaster of Paris?

He'd decided yesterday, after quizzing Bruin and Patterson, that the men had had no involvement in the killings of Dudgeon and Bagshot. They'd also been open in telling him the whole story of how they ended up on the barge on the River Lee Navigation canal, the part that their debt to Gerald Carr had played in it, and their rescue from having their fingers chopped off, by the intervention of this Michaels bloke, the same one who was now dead on a mortuary table. Jarrett was certain they'd had nothing to do with bumping off Michaels and dumping his body in Piccadilly Circus, because last night they'd both been at their job at Tussauds, keeping watch on the museum, as verified by Tussaud himself, the cleaners, and the local beat copper who'd stopped to chat to them through an open window.

* * *

Daniel left Abigail to sort through her notes on her previous trips to Egypt to prepare for her lunch meeting with Doyle and returned to the offices of *The Telegraph* in the hope of catching Joe Dalton. He was lucky, Joe was there, but just about to leave.

'A dead body's been dumped at the base of Eros in Piccadilly Circus,' Dalton told him. 'I'm on my way to see Inspector Jarrett at Scotland Yard.'

'Is this to do with the bank robberies?' asked Daniel.

'I don't think so,' said Dalton. 'If the gossip I hear is right, it's more likely to be this bloke you were talking about who's involved in the Tussauds business. This Michaels character.'

'Michaels!' exclaimed Daniel. 'Can I come with you?'

'Only as far as the front door of the Yard.' Dalton smiled. 'I'm told you're barred.'

'I am, but I need to talk to you, so we can talk on the way. And, after you've seen Jarrett, maybe I can buy you a coffee?'

'Okay, but not at Freddy's,' said Dalton. 'It won't do my reputation at the Yard any good to be seen associating with you.' As he headed for the exit with Daniel following, he asked, 'What did you do to upset Superintendent Armstrong so deeply that he bars you from the Yard? I remember it wasn't that long ago you saved his life.'

'Armstrong sees me and Abigail as competition. Not helped by you and your colleagues in the press praising us and comparing us favourably with Armstrong and Scotland Yard.'

'The purpose of the press is to hold the establishment to account,' said Dalton.

'I thought it was to report news,' said Daniel.

'There's that as well,' agreed Dalton. 'I shouldn't worry, Daniel. You've been here before with Armstrong. He gets upset and then it blows over. So, what did you want to talk to me about?'

'We went to see Caroline Dixon yesterday.'

'Ah! Great woman.'

'So you said, but she threw us out and told us not to come bothering her again.'

'You must have said something to upset her.'

'We did when we asked if she could throw any light on who might have been involved in what happened at Tussauds.'

'You asked her that?'

'We've been asking everyone involved in the wax business – or wax *artistry*, which is the preference of Maurice Greville – to try to make sense of what happened.'

'She wouldn't like that,' said Dalton.

'She didn't. As I said, she asked us to leave.'

'It's because that life is behind her now. In the past, and she doesn't like to be reminded of it.'

'That's what Abigail said.'

'And Abigail is right. You have to understand that Mrs Dixon has re-invented herself. She's no longer a menial worker in wax, but someone who is bringing about a revolution in health standards in this country with her support for the Nightingale Fund. And not just in this country; the Nightingale Fund is training nurses across the world.'

'Tell me about the fund,' said Daniel.

'I assume you already know about Florence Nightingale's work.'

'I know about what she did in Crimea,' said Daniel. 'The Lady with the Lamp. Saving the lives of soldiers.'

'The really important stuff came later as a result of her experiences in Crimea,' said Dalton. 'Especially her emphasis on hygiene and nutrition. Did you know that the improvements Nightingale made in the military hospitals in the Crimea reduced the death rate from forty-two per cent to just two per cent?'

'No,' admitted Daniel.

'Nightingale identified the cause of most deaths to be the result of poor or non-existent hygiene, bad nutrition, stale air, and the overworking of soldiers. During her first winter at Scutari in Turkey, four thousand soldiers died there, and ten times more died from illnesses such as typhus, cholera and dysentery than from battle wounds. She was so appalled by the conditions at the military hospitals that she persuaded the British government to get none other than the great Isambard Kingdom Brunel himself to design a prefabricated hospital that could be built in Britain and transported to the war zone. That first hospital at Renkioi had a death rate of less than one tenth of the death rate at Scutari.'

'Impressive!' said Daniel.

'The key to her work was having properly trained nurses who were aware that hygiene and nutrition were the keys to recovery of patients. When she first went to the Crimea in 1854 she took with her thirty-eight women volunteer nurses that she'd trained herself. It was those nurses that kept people alive, and Nightingale reasoned that if this could be done in times of war it could also achieve the same result in times of peace. As result, the Nightingale Fund was set up to train nurses, and when people realised the importance of the work she was doing, money poured in. In 1860 the fund had raised enough money – £45,000 – to set up the Nightingale Training School at St Thomas' Hospital, and those first trained nurses went out across the nation to establish her nursing principles in hospitals, including: Cumberland, Liverpool, Edinburgh. Trained nurses went abroad to spread the word. America's first nurse, Linda Richards, was trained by Nightingale and went on to develop nursing schools across the United States.'

'I've never heard you so eloquent,' said Daniel. 'You sound like one of those religious converts you see on soapboxes at Hyde Park Corner.'

Dalton glared at Daniel.

'I am proud to spread the word of what Nightingale has done,' he said sharply. 'Not just for soldiers but for the whole population. Her emphasis on hygiene forced the government to introduce mains drainage, which saved the lives of hundreds of thousands of ordinary people. Millions, in fact, when these same issues were addressed across the world. It's that which will be her legacy, not just being known as the Lady with the Lamp.'

'I've offended you,' said Daniel. 'For which I apologise. I meant no disrespect, Joe.'

Dalton nodded. 'I'm sorry if I seemed sharp with you, but I believe in what she's doing, and those who are supporting her, like Caroline Dixon.'

Feather, accompanied by Sergeant Cribbens, returned to Billings Bank to find it very busy with customers, all of whom seemed happy to queue and wait for one of the counter positions to be free. There seemed to be no sense of impatience to be served; instead there appeared to be quite a lot of intense whispered gossip going on in the queues.

'Any bets that most people are here just so they can say to their neighbours and friends they went to the bank that had been robbed,' Feather muttered to Cribbens.

'Rubberneckers.' Cribbens scowled in disapproval. 'You get the same when there's been a fatal accident, everyone turns up to gawp at where it happened.'

They made their way through the crowd to the manager's office and knocked at the glass in the door. There was a pause before the door opened, during which time they heard the sound of keys being turned in locks and bolts being slid into place.

'Shutting the stable door after the horse has bolted,' murmured Feather.

The door opened and the anxious face of Septimus Morris peered out, the anxiety gave way to relief when he saw who his visitors were.

'Inspector,' he said. 'Please, come in.'

'Thank you, sir. This is my sergeant, Sergeant Cribbens, who'll be working with me on the investigation into the events that took place here.'

Morris nodded a brief greeting to the sergeant, then concentrated his attention on Feather. 'Do you have any news, Inspector?'

'Not yet, sir, but we are following definite lines of enquiry.'

'What lines?'

'At this moment, it's too early to say. But I'd like to talk to Mr Crum again, if I may, to clarify one of two things.'

Morris's face showed unhappiness as he said, 'I'm afraid Mr Crum is no longer available.'

Feather regarded him, puzzled.

'What do you mean?' he asked. 'Has he left the bank?'

Morris shook his head, then lowered his voice to almost a whisper as he said, 'Mr Crum drowned last night. He was found in the Regent's Canal. Reports suggest he was . . . intoxicated.'

'Drunk?'

'If you prefer, yes. I don't understand it; when he applied for employment here he stressed that he was a teetotaller to impress us with his personal responsibility.'

'Which police station dealt with the incident?'

'Camden Town in Parkway. They were the ones who called to advise us of the tragedy. Everyone here is terribly upset, especially in view of . . . what happened.'

'Yes, I understand,' said Feather sympathetically. 'Do you have his address? I'd quite like to talk to his family.'

'He lived with his widowed sister, a Mrs Pugh,' said Morris. 'I believe the police from Camden Town have already advised her of his tragic demise.'

'Thank you,' said Feather as Morris opened a drawer for Crum's details and wrote down his sister's address. 'Did Mr Crum show any signs of disturbance since the – er – event here yesterday? Was there any sign that he might try to take his own life?'

'No, absolutely not,' said Morris. 'He was upset by what had happened, but we all were.'

'Thank you, Mr Morris,' said Feather, taking the address from him. 'I'll report back to you when we have any information.'

As he and Cribbens left the bank, Feather said, 'Well, Sergeant, what do you make of that?'

'You said he was on edge when you talked to him,' said Cribbens.

'I did.'

'And defensive.'

'He was.' Feather nodded.

'Sounds like guilt to me, sir. What do you think? He topped himself?'

'Or someone helped him on his way,' said Feather. 'Let's see what Camden Town nick have got on it, and then we'll see what his sister has to say.'

Daniel was sitting in an Italian coffee house a short distance from Scotland Yard – one further away from the building than Freddy's and not so frequented by the local police, when Joe Dalton joined him.

'It's Michaels, sure enough,' confirmed Dalton, sitting down. He turned and gestured to the woman behind the bar, who smiled and nodded as she set to work preparing a coffee for him, her easy manner proving to Daniel that this was an establishment at which Dalton was a regular.

'Why are you here, covering this, instead of Robert Peake?' asked Daniel. 'I thought he was doing the Tussauds story and you were writing about the bank robberies.'

'I'm doing both at the moment,' said Dalton. 'Peake's ill with a bad cold. He wanted to come in, but I told my editor we couldn't have him in or the whole office could catch it. That's one of the things I learnt from writing about Nightingale. Hygiene and prevention.'

'So what did Jarrett tell you?'

'It seems that Michaels was killed by someone pouring plaster of Paris down his throat and letting him choke to death.'

'Plaster of Paris?' echoed Daniel, bewildered. 'That's a new one for me. I've never heard of anyone being killed that way before.'

'Nor me,' said Dalton.

'Did Jarrett have any information on Michaels? There's some confusion as to if that was his name. I met someone who did business with him who told me he said his name was Stafford.'

Dalton shook his head. 'What else have you got on this Michaels character? Or Stafford?'

'I believe he was tied up with a local crook called Gerald Carr.'

'Gerald Carr?' said Dalton with a shudder.

'You've heard of him?'

'Everyone's heard of him,' said Dalton.

'But I've never seen anything about him in the pages of the newspapers.'

'That's because they value their fingers too much.'

'Ah, you've heard about that,' said Daniel. 'Have you ever met him?'

'No, and I've no wish to. You?'

Daniel nodded. 'When I worked at Scotland Yard. Abberline pulled him in on suspicion of murder. We had to let him go. He had an alibi with plenty of witnesses, plus someone else turned up who said they did it.'

'A fall guy?'

'Definitely. We were fairly sure that Carr threatened his wife and family to make him come in and confess.'

'What happened to the man? Was he convicted?'

'No, he was killed in prison while he was on remand awaiting trial.'

'Carr?'

'That's what we all suspected, but we couldn't prove anything.'

'He sounds like the sort of character who eliminates people who could land him in trouble if they opened their mouths.'

'That's about the size of it,' said Daniel.

'D'you think he's the one who did Michaels? And the two watchmen at Tussauds?'

'Michaels, possibly, if Carr thought he was cheating him. But why the two watchmen?'

'Because they knew too much.'

Daniel shook his head. 'It doesn't make sense, Joe. The two watchmen were involved in something with Michaels, some criminal undertaking, but whatever they were up to never came to fruition. It was unfinished business, by all accounts. So why kill them before it was all done and dusted?'

CHAPTER TWENTY

Daniel sat in the office of Isobel Morton, owner of Morton's of London Wax Museum and gave her an apologetic smile.

'I'm very sorry to trouble you again, Mrs Morton,' he said, 'but I'm intrigued by this business of young Thomas Tandry.'

Isobel Morton, a tall, statuesque woman in her sixties with coiffured hair dyed a shade of purple, looked back at him, her expression equally concerned. 'I've been worried about him ever since he vanished,' she said. 'I've reported his disappearance to the police, but they don't seem unduly concerned. They say they'll look into it, but they also tell me that many young boys of his age vanish, as if that explains it. I've told them that he wasn't that kind of boy.

He'd never done anything like that before.'

'How long has he been with you?'

'Four years,' said Morton. 'We took him on when he was nine, and that's why I can't believe he disappeared of his own accord. He had less than a year to do to complete his apprenticeship, and I'd already told him he had a job here with us at Morton's. There was no reason for him to vanish.'

'Had here been any disagreements between him and any other members of your staff lately?'

'No, absolutely not. If there had been I'd have known about it. We are very close here, almost like a family. He's grown up with us. Yes, Thomas was ambitious, but to the best of my knowledge no one at any other establishment that works in wax had approached him about working for them. And if they had, I'd have known about it. The world of wax is a very small world, Mr Wilson.'

Inspector Feather and Sergeant Cribbens stood at the reception desk just inside the door of Camden police station and listened to the duty sergeant as he related the events of the previous night.

'Eight o'clock it was when the local beat copper was alerted to the fact that there was a man floating in the canal. He pulled the man out with the help of passer-by, but the bloke was a goner. Luckily he had a wallet in his pocket with his name and address in it, so we were able to find out who he was. Most time when bodies are pulled out of the canal there's no knowing who they are. And if they've been there for a day or two it's even harder to identify them. The head swells up and they get bloated—'

'Yes,' interrupted Feather with a genial smile. 'I've seen a few in my time. Not pleasant.'

'Arthur Crum, his name was. But you know that already.'

'Yes, the bank told us,' said Feather. 'They also said he was drunk.'

'Indeed he was. I don't know how much he'd put away, but he reeked of it.'

'What did his sister say when she was told? Did she give any idea of why he might have wanted to do away with himself?'

'No. I didn't see her myself, but the copper who did told me she was in a state of shock when he told her. She couldn't believe it. Insisted he was a teetotaller, never drank alcohol of any sort.'

'Never drank alcohol of any sort,' mused Feather as they walked away from the station.

'They all say that,' said Cribbens. 'My neighbour says he signed the pledge and he never touches a drop, but at least once a month I find him lying drunk outside his front door. "It's the devil," he said to me once as I picked him up. "It gets inside a bottle and calls to me."'

Arthur Crum's sister, Mrs Esmerelda Pugh, lived at Chalk Farm, a brisk stroll from Camden Town police station, and she was still in a state of shock and distress when Feather and Cribbens arrived at her house in a small terrace in one of the back streets.

'I don't understand it!' she said, and she dabbed at her tears with her handkerchief. 'What was Arthur doing by the canal? He hated the canal. Said it smelt bad and had all sorts of things in it. He was very fastidious, was Arthur. Very particular about things like that. Cleanliness.'

'And you say he was a teetotaller?'

'He was. And strict about it! He loathed alcohol. Said it muddled the mind. But the policeman who came to tell me the news said he was drunk as anything. Too drunk to walk properly, he said, that's what they thought had happened. He was so drunk that when he was walking beside the canal he fell in. But that's wrong on so many counts. He never drank. And he'd never have been walking beside the canal.'

'Pardon me for asking, Mrs Pugh, but had anything happened lately to unsettle him?'

'Only the bank robbery, that made him very upset. Not so much the robbery but the fact he was questioned by the police. He said the inspector who quizzed him was rough in his manner, aggressive and nasty.'

'So the fact he was questioned may have unsettled him enough to—'

'No!' she said quickly. 'If you're thinking he did it deliberately, you're wrong. Arthur would never do something like that. He always said that life is God's gift to us, and those who take their own life are committing one of the biggest sins against almighty God that a man can do, for which they would burn in hell for all eternity.' She wiped her eyes again. 'Arthur had very strong opinions about lots of things.'

'Had anything changed for him lately?' asked Feather.

'In what way?'

'Well, had he recently come into money, for example.'

For the first time, she looked awkward. 'Well, now you

come to mention it, it did seem to me that he had more money than he usually had. Not lots, but enough to buy me a little treat now and then. Nothing special or big, just some chocolates. He knows – knew – I like chocolates, but as a widow I haven't got the money to waste on fripperies. Not that he didn't pay his way. He did. He was very good like that, was Arthur.'

'When did this happen? The chocolates?'

'About two weeks ago. And then, last week, he bought me a handkerchief. A lovely one it was. Lovely material with edging.' She gave a thoughtful frown. 'To be honest, I wondered what had brought this on. Really, Arthur was a rather frugal person, not given to fancy things.' She hesitated, then said, 'I wondered whether he hadn't met some woman and that's what had changed him. Softened him, so to speak.'

'Did he talk about this woman?'

'Oh no. And I might be wrong. But it's just that . . . well, he seemed different. And then once, when he came home from somewhere – and he didn't say where he'd been – I could have sworn there was an aroma of perfume on him.'

'What sort of perfume?' asked Feather. 'Cheap perfume? Expensive?'

'Oh, very expensive!' said Mrs Pugh. 'That's why it struck me. And it made me wonder if Arthur hadn't got involved with someone who was above his station. You know, that maybe he was out of his depth. And maybe that's what happened to make him . . . do something so out of character. That whatever and whoever this woman was, that somehow it had gone wrong.'

* * *

Daniel stood in the kitchen of Mrs Wicksteed's house as she prepared a stew.

'I make sure that all my charges are well fed,' she said. 'I give them porridge for breakfast and a good hot meal when they come home.'

'How many lodgers do you have?' asked Daniel.

She looked at him with disapproval.

'I don't speak of them as lodgers,' she told him. 'They are my guests. The one thing I stipulate is that they are in employment. I have five with me at the moment, since Thomas disappeared.' She shook her head in disbelief. 'I still can't get my head round that. He was always so steady. As all my charges are. In answer to your question, I usually have six at a time: three girls and three boys. I have two rooms, very clean, and they share a bed, three boys in one, the three girls in the other.'

'And have there been any issues between Thomas and any of the others lately? Rows? Disagreements, that sort of thing.'

'No,' she said firmly. 'The thing is, Mr Wilson, that these children are either orphans, or ones whose parents can't look after them. If it wasn't for me taking them in they'd be in the workhouse or on the streets. They know that and they're grateful. If any of them ever does anything like have a tantrum – which happens very, very rarely – I remind them of that fact, and the awful fate that awaits them if I have to ask them to leave.'

'Yes, I see,' said Daniel.

'It's a system that works,' said Mrs Wicksteed.

'And the children pay you for their rent and keep from their wages?'

'They do. Although it's barely enough to cover the costs, so the local church contributes, on the understanding that the children attend services on Sunday.'

'On the day that Thomas disappeared, was there anything unusual about him? Anything that suggested he was planning to run away?'

'Absolutely not. He had his porridge as usual, then he set off to walk to work. He's normally home by five o'clock. When he hadn't arrived by half past five I sent one of the others to Morton's wax museum to see if anything had happened to him. If he'd been taken ill, or something. When the child came back – Stanley Hopkiss it was – he had Mrs Morton with him, who was most disturbed when she heard that Thomas hadn't arrived home.'

'Yes, I've spoken to Mrs Morton and she told me how worried she was about him,' said Daniel. 'She told me she'd reported his disappearance to the police.'

'Who have done nothing in response,' said Mrs Wicksteed, again with heavy disapproval.

'What do you think has happened to him?' asked Daniel.

'I have no idea,' she said. 'The only thing I can think of is that someone's abducted him. It does happen to children, you know. Especially those who look young. And Thomas did look young, being particularly small for his age.'

Inside the dining room at the Langham Hotel, Abigail supped her French onion soup, while Doyle tucked into his starter of partridge with pears, elaborating on the proposed expedition to the sun temple in between bites.

'I'm curious if we might find much there,' he said. 'You

know, ancient artefacts. Will there be any for us?'

'I think that's quite likely. There are quite a few different opinions about how long Niuserre reigned for, with some saying it was for over thirty years, while others believe he was only on the throne for perhaps ten. My own feeling is to opt for the longer period based on the number of pyramids he built: three for himself and his queens, plus a further three for his father, mother and brother, all of them in the necropolis at Abusir. He also built the largest surviving temple to the sun god Ra. If you consider that in addition he completed the Sun Temple of Userkaf in Abu Ghurob and the valley temple of Menkaure in Giza, all of this will have taken many years, it indicates towards the longer reign.'

'Has there been much work done on the sun temple already?'

'Only relatively superficial examinations. Do you know about the work of Karl Lepsius?'

'No,' said Doyle. 'Is he important?'

'He's generally considered to be the greatest Egyptologist.'

'Then he's the man for us!' exclaimed Doyle. 'How can we contact him?'

Abigail smiled. 'Through a medium, if you believe in that kind of thing. Lepsius died in 1884.'

'Ah,' said Doyle.

'He and his team spent three years from 1842 exploring most of the pyramid sites of Egypt. It's only now, after his death, that his very detailed notes are going to be published, with the first volume due to appear next year.'

'But he visited Abu Ghurob?'

'He did. In his work he listed the pyramid that Niuserre

built for one of his queens, or possibly the queen of his brother, Neferefre, something that's still being debated, as pyramid number twenty-four. Another rather unusual construction, which looks like two pyramids squashed together, and is on the south-eastern edge of the necropolis is known as Lepsius XXV.'

'But did he explore the sun temple?'

'As I mentioned earlier, there are two sun temples at the site. The one Niuserre built himself, and the one he completed which was begun by Userkaf. Both are dedicated to Ra. Am I right in thinking it's the god Ra that you're interested in?'

'It is indeed!' said Doyle. 'From what I've read of ancient Egyptian religion, Ra seems the most important.'

'Along with the sky god, Horus,' said Abigail. 'Often you'll find the two gods merged into one and called Ra-Horakhty. But I agree that Ra had prime of place, as befitted the god of the sun. The Egyptians believed that Ra ruled all parts of the created world, that he created every form of life, including humans.'

'And we might well find examples of his power inside the sun temple at Abu Ghurob,' said Doyle, his face lighting up with excitement at the thought.

'We might find examples that showed the Egyptians' *belief* in his powers,' said Abigail, her tone cautious.

'Tell me about the pyramids,' urged Doyle.

'What, exactly?' asked Abigail.

'Their restorative powers. That's what I was told they were for, not just as burial tombs to honour the pharaohs.'

'Yes, that's true,' said Abigail. 'That's what the ancient

Egyptians believed. You have to know that the Egyptians believed that the human form is made up of different components, the chief of which are the ka, which is seen as the life force, the ba, which is viewed as the soul, and the physical body. In death these become separated. The pyramid was seen as a cosmic machine which unites the parts which had become separated, and when these parts were unified an akh was the result, a being of light, a powerful living embodiment of the pharaoh in the afterlife as a god.'

'Rebirth,' said Doyle.

'Yes,' said Abigail. 'Although what I've given you is very much an abbreviated version of the process.'

'There has to be a reason for the tales told, especially about Ra,' said Doyle. 'Surely no belief system lasts for that many thousands of years unless it's based on something real.'

'Humans have the ability to ascribe supernatural events to many that are often explained by science,' countered Abigail. 'Your Sherlock Holmes stories often show that, when there is a crime committed and the only answer seems to be a supernatural agency at work, until your hero explains the concrete reality of what happened.'

'Pish to Holmes!' said Doyle dismissively. 'I'm saying that there might be more to these beliefs than just folk tales. There might be something real and tangible behind them.' He leant forward intently. 'I have been a member of the Society for Psychical Research for the last three years, and long before I joined I was aware of extraordinary events taking place that could not be explained in practical terms.

The dead do talk to us. I have experienced this myself at seances conducted under the strictest rules of observation. No trickery. Remember what Shakespeare said in *Hamlet*: "There are more things in heaven and earth, Horatio, than are dreamt of in your philosophy".' Who is to say the sceptics are right, or that modern mediums and the ancient Egyptians are wrong?'

Inspector Jarrett and Sergeant Pick made their way through Scotland Yard reception and then out through the back door to the rear courtyard, where the carriages, vans and horses were kept. They found the stable master, Bill Harris, polishing the lamps on one of the carriages.

'Ah, Harris!' said Jarrett imperiously. 'I want a van made ready.'

'Certainly, Inspector. How big?'

'Big enough to bring back at least half a dozen prisoners,' said Jarrett. He gave a wink and added with a smug smile, 'We're going after Gerald Carr.'

'Carr?' said Harris, impressed. 'If you want one with cells in you'll have to wait until one comes back in. They're all out at the moment.'

Jarrett shook his head. 'No, just one with benches in it will do. We'll have them handcuffed to the bars inside, so they won't cause any trouble.'

'I'll get one ready for you,' said Harris. 'Give me ten minutes to get the horses in and reined up.'

'We'll be back in ten minutes,' said Jarrett. He headed back to the main building, Sergeant Pick trailing along beside him. 'Right, go and pick two good uniformed men to come with us,' he said.

'Yes, sir,' said Pick. Then, warily, he added, 'Do you think that was wise, sir?'

'What was wise?' asked Jarrett.

'Telling Bill Harris where we were going. I've heard rumours that he earns backhanders from tipping off people if a raid's about to take place.'

'Nonsense!' snorted Jarrett. 'I've known Bill Harris for years. And one thing I've learnt, Sergeant, it does to impress the non-uniform staff with what we do. It makes them feel involved.'

'Yes, sir,' said Pick.

'Now go and fix up those uniforms.'

'Yes, sir,' said Pick.

Back at the vans, Bill Harris was scribbling a note on a piece of paper. As soon as he finished it, he nipped out the rear entrance to where the hansom cabs were lined up, waiting for custom. He spotted the driver he wanted at the rear of the queue and hurried over to him.

'Get to Gerald Carr's yard in Somers Town and give him this,' he said. 'Urgent.'

Daniel stood in the cellar at Madame Tussauds museum and looked around at the brick walls and the solid cement floor. His hopes of finding any clues as to what had happened to young Thomas Tandry were drying up, so he had returned to the museum. He was sure that this place held the key to the murder of Dudgeon and Bagshot. Despite what both Abigail and John Feather said, he felt in his bones it was to do with the fact that Michaels had arranged for them to work at Tussauds because they were tunnellers, and Tussauds was only two shops away from a bank. Yes, he and Abigail had examined the walls, but that had only been a superficial look; any proper investigation had been impossible because of the crates containing the surplus wax mannequins which were stored against the walls.

He left the cellar and made his way upstairs to Tussaud's office and found the museum manager at his desk.

'Mr Tussaud, I wonder if I can have your permission to examine the cellar here at the museum.'

'I thought you already had,' said Tussaud, puzzled.

'A surface examination only. With your permission I'd like some of the crates that are stacked against the walls moved away.'

'Why?'

'It's this business of Dudgeon and Bagshot being tunnellers. You know about the bank robberies that have been taking place?'

'Of course, but those have been where a bank is next to a cellar. The nearest bank to us is two shops apart, with solid earth between.'

'Exactly, sir. And tunnellers dig through solid earth.'

'Not that distance, surely.'

'Dudgeon and Bagshot worked on the Gasworks Tunnel just north of King's Cross station. That tunnel was 1,590 feet long. The distance from Tussauds to the bank is much shorter than that.'

'But surely it would take more than two men.'

'Not necessarily, sir. Yes, to dig a tunnel a railway train can pass through, but not for a man to crawl through.'

'But there'd be spoil from the digging,' pointed out Tussaud. 'How would they get rid of it?'

'I'm sure there are ways,' said Daniel. 'Please, Mr Tussaud, I may be wrong, but I need to know. I only need the crates moved away from the east wall.'

'Why that one?'

'Because it's the one that faces in the direction of the bank.'

'You feel it's a possibility?'

'I do,' said Daniel.

'Very well,' said Tussaud. 'I'll have those crates moved away from the wall. I'll detail two men to do it now.'

'Thank you,' said Daniel.

As he walked back down to the cellar, he thought ruefully: *If I'm wrong and there's nothing, I shall be thought of as an idiot. And if it gets back to Scotland Yard, I'll never live it down.*

Feather and Cribbens walked away from the Mayfair branch of Paget's Mercantile Bank, still taking in what they'd just been told by the manager about the tragic accident that had led to the death of Derek Parminter a week before.

'He seems he fell in the canal and sadly drowned,' the manager had told them.

'Which canal?' asked Feather.

'The Grand Union, the section that runs parallel to Royal College Street in Camden Town. Do you know it?'

'I do,' said Feather. 'Did Mr Parminter live in Camden Town?'

'No,' said the manager. 'He lived in Kentish Town. I don't know what he was doing in Camden Town. Visiting someone, I expect.'

225

'Do you have his last address?'

'I do,' said the manager.

'Did he have family?'

'I believe he was a bachelor who lived in lodgings.'

With that, the manager had checked his records and handed Feather an address in Kentish Town.

'So, Sergeant,' said Feather as they returned to the police van. 'What do you think of that? Two bank clerks, both fall into the canal, one at Regent's Park, the other in Camden Town.'

'I think it smacks a bit too much of a coincidence,' said Cribbens.

'So do I,' agreed Feather. 'Especially as both seemed very edgy when they were quizzed about the bank raids.'

'Think someone bumped them off, sir?'

'Unless clumsiness while walking along canal towpaths is a sudden popular new trend amongst blank clerks. We'll talk to Parminter's landlady and see what she has to tell us about him.'

Daniel looked at the bare east wall of the wax museum's cellar, fully exposed now the crates had been moved into the centre of the floor. Shutting the cellar door to cut out any external noise, he crouched down and began to knock against the brickwork, listening out for any change in the sound which would indicate a hollowness behind the bricks. Slowly, he worked his way along the length of the wall, tapping and listening. There was no change in tone.

Am I wrong? he asked himself in angry desperation. *Are Abigail and John right, that I'm clutching at straws over an obsession, chasing shadows?*

He stood up and looked at the bricks. They were smeared with the dirt of ages, as was the lime mortar between the bricks.

Would they need to start a tunnel from the floor level? wondered Daniel. It would be easier to open an entrance at about waist or chest height and then climb in.

Once more he worked along the length of the wall, this time at waist height, knocking against the bricks, listening hard. It was when he reached the middle of the wall that he heard a change of tone as he knocked, a sound slightly higher. Or was it his imagination? Wishful thinking?

He knocked again at the particular brick, listening intently. He was sure the tone was higher. He began to knock at the wall around the suspect brick, and soon felt he'd identified a patch of the wall which suggested a hollow behind it. He chose the centre of the patch and, taking a penknife from his pocket, began to scrape with it at the mortar, which started to crumble as he penetrated the surface. More digging saw the mortar fall away easily and he was able to pull out the brick. The mortar around the adjacent bricks was also loose, and soon he had five bricks out on the floor at his feet, exposing a hole. He pushed his hand into the hole. There was nothing there, no solid earth, just vacant space.

He pulled more bricks out, stopping when he exposed solid earth behind any of them, and soon he had revealed a large hole, big enough for a man to be able to climb into.

There were two candles lying just inside the hole, one of which was half burnt. Daniel lit it and held it into the hole, and saw that it was indeed the start of a tunnel which was already some way into the solid earth. The ceiling and sides of the tunnel were kept in place by slats of wood.

I was right! thought Daniel exultantly.

CHAPTER TWENTY-ONE

The police van drove through the gateway, past the tall wooden gates standing open, and pulled to a halt in the centre of the sprawling yard that was Gerald Carr's base of operations in Somers Town. The yard area was edged on two sides by barn-like wooden buildings, the doors of which were all shut. In the side furthest from the entrance gates was a two-storey brick building, stairs leading up from the yard to the top storey.

Telling the two uniformed constables to wait in the van, Jarrett and Sergeant Pick descended from it.

'You been here before, Sergeant?' asked Jarrett.

'No, sir,' said Pick.

'That top floor is where Carr lives.'

'It all looks pretty run-down and shabby,' commented Pick. 'The paint's flaking off all the woodwork, including the two main gates. And it all looks dirty.'

'Carr doesn't care what it looks like, or what people think of him,' said Jarrett. He gave a shout: 'Gerald Carr! We want to talk to you!'

There was a pause, then the door of one of the barns opened slightly and a man looked out.

'Here's someone I know,' grunted Jarrett. 'Foxy Wood! Come over here!'

Hesitantly, the door opened wider and a small, thin, rat-faced man sidled out.

'I nicked him five years ago,' muttered Jarrett. 'Robbery with violence. Never got it to stick, though. None of the witnesses were willing to talk.'

Foxy Wood approached them warily.

'Remember me, Foxy?' asked Jarrett.

The small man nodded sourly.

'We've come to talk to your boss.'

'Mr Carr isn't here,' said Foxy.

'Come off it, he's always here,' snorted Jarrett.

Foxy shook his head.

Jarrett frowned, puzzled. 'Where is he, then?'

'I don't know,' said Foxy.

Jarrett leant towards the smaller man, scowling. 'See here, Foxy, I don't take to being lied to. Gerald Carr never leaves here unless it's for something very important. He doesn't need to. He lives here, and anything he wants – or anyone – they come to him.'

'I'm telling you the truth, Inspector. I don't know where he is.

230

He told me he had to go somewhere, and he went.'

'When was this?'

'A couple of hours ago.'

'And where's everyone else? The rest of his mob?'

Foxy shrugged. 'Don't know. They weren't here when I arrived.'

Jarrett looked at the buildings around the yard. 'I think we'll take a look. Just in case he might've returned while your back was turned.'

'Help yourself,' said Foxy. 'But he ain't here.'

'We'll see,' said Jarrett. He called the two constables from inside the van. 'Constable Evans, you go with the sergeant and search the buildings on that side. Constable Butler, you come with me.'

As Jarrett and PC Butler headed for the ramshackle barns, Sergeant Pick had to bite his lip to stop from saying, *You might almost think Carr knew we were coming.*

Derek Parminter's landlady apologised to the two policemen. 'I'm very sorry, but I don't know anything about Mr Parminter's social life or his habits, or who his friends might have been. He was a good tenant. Never gave any trouble. Always on time with his rent. Kept to the rules of the house.'

'Which are?'

'No one of the opposite sex in lodgers' rooms.'

'How many lodgers do you have?'

'Three. Two men and a middle-aged lady. Mr Parminter was a bank clerk, Mr Ostred is a shipping clerk, and Miss Wimpole is a librarian. All very respectable.'

'Would it be possible to look at Mr Parminter's room?' asked Feather.

'It's not his room any longer,' said the landlady. 'I let it shortly after I heard the news about his death to Mr Pringle, an accounts clerk. My rooms are in high demand. Most of my lodgers stay with me for a long while.'

'How long was Mr Parminter with you?'

'Just over a year.' She gave them a puzzled look. 'I can't think why he ended up in the canal as he did. The police suggested he'd been drinking, or perhaps he'd been depressed, but I told them that nothing could be further from the truth. Mr Parminter was never the worse for alcohol in all the time he was here, and he never gave any sign of depression. The opposite, he was always cheerful.'

'Do you know what he might have been doing in Camden Town?'

'No. But then, as I said, I didn't enquire about his habits.'

'Do you know if there was woman in his life?' asked Feather. 'Anyone he'd started seeing not long before he died?'

'If there was, he certainly didn't bring her here,' she said, indignant at the suggestion.

Daniel and John Tussaud stood in front of the hole in the cellar wall. Tussaud look stunned.

'What does it mean?' he asked, bewildered.

'It means that Mr Dudgeon and Mr Bagshot were attempting to tunnel to the vault of the bank before they were killed.'

'Do you think that's why they were killed?'

'I do,' replied Daniel.

'But who by? Who would have known what they were up to?'

'A man called Michaels,' said Daniel. 'Did they ever mention him?'

'No. Who is he?'

'He's the man who persuaded Mr Bruin and Mr Patterson to leave at short notice. His body was recently discovered in Piccadilly Circus, not far from Greville's wax museum.'

'Greville's?' Tussaud looked even more perplexed. 'How do Greville's fit into this?'

'I must admit, I don't know,' admitted Daniel. 'But I'm hoping we might find out more once we share this latest information with Scotland Yard.'

'I shall send a note to Inspector Jarrett at once, informing him of this and requesting he come to see it.'

'Can I ask you to send your note to Inspector Feather,' said Daniel.

'I thought Inspector Jarrett was in charge of the case.'

'He is,' said Daniel. 'But Inspector Feather is in charge of investigating the recent bank robberies. He's the one we need to inform first, and we'll leave it to him to tell Inspector Jarrett. I think you'll find that's the proper protocol.'

Inwardly, Daniel was thinking, *And also because there's no need for Mr Tussaud to know we're currently barred from Scotland Yard.*

Daniel was standing in the lobby of the museum with John Tussaud when the messenger returned from Scotland Yard.

'Inspector Feather is out on an investigation,' he told them. 'I left your message for him.'

'In that case I'll leave you,' Daniel said to Tussaud. 'When Inspector Feather arrives, show him the tunnel in the cellar, and then ask him if he'd come to see me at my house.'

Daniel left the museum and had just begun to walk along Marylebone Road in the direction of Warren Street when his path was stopped by two men, one of them smiling broadly in a cheery greeting.

'Daniel Wilson?'

Daniel tensed, on his guard. There was something about the man that gave the lie to his apparent bonhomie, especially as his companion remained grim and unsmiling.

'Possibly,' he said.

The smiling man turned to his companion and chuckled. 'Possibly!' he laughed. 'What a card!' Then he turned back to Daniel, still smiling. 'We hear you're looking into these murders at Tussauds wax museum.'

'Do you,' said Daniel warily.

'We do. And we're here to tell you to stop.'

'For what reason?'

'For reason of your good health.' Then the smile disappeared from the man's face to be replaced by a look of menace. 'Or, more to the point, for the good health of your partner, Miss Fenton. It would be a great pity if a good-looking woman like that suffered something like a vitriol attack. Terrible stuff, vitriol. Burns the skin. Even worse if it gets in the eyes.'

Daniel glowered at the man.

'If you touch one hair of her head . . .' he snarled.

'We wasn't thinking of her head.' The man grinned lewdly.

Daniel suddenly launched himself at the man, determined to wipe that nasty smirk from his face, but he hadn't spotted the other man moving behind him, and he felt a thunderous blow to the side of his face that felled him to the pavement.

Momentarily addled, he was aware of the cosh being swung in front of his face, before it smacked onto his head.

'This is a warning from Gerald Carr,' he heard the man say. 'Forget about the wax business or else it'll be the worse for both of you. Especially for your lady friend.'

Abigail left the Langham Hotel and walked down Portland Place to Oxford Circus, making for a particular bookshop with a good stock of practical books on the pyramids of Egypt. If she was going to lead this expedition of Conan Doyle's – and she'd now decided that she would – then she wanted to find out everything that had been written about the temple of Ra at Abu Ghurob. It had become obvious during her conversation with Doyle that their ambitions for this expedition were different, Abigail's practical, while Doyle's interest was almost religious, in as far as the pagan religions of ancient Egypt were concerned. *I should have been aware of his interest in the supernatural when I read his Egyptian stories*, she told herself. Because her mind was full of their recent conversation she wasn't paying attention to the people crowding the pavement. In fact, she'd moved to walk along the kerb to avoid the crush, and she was shocked to feel a sudden push in her back that sent her stumbling forward into the road, right into the path of two heavy horses pulling a wagon, their massive metal-shod hooves rising up as they reacted to this sudden apparition, and then crashing down towards her . . .

CHAPTER TWENTY-TWO

Desperately, Abigail rolled out of the path of the two horses, and just in time, as the great hooves smashed onto the cobbles close by her head. Abigail pushed herself up as the wagon driver looked down at her, concern on his face as he held on to the reins to calm the horses.

'Are you all right?' he called.

Abigail looked down at herself, her long coat smeared with horse manure from the road.

'Someone pushed me!' she said to him, angry.

A crowd had gathered, men spilling into the road to see if she was all right and to offer their help.

'Thank you, but I'm fine,' Abigail told them. In truth, she wasn't. Her elbow hurt where it had hit the road, and she was furious at the fact that she was covered in horse dung. And most of all, she was angry that someone had pushed her into the road right in front of the oncoming heavy horses. She looked towards the people on the pavement, watching her anxiously. Was it one of them? If so, there was no expression of guilt or malicious triumph on any of the faces. Whoever did it had vanished. But who? And why?

She shook her head as hands were offered to lead her back to the pavement.

'Honestly, I'm fine,' she insisted, waving away the offers of assistance. 'I'm just shaken. Thank you.'

She stepped back to the pavement. There'd be no bookshop visits for her today. She needed to get home and clean herself.

John Feather worked his way backwards out of the hole in the cellar, his hand protected from the burning candle he held by a stout cloth wrapped round his fingers, and joined John Tussaud and Sergeant Cribbens.

'It's a tunnel right enough,' he said.

'How far does it go?' asked Tussaud.

'Without the aid of a measuring stick I can't be sure. We'll get someone in who can answer that question properly. But it's certainly quite a way in already. And properly constructed, with wooden sections at the sides supporting the roof slats.' He looked at Tussaud. 'There's no doubt in my mind they were heading towards the bank.'

'Yes, that's what Mr Wilson said.'

And I told him he was clutching at straws, thought Feather ruefully. *And not just me, Abigail said the same thing.*

'For the moment, Mr Tussaud, I suggest you move a couple of these crates back against the wall to block the entrance to the hole. I'll arrange for an engineer to come and investigate it properly, and then we can arrange for it to be filled in.'

'Yes please,' said Tussaud. He looked at the hole in wonder. 'To think this was going on the whole time and no one had any idea.'

Feather and Cribbens made their way out of the cellar and headed upstairs to the ground floor.

'Looks like Mr Wilson was right, sir,' said Cribbens.

'It does indeed,' said Feather. He looked at his watch. 'Right, that's us finished for the day. Head back to Scotland Yard in case there's any new messages about the bank robberies.'

'Right, sir. And if there are?'

'Bring them to me at Daniel Wilson's. You know his house?'

'I do.' Cribbens nodded. Then he looked doubtful. 'Is that wise, sir? Superintendent Armstrong says we're barred from having anything to do with him and Miss Fenton.'

Feather gave him a wink. 'I have a special dispensation from the superintendent. I'm allowed to call on him, providing no one else at the Yard knows about it. So, officially, you don't know. And, if you're asked, I just went home.'

'Yes, sir.' He gave Feather a puzzled look. 'It's all a bit odd, sir, if you don't mind my saying so.'

'I don't mind you saying so at all, Sergeant. In fact, that's my opinion as well. But ours is not to reason why, Sergeant. Ours is just to go through the motions. If I don't see you later, I'll see you in the morning at the Yard.'

Daniel stepped down from the hansom cab. He'd originally set out to walk home after being attacked, but his head ached. *If I'm going to collapse I'd rather do it in a cab than tumble down in the street*, he'd decided. The pain in his head from the blow had eased slightly by the time the cab pulled up outside his small terraced house in Camden Town. Luckily it had been a warning, not a murderous attack, although the end product seemed not much different to him. A glancing blow to his cheek followed by a harder one to the back of his head. He was lucky that he'd been told by a doctor that he had a particularly thick skull. And the blows, although hard enough to hurt, could have been worse.

He walked into the house and called, 'Abigail!'

'I'm out here!' came the shouted response.

Daniel walked through the kitchen, then the scullery, and into the small back yard, where he found Abigail with a pail of soapy water, sponging her long coat, which had been pegged to the washing line, but there was still the familiar aroma of horse manure.

'What's happened?' he asked.

Abigail had been weighing up what to tell Daniel all the way home. If she told him she'd been pushed into the road, he'd get overprotective of her. And, on reflection, she wondered if she hadn't leapt to the wrong conclusion. The pavement had been crowded. People were jostling to get through the crush.

'I fell into the road,' she said. 'Right into a pile of horse manure.' Suddenly her expression showed alarm as she saw the livid bruise on the side of his face. 'My God, what's happened to you?'

'I was attacked by two men, with a message for me from Gerald Carr,' said Daniel bitterly. 'Correction, a message for *us*. They threatened harm to you if we didn't stop looking into the murders at Tussauds.' He frowned as he regarded her inquisitively. 'You're sure you fell? I've never known you stumble before.'

Abigail hesitated, then admitted, 'It's possible I was pushed.'

'My God!' exclaimed Daniel.

'But it can't be the same people,' added Abigail quickly. 'You said they warned you what might happen to me if we didn't stop. They'd hardly launch an attack on me at the same time.'

'You don't know Gerald Carr,' said Daniel. 'He'd do it to drive his point home.' He looked at her earnestly as he said, 'You can't stay here. In London, that is. I think you ought to go to Cambridge and spend time with your sister, Bella.'

'No,' said Abigail firmly. 'I'm not leaving.'

'Why not?'

'Would you run away if the positions were reversed?'

'It's not running away. You're always saying you'd like to pick up your relationship with Bella. It's been almost three years since you last saw her.'

'Daniel, don't dissemble,' said Abigail sternly. 'We are partners. Whatever happens we face things together.'

'You don't know Gerald Carr. He's clever. For all his malevolence he's never been convicted of any offence. And he's absolutely ruthless. He thinks nothing of killing people if they pose a threat to him. There is a very real possibility that he's behind the murders at Tussauds, hence the warning to us to back off.'

'Do you think he's responsible for the murders?'

'I didn't before today. I thought it was a rival gang of bank robbers, but after this . . . I'm not so sure.'

'Go in and put the kettle on,' she said. 'I'll just finish cleaning my coat and then we can have a cup of tea and talk things over.'

'What is there to talk over?' demanded Daniel. 'You're in danger.'

'And from now on I'll be on my guard,' she told him.

'But . . .' Daniel started to protest.

'Put the kettle on,' repeated Abigail. 'I'm in desperate need for a cup of tea.'

Resignedly, Daniel entered the house and put the kettle on the kitchen range. *There's no arguing with Abigail*, he reflected ruefully. It was the same when they'd been in Manchester and her life had been threatened, but she'd refused to hide away. *All I can do is let John Feather know the danger, and between us we'll do our best to keep an eye on her.*

Abigail came in from the yard, wiping her hands, just as the kettle came to the boil and Daniel set about making tea.

'I found a tunnel at Tussauds,' he told her as he poured the boiling water into the pot.

She looked at him in bewilderment. 'A tunnel?'

'In the cellar. It's only partially made, but it definitely heads in the direction of the bank.'

Abigail sat down, stunned. 'So you were right.'

'I was,' said Daniel. 'But we still need to get it confirmed. I got John Tussaud to send a message to John Feather, telling him about it. John was out on his investigation, so I asked for him to come here after he's examined the tunnel so far.'

'So they were planning to rob the bank. Dudgeon and Bagshot, and Michaels.'

'Along with Gerald Carr, as I get the impression he was in partnership with Michaels.'

'So why would Carr want to kill Dudgeon, Bagshot and Michaels?' asked Abigail.

'I don't know,' said Daniel. 'That's what puzzles me. That's why, until I was attacked today, I didn't think of Carr as being responsible for the deaths.' He poured tea for them both, then asked, 'By the bye, with all that's gone on, I forgot to ask how your lunch went with Mr Doyle.'

She gave a wry smile. 'I think that he and I have different agendas about this expedition.'

'Oh? How so?'

'I think he's hoping to find confirmation for the supernatural aspects of Egyptian religions. You know, re-animation, for example. Life after death. Eternal life.'

'Surely not. Mr Doyle is one of the most practical people there is, and very down-to-earth. Look at his Sherlock Holmes stories: practical answers to apparently supernatural events.'

'But then you have to look at his other stories. The Egyptian ones. I think he's searching for something.'

'Something other-worldly?'

'I could be wrong, but that was the impression I got.'

'Will that affect the expedition you've been talking about, if you and he have different agendas?'

'No,' said Abigail. 'We might interpret what we find

differently, but that won't stop us gathering information and materials from the site. For me, any expedition must be approached with an open mind, and I hope that Mr Doyle feels the same.'

There was a knock at the door.

'That might be John,' said Daniel.

It was, and he returned from answering the door with the inspector behind him.

'You're just in time for tea,' said Daniel.

Feather stopped and sniffed suspiciously. 'What's that smell?'

'Horse dung,' said Abigail ruefully. 'I got it off my coat but some got in my hair.'

Feather looked at her, puzzled. 'What are you doing putting your head in horse dung?'

'I didn't do it deliberately,' said Abigail. 'I fell in the road.'

'She was pushed,' said Daniel, grim-faced.

They told him their experiences that afternoon: Abigail being pushed in front of a wagon in Oxford Street, and Daniel being attacked as he left Tussauds. 'They said it was a warning from Gerald Carr, which suggests he's behind the three murders.'

'Possibly now five,' said Feather. And he told them about Arthur Crum and Derek Parminter. 'I think they were each passing information to the bank robbers to let them know when there was a sizeable amount in the vault worth robbing. And both were killed to make sure they didn't reveal who was behind it. Oh, and I saw the tunnel in the cellar at Tussauds. You were right.'

'It was the only logical answer as to why Dudgeon and Bagshot, two tunnellers, had been brought in to replace Bruin and Patterson.' Daniel shrugged. 'But, if it's any consolation, I had my doubts. It did seem a long way for two men to dig a tunnel. Did you go inside it?'

'I did,' said Feather. 'I'm going to get an engineer to do a proper inspection of it tomorrow, tell us how long it is so we can work out how much time they'd have needed to get to the bank.'

'The puzzle is why all these people are being murdered.' Daniel frowned. 'The two bank clerks I can understand, to stop them talking about who they told about the amount of money in their respective bank vaults. But that means they were killed by the people breaking through from the cellar next door. And I can't shake the idea that there are two different gangs at work: one who breaks into the next-door bank, and one behind the tunnelling long distances. We know that Gerald Carr is involved with the tunnelling gang through Michaels, but what's his connection to the other bank raids?'

'He's surely connected to the murders at Tussauds,' said Feather. 'The men who attacked you said the warning came from him, and to stop looking into those murders.'

'But what's his connection?' asked Daniel. 'Why would Carr have the two nightwatchmen and Michaels killed? Especially before the tunnelling is completed. It doesn't make sense.'

'Maybe there aren't two rival gangs?' suggested Abigail. 'Maybe it's all one big gang doing both?'

'Possibly,' said Daniel. 'But it doesn't explain why

they're killing their own people.' He looked at them, grimly determined. 'We need to question Gerald Carr.'

'Inspector Jarrett's been tasked with bringing him in,' said Feather.

'When he does, I'd like to be part of the team that questions him,' said Daniel.

Feather looked doubtful.

'I can't see Armstrong agreeing to that,' he said. 'You know how set he is against you.' He sighed. 'But I'll mention it. See what I can do.'

'Thanks, John,' said Daniel. 'After all, he must see that we're all on the same side.'

'He just sees that he's compared in the press with you two unfavourably,' said Feather.

After Feather had gone, Daniel and Abigail discussed the weighty problem of Gerald Carr.

'He holds the key to this case,' said Daniel. 'And if Armstrong isn't going to let us in when they bring him in, I'll just have to find a way to talk to him myself.'

'Is that a good idea?' said Abigail doubtfully. 'You've just had first-hand experience of him already today. The next time it might be more than just a warning. Why not wait and see what he tells Jarrett? I'm sure John Feather will tell you.'

'Because I don't think that Jim Jarrett will ask the right questions,' said Daniel.

'Can't you give John a list of the questions you want asked?'

'It doesn't work that way,' said Daniel. 'There are protocols to follow. It's Jarrett's case.'

'Surely not now they've found the tunnel at Tussauds. That's John's case.'

'Yes, you may be right,' agreed Daniel. 'But I'd still like to be there when Carr is questioned. It's not just the answers he'll give, it's how he says them. His manner. His body language. His hand movements. That's what a proper questioning is about.' He sighed. 'I still think the only way for me to find out what I want is to be face to face with Carr.'

'And say he kills you?' demanded Abigail.

'That could be a drawback,' said Daniel. 'Which is why it's down to me to make sure that doesn't happen.'

CHAPTER TWENTY-THREE

Gerald Carr stood at the window overlooking his yard. Locky and Lard, his two bodyguards, should be arriving about now and ringing the bell for him to open the gates and let them in. As he stood there he heard the unmistakeable sound of two shots being fired outside his gates, followed by the big brass bell in the yard ringing as the rope outside was pulled. Two shots! Locky and Lard must have come across someone dangerous. Perhaps more than one, as two shots had been fired.

Carr hurried down the wooden stairs to the yard and across it to the gates. It was important to get the dead bodies dragged inside the yard before people started poking their noses in. The bell had stopped ringing now and there was no more shooting, which suggested that Locky and Lard had dealt with the problem, whatever or whoever it had been. Carr unlocked the padlock and pulled the two bolts, then pulled the first of the gates open. He began to step out, then stopped in shock. The bodies of Locky and Lard lay face down on the pavement; both had been shot in the back. As he stared at them, bewildered, he was suddenly aware of a flicker of movement on the other side of the road, and he darted back into the yard just in time as a bullet smashed into the wood of the gate, right where he'd been standing.

Hastily, he pushed the gate shut and slammed the bolts home, then ran to a large gong suspended from a frame close to the gates. He picked up the long-handled mallet and hit the gong hard, once, twice, three times, the sound echoing from the yard into the surrounding streets. It was a sound that his men who lived nearby would recognise, the alarm that the yard was under attack. Who would dare to do this?

And then the answer hit him. First those two watchmen, then Michaels, and now him. For the first time in his life – well, in his *adult* life – Gerald Carr knew he wasn't safe. He had to do something he'd never done before if he was going to save himself.

Superintendent Armstrong sat behind his desk looking up at Feather as he told him about the tunnel that had been discovered the previous day in the cellar at Tussauds Museum. 'So, it looks as if Wilson was right and the murders at Tussauds are connected with the bank robberies.'

Armstrong sat, processing the information, a scowl on his face.

'It may just be coincidence,' he said at last. 'Get someone in to check this alleged tunnel out. It could be just subsidence behind the wall.'

'I examined it myself. There are wooden slats in it supporting the ceiling and sides. It's definitely a tunnel. At least, part of a tunnel, and it's heading in the direction of the bank two shops away.'

'Get someone in to look at it, anyway. Someone who knows about tunnels. They can tell us how far it goes.'

'Yes, sir,' said Feather.

He turned and was about to leave, when Armstrong called him back.

'On second thoughts, we can't afford delays on either case. Important people are watching us. Get someone in to check this alleged tunnel, but at the same time bring Wilson in. We need to talk to him.'

'Just him? What about his partner, Miss Fenton?'

'Bring her in as well. They work together; what he knows she knows, and vice versa. Bring them both in, and tell Inspector Jarrett to come in as well. Set up a meeting here for this afternoon.' As Feather once again made for the door, the superintendent shouted after him, 'And keep it out of the papers! If these two cases do turn out to be connected, I want Scotland Yard to get the credit, not Wilson and Fenton! We'll tell the press about it in our own time, and in our own way.'

Gerald Carr watched as two of his men loaded the bodies of Locky and Lard onto the back of an open wagon and covered them with a large, oiled cloth.

'Put them in the usual place,' he said.

'The usual place' was a large area of marshy ground that a friend of Carr's owned not far from St Pancras railway station, a convenient place for many things to disappear, including bodies.

Carr turned to the others who'd come, summoned by the gong.

'I want a carriage, something that looks like a hansom cab but doesn't have any numbers on it,' he told them.

'There's one at Harry Towb's,' said one of the men.

'Go and get it,' said Carr. As the man left on his errand, he addressed the others: 'Iggy and Joe, you're coming with me.'

'Where to, boss?' asked Iggy.

'On an errand,' said Carr. 'Foxy, you stay here and keep an eye on the yard until I get back. The rest of you can clear off home.'

'Don't you want us to make enquiries as to who the shooter was who bumped off Locky and Lard, Mr Carr?' asked Foxy.

Carr shook his head. 'I know who it was,' he said. 'I'm dealing with it.'

From his vantage point behind a large wagon parked by the kerb, Daniel continued to watch the activity in Carr's yard. He'd come to Somers Town intending to find a way of getting to meet Carr face to face, and had found the place a hive of activity with one wagon drawn by a large heavy horse in the yard, onto which two dead bodies had been loaded and covered with an oiled cloth, and men bustling to and fro, some of them armed, while Carr stood in the middle of the yard directing operations. What had happened? How had the two men died? Had Carr killed them?

As he watched he saw a small carriage approach the yard from the end of the road, drawn by a single black horse. The carriage pulled up outside the entrance to the yard and a man got out of it and went into the yard, returning a short while later accompanied by Carr and two tough-looking men. The three men climbed into the carriage, and, as soon as the doors had shut, the driver flicked the reins and the carriage moved off. Once the entrance was clear of the obstruction by the carriage, the heavy wagon with the bodies on board trundled towards the entrance and then rumbled out into the roadway. The men who remained milled around together, talking in murmurs too low for Daniel to catch what was being said, but he could tell from the worried expressions on their faces that something had gone seriously wrong here. And, with Carr gone, there was no use in him hanging around to find out what it was.

Daniel headed along the road, and as he neared the junction at the end he had to stop to let an elderly woman who was doubled over, wearing a cape with a hood and using a walking stick to hobble along, pass him. Instead she stopped.

'Pardon me, madam,' said Daniel, and he moved to one side.

'You're very polite, young sir,' said the woman, and she stood up, straightening herself, and threw back her hood.

'Abigail!' Daniel cried in surprise. 'What are you doing here?'

'After what you told me about Gerald Carr, you surely didn't expect me to allow you to just walk into danger, with the possibility of you being killed, without coming along to keep an eye on you.'

'But what could you have done if things had gone badly?'

'I would have done something,' said Abigail. 'I don't know what, but something. Possibly to do with this.'

And she clicked the handle of the walking stick and pulled on it to reveal a sword blade within the actual stick.

'A sword stick?!' said Daniel, incredulous. 'When did you get hold of this?'

'I brought it with me from Cambridge. It belonged to an uncle of mine who left it to me in his will. He said it would offer me protection on my foreign travels.'

'Why didn't you tell me you had it?'

'I don't know. I thought you might laugh at me.'

'Why would I laugh at you?' He looked at her warily. 'How many other things have you been hiding from me? Weapons, I mean.'

'None,' she told him. 'This was all, and I've never had cause to use it. But today, after what you said, I thought it might be of some use.'

'Against Gerald Carr and his gang?'

'The threat of a woman armed with a sword would be enough to make them take pause,' she said. 'So, what happened? Did you see Carr?'

'I did, but not to talk to. He's just been driven off in a carriage. And two dead men were on that wagon that trundled away just now.'

'Dead? How? Did Carr kill them?'

'I don't know,' admitted Daniel. 'But with Carr gone, I think we'll have to pass this on to Inspector Jarrett and let him make his enquiries.' He smiled. 'I feel that might be more productive than you going in there and threatening people with your swordstick. And safer.'

Marion Budd stood outside the large building that was Madame Tussauds waxworks museum and she could feel her heart pounding. He was in there. Her Daniel. At least, she hoped he was. This was where her uncle John said he was spending most of his time, investigating the murders there. She knew in her heart that Daniel was the one for her. She knew it as soon as she'd seen him again after all these years. Before she'd just been a young girl, but now she was a woman. Yes, she was younger than him, but that didn't matter; she knew most women who got married had husbands much older than them. And she was sixteen. That was almost elderly by comparison with some of the women she knew. There'd been at least four girls in her home village who'd been married at thirteen and mothers at fourteen. Sixteen was old.

She knew now she'd been wrong to push Abigail the way she had so that she fell in front of that horse. She'd only meant to frighten her so that Abigail might leave London, but she could have been killed, and if that had happened Daniel would have been overcome with grief. He might even have left London himself, and Marion would lose him. She wouldn't make that same mistake again. Nor would she make the same mistake she'd done with the Reverend Wattle. She'd been wrong about the Reverend Wattle. She'd thought he loved her, the way he'd looked at her, smiled at her, been so kind to her, so caring. But when she'd told him how she felt about him, instead of taking him in her arms as she'd hoped, he'd stared at her in shock. Then he'd panicked and told her mother what she'd said. She couldn't let that happen with Daniel. She had to be more careful. No, she'd just call on him, talk to him, smile at him, let him know by little things how she felt about him, how much she loved him.

She made her way to the entrance and walked in. A young man wearing a uniform politely stopped her and, pointing towards the box office, said, 'You need to buy a ticket first.'

'I'm not here to see the waxworks,' said Marion. 'I'm here to see Mr Daniel Wilson. The one investigating the murders here. I've got a message for him.'

Even as she said it, her heart sank. Why had she said that last bit? She didn't have a message for him. She'd have to make one up. Tell him that her aunt and uncle had told her to call and invite him to tea. But then she'd have to pretend to them that they'd said that to her.

I'll tell them I thought they said it, she decided.

But then the young man dashed her hopes. 'Mr Wilson isn't here at the moment,' he told her. 'Nor Miss Fenton.'

I don't care about Miss Fenton, she thought angrily. Aloud, she asked, 'When will he be here? Later today?'

'I don't know,' he said. 'I don't know if there are any plans for him to be here today. But I'll give him a message if he comes in. Who shall I say was asking for him?'

'There's no need,' she said, doing her best to hide her deep disappointment. 'I'll see him later at home.'

And she turned and walked out, thinking, *Yes, I'll see him at his home. And we can have tea together.*

'Are you all right, Mr Greville?'

Doris, the Greville's museum box office attendant stood in the doorway of Maurice Greville's office and regarded her employer with concern. He'd been looking worried these last two days, ever since that man had been found dead at the foot of Eros.

'Of course I'm all right,' Greville snapped back petulantly. 'Why shouldn't I be?'

'Well, it's just that you haven't seemed to be yourself these last couple of days. It's like something's on your mind, and I wondered if it was due to the man who was found dead just outside.'

'Why should it be?' he demanded angrily. 'I didn't know him!'

'There's no need to bite my head off,' said Doris, offended. 'I'm only saying it because I'm worried about you. Maybe it's not that. Maybe you're sickening for something.'

'I'm not sickening for something,' snapped Greville. Then his tone softened. 'I'm sorry, Doris. I didn't mean to snap. Maybe you're right, perhaps I am coming down with something.'

'You could always go home and rest. I'm all right looking after the box office. And Wally the attendant is here if needed. We can hold the fort.'

'No. I'll stay.' He forced a smile he didn't feel. 'Sometimes work is the best medicine. If I go home I'll only feel sorry for myself and get miserable.'

'Perhaps you ought to get married again,' suggested Doris. 'I know you had bad luck last time, but there's plenty of good women out there.'

Yes, and I know one who'd like to get her feet under my table, thought Greville. Aloud, he said, 'Yes, what you say is true, Doris, and maybe I will one day.' He forced a smile at her again. 'You've always been very dear to me.'

He saw her blush and knew he'd said the right thing. Then he gave a heartfelt sigh and said apologetically, 'But right now I think I'm better off alone, doing some work to take my mind off things.'

'What sort of things?'

'This Jack the Ripper display. I'd really hoped that Mr Wilson and Mr Abberline would be helpful, but they seem very reluctant.'

'I'm sure they'll agree given time,' said Doris. 'Not everyone likes the idea of being shown in wax. Policemen, especially. Wold you like me to get you anything? A cup of tea?'

'No thanks, Doris. Thank you so much for the way you are to me. And I am sorry for the way I was before.' He smiled again. 'I don't deserve you.'

She blushed again, and then left, pulling the door shut behind her.

I'm going to have to sort things out with her, he decided. *But right now I've got bigger things to worry about.* Doris had hit the nail right on the head: the dead man who'd been found at the bottom of Eros, staring directly at Greville's museum. It had been a message, obviously aimed at him. Someone had killed Harry Michaels and left him staring at Greville's place. Who had done it, and how much did they know? And just how much danger was he in right now?

Inspector Jarrett and Sergeant Pick had chosen to travel to Somers Town by hansom cab. After their previous experience, when they'd found Carr's yard empty except for Foxy, Jarrett was taking no chances. Although he didn't believe what Pick had suggested, that Carr had been given advance warning of the raid by Bill Harris, this time he'd told no one at Scotland Yard of his plans, except Superintendent Armstrong. But once again, as he and Pick made their way past the two tall wooden gates into the yard, he was bewildered to find it empty. Well, almost empty. As before, he spotted Foxy Wood inside one of the barns.

'Foxy!' he bellowed. 'I can see you! Come here!'

Foxy shuffled his way out of the barn into the yard.

'Back again, Inspector?' he asked.

'Where is everyone?' demanded Jarrett.

'Out,' said Foxy.

'Where's Gerald Carr?'

'He's out as well. Just like last time.'

Jarrett looked at Foxy, a scowl on his face, but inside his head his mind was racing. What was going on? Carr never left the yard, yet twice now he'd been out. At least, that was what Foxy claimed. It was impossible. Something wasn't right.

'Right,' he said determinedly. 'We're going to search the whole place. Not just the barns but Carr's private quarters as well.'

'You can't do that,' said Foxy defiantly. 'He's got his personal things in there.'

Jarrett leant menacingly towards Foxy. 'I am the police,' he stated. 'I am from Scotland Yard.'

'Don't you need a warrant?' demanded Foxy.

Jarrett held his fist under Foxy's nose. 'This is my warrant.'

To Pick, he said, 'Sergeant, take him into one of the barns and tie him to something. Wrists and ankles. I don't want him interfering while we take a good look round.'

'I'll put in a complaint,' warned Foxy.

'You do that,' said Jarrett. He gestured round the empty yard. 'There's no one here but us. It'll be your word against two highly respected officers from Scotland Yard who'll say you had to be restrained to stop you interfering with the proper process of a police investigation.'

Foxy hesitated, then shrugged. 'Tie me up, them,' he said. 'Much good may it do you. You won't find Mr Carr here. He's out.'

'Tie him up, Sergeant,' growled Jarrett.

There was an envelope on the doormat waiting for Daniel and Abigail when they arrived home.

'It's from John Feather,' announced Daniel. 'We've been invited to a meeting this afternoon at Scotland Yard.'

'Will we be allowed in?' asked Abigail.

'We will.' Daniel nodded. 'John says our meeting will be with him, Superintendent Armstrong and Inspector Jarrett.'

'Something important must have happened to make Armstrong change his mind and allow us in.'

'The tunnel we found at Tussauds,' said Daniel.

'The tunnel *you* found at Tussauds,' Abigail corrected him.

He smiled. 'I'd always thought I dislike people who say "I told you so", but today I'm feeling more receptive to the thought.'

'I think the word you're looking for is "smug",' she said.

She went to him and kissed him. 'But I love you, you smug, brave man.'

'How much?' he asked with a grin.

'If you carry me upstairs and undress me, very slowly, I'll show you,' she said.

Jarrett and Pick left the yard, watched by Foxy. There had been no sign of Carr, or anyone else, anywhere at the yard, not in the living area, nor in any of the other buildings.

'I don't understand it,' Jarrett said as Foxy shut the tall gates behind them. 'That place is where Carr feels safe. He knows there are lots of people who'd like nothing better than to see him dead. And where are all his men? That place is usually buzzing with them. Today, there's only Foxy there.'

'Just like last time,' said Pick.

Jarrett shook his head. 'I know what you're suggesting, Sergeant,' he growled, 'and to me this shows it can't have been Bill Harris who tipped him off last time, because Harris didn't know we were coming here now. So either someone else is giving Carr the wink about when the police are coming, or there's something odd going on.'

'Perhaps we need to try and find some of his men,' suggested Pick. 'Hopefully they might be more informative about Carr's whereabouts than that bloke, Foxy.'

'We will, but not today,' said Jarrett. 'Right now we've got to get back to the Yard. The superintendent wants me there for a meeting.'

'Oh? Who with?'

'Him and Inspector Feather, and that pair of so-called

private investigators, Wilson and the Fenton woman.'

Pick looked at him, puzzled. 'I thought they was barred, sir,' he said.

'So did I,' said Jarrett sourly. 'The trouble is you can't trust anyone when it comes to orders from the top.'

CHAPTER TWENTY-FOUR

Superintendent Armstrong sat behind his desk and looked at the four sitting opposite him: Inspectors Feather and Jarrett, and Daniel and Abigail. He did not look particularly happy, but then, thought Daniel, the superintendent rarely did. There had been no mention of he and Abigail having been barred from Scotland Yard until this moment, and Daniel knew that if he and Abigail raised the matter, it would be denied. The important thing was that they were here, and included in the investigation.

'I decided it was time for this meeting because, from information received, it appears that the two cases – the murders at Madame Tussauds and the recent bank robberies – may be connected, and solving one could lead to the arrest of the culprits perpetrating the other.

'As you know, the bank robberies were carried out by the thieves knocking through to the bank vaults from the cellar of an adjoining shop at night, while the shop premises were empty. It's now been discovered that a similar, though more elaborate version, of that same technique was being planned at Madam Tussauds. A partially-dug tunnel has been discovered in the cellar at the wax museum, aimed towards a branch of a bank just three shops distant. The tunnel was discovered by Mr Wilson when he made an examination of the cellar at the museum, and Inspector Feather, who's in charge of the investigation into the bank robberies, has confirmed its presence.'

He looked towards Feather, who took up the story. 'I got hold of a tunneller, a former miner. He confirmed it's definitely man-made as shown by the wooden slats supporting the sides and the ceiling of the tunnel. According to him it goes about halfway beneath the shop next door. He estimates that if they dug that in two weeks, then it would have taken them another five weeks to get to the bank.'

'Where did they get the lengths of wood from every night?' asked Jarrett. 'Surely someone would have noticed them bringing in that much wood.'

'My guess is that they were kept in one of the crates stored in the cellar,' said Daniel.

'And getting rid of the spoil they dug out?'

'There's a patch of waste ground behind the museum. I expect it went there.'

'So it looks as if these were the same people who did the

bank jobs,' said Armstrong.

'I don't think so,' said Daniel.

Armstrong and Jarrett looked at him, puzzled.

'It has to be,' said Jarrett. 'It's the same method. Knock through into a bank vault from next door.'

'But this wasn't from next door,' pointed out Daniel. 'It was tunnelling, and taking much longer than an overnight job.'

'But still the same people, surely,' said Armstrong.

'No,' said Daniel. 'I think we're dealing with two different and rival gangs here. One does the bank jobs by breaking through a cellar wall, while the other aims to do it by tunnelling, this last being masterminded by Harry Michaels.'

'But so far the only tunnel that was started never got finished,' said Jarrett.

'Exactly,' said Daniel. 'That's why I said *rival* gangs. In some way, the gang who break through from cellars found out that another mob was planning to do the same, but using tunnellers.'

'Why would they do that when it's much harder than knocking through from a cellar and takes so much longer?'

'I think Michaels reasoned that sooner or later the bank authorities would put in protection if there was a cellar adjacent to their vault. He decided to go one better and tunnel into bank vaults where the nearest cellar was just one or two shops' distance away. Realising that tunnelling like this would take time, his plan was to install men as nightwatchmen at a suitable premises, and they would then tunnel through. It's possible that Dudgeon and Bagshot were his first employees after he met them in a pub and heard about their exploits as engineers.'

'And he was killed because . . . ?'

'Because he was treading into someone else's territory, the bank robbers'. That's who the message of the murders is aimed at: to anyone thinking of copying Michaels and tunnelling into banks, copying their method but going one step further. I think Dudgeon and Bagshot were killed for the same reason. To send a message to their rivals to stop.'

'A bit more than a message,' said Armstrong sourly. 'By killing Dudgeon, Bagshot and Michaels, they've put a complete stop to it.'

'Not if there's someone behind Michaels,' said Daniel. 'Think about it, it will have cost quite a bit of money to pay Dudgeon and Bagshot for two weeks, to pay wages for non-existent work to Bruin and Patterson, to hire the barge on the Lee Navigation. I think, when we look into Michaels, or whatever his real name was, we'll find he was a chancer with no big money of his own. He had a backer.'

'Gerald Carr!' said Jarrett.

'Exactly,' said Daniel. 'The man who apparently got paid by Michaels to clear Bruin and Patterson's debt.'

'So Carr was behind this tunnelling business,' said Armstrong.

'I think Michaels had the idea, but I'm betting that it was Carr who put up the money.'

Armstrong looked at Jarrett. 'Have you found Carr yet, Inspector?' he asked.

Jarrett shook his head. 'I called at his yard earlier and he seems to have done a runner.'

'Miss Fenton and I were there this morning,' said Daniel. 'We saw what appeared to be the bodies of two men loaded onto a wagon in his yard, and then Carr appeared with two of his men – his bodyguards – got into a carriage and drove off.'

'There were no bodies when myself and Sergeant Pick arrived,' said Jarrett. 'No wagon, either. Nor any of his men, except for the one they call Foxy.'

'Bring him in, Inspector. We'll put the squeeze on him and find out about these dead men, and where Carr went to.' He turned to Daniel. 'You're sure about these dead men in the wagon?'

Daniel nodded.

Jarrett got up. 'I'll go and get Sergeant Pick to bring in Foxy.'

'No, not yet. Wait till we've finished. Sit down, because I'm sure there's more to come, and I want all of us to know what's happening.'

Jarrett resumed his seat. Armstrong looked towards Feather. 'You have more deaths to report as well, I believe, Inspector.'

'Yes, sir,' said Feather. He told them about Arthur Crum and Derek Parminter. 'I'm fairly sure they told the crooks when the bank vaults would be holding particularly large sums of money. It looks as if both men were bribed for the information, with possibly one of them being seduced by a woman into passing it on. Both men died, each apparently drowning accidentally in a canal, which is too much of a coincidence. We're still trying to find out who they were in touch with.'

'I'm still not convinced that Carr isn't behind the killings,' said Armstrong. 'We know what he's like. Absolutely ruthless. He's perfectly capable of killing people if he thought they were double-crossing him. Or just to shut them up about his involvement.'

'If that was the case, Bruin and Patterson would be dead,' pointed out Daniel. 'They knew about Carr's involvement with Michaels. But they didn't know it was all part of a plan to rob banks. I still believe it's this rival gang who've done the killings. And not just Michaels and the two watchmen, but the bank clerks.' He looked at Feather. 'You said both men seemed edgy, as if they might crack under pressure.'

'That's right,' said Feather.

'So, if you're right, who's this rival gang?' asked Armstrong.

'Whoever they are, I'm sure that someone in it is connected with the wax business.'

'Just because one of the dead watchmen was covered in wax?' asked Armstrong, obviously doubtful.

'And Michaels was killed with plaster of Paris, which is also used by the wax modelling trade,' added Daniel.

'Louis Tussaud!' exclaimed Jarrett with a note of triumph. He turned to Armstrong. 'Remember, I said so, Superintendent.'

'I don't think so,' said Daniel. 'Louis Tussaud doesn't fit.'

'Who does?'

Daniel hesitated, then said, 'Caroline Dixon.'

Armstrong stared at him. 'Caroline Dixon! The rich philanthropist? The one who's bankrolling Florence Nightingale?'

'Yes,' said Daniel.

'That's insane!' burst out Armstrong. 'You're suggesting that a woman like that bangs through to bank vaults from shop cellars?'

'I'm suggesting that she hires men to do it.'

'But why? She's rich! Very rich!'

'How did she get to be so rich?' asked Abigail.

'Her husband left her money.'

'How much did he leave her?' pressed Abigail.

'I don't know,' said Armstrong.

'It's possible,' put in Feather thoughtfully.

Armstrong looked at him, annoyed.

'What's possible?' he demanded angrily. 'Caroline Dixon?'

'The sister of one of the bank clerks who died said her brother had recently got involved with a woman. A woman who could afford very expensive perfume.'

'That means nothing!'

'It does because he died soon after the bank robbery. I believe he'd been seduced by some rich woman into passing on details of when there'd be enough money in the bank to make it worth robbing.'

Armstrong shook his head. 'No,' he said. 'Caroline Dixon is a respectable figure. She's revered for what she does for the Florence Nightingale Fund by the most eminent people in society. She's been at guest at the prime minister's, for God's sake! Both at Downing Street and at Chequers. She's been received by the queen at Buckingham Palace.'

'There are plenty of examples of people in high society whose wealth is founded on fraud and criminal activity,' continued Abigail. 'At least look into her late husband's finances. Find out if he really did leave her as rich as everyone believes. If he didn't, then I think you'll find the money she pours into the Nightingale Fund is more than can be raised by social get-togethers at her house. The apparently wealthy are notoriously mean with their money.'

Armstrong deliberated on this, then said, 'All right. Inspector Feather, you're in charge of the bank raids, you look into the late Mr Dixon's financial affairs. But discreetly. *Very* discreetly.'

'Yes, sir.'

The superintendent turned to Inspector Jarrett. 'Inspector, you're to keep looking for Gerald Carr. In my view he's still more likely as the person at the heart of this. You can start by bringing in Foxy and seeing what you can get out of him.'

'Yes, sir,' said Jarrett.

'What do you want us to do?' asked Daniel.

'Nothing,' said Armstrong firmly. 'You're here on sufferance because you found the tunnel. This is a police operation. You stay out of it.'

'We can hardly do that. We have a duty of responsibility to our client, Mr Tussaud. He was the one who hired us to look into the murders and find out why they were done, and who by. John Tussaud now knows about the tunnel in the museum cellar.'

Armstrong fell silent, then said, 'All right, you can mention we think it's connected to the bank robberies. But not a word about Caroline Dixon, is that clear?' He gave a nod of his head to indicate the meeting was over. 'Right, let's keep in touch. If any one of you gets any information at all about either the bank robberies or the murders at Tussauds, let me know and I'll make sure it's shared. But be careful. With this many people already dead, we're dealing with some very dangerous people.'

'Yes we are,' said Daniel. 'I was attacked by two men who told me they work for Gerald Carr, warning me off investigating the murders. They threatened to harm Abigail if I didn't desist. And Abigail was pushed under a wagon in Oxford Street. Luckily she just managed to get out from under the hooves of the wagon's horses.'

'Did you report this?' demanded Armstrong.

'We're reporting it now,' said Daniel.

'It's a bit late now,' growled Armstrong.

'We weren't sure where we stood with Scotland Yard,' added Daniel.

Armstrong didn't reply; instead he scowled and gave a grunt and gestured for them to leave. As they all got up, the superintendent said, 'One moment, Inspector Jarrett. I need to talk to you before you go.'

Feather, Daniel and Abigail left the office, and Jarrett resumed his seat.

'You wanted to tell me something else, Superintendent?' he asked.

'Yes. Why didn't *you* find that tunnel in the cellar at Tussauds?' Armstrong demanded.

'There was no reason for it to be there,' protested Jarrett.

'There was a bank not far away.'

'Three doors away! With no cellars in between, just solid earth.'

'Dudgeon and Bagshot were tunnellers. You knew that as well as Wilson.'

'No one could have thought anyone would do such a thing. Inspector Feather said it was out of the question. And so did Wilson's own partner, Miss Fenton. I know because Inspector Feather told me.'

'But it's what they were doing,' grated Armstrong.

'No one could have known!' Jarrett defended himself.

'Wilson did,' snapped Armstrong. 'From now on we find out everything that Wilson and Fenton are up to, and we act on it.'

'Say it's wrong information?' protested Jarrett. 'Wilson isn't always right.'

'If it's wrong, we make sure they get the blame. If it's right, we get the credit.' He gestured towards the door, dismissing the inspector. 'Now go and bring in Foxy and squeeze him.'

CHAPTER TWENTY-FIVE

Daniel, Abigail and John Feather sat in Feather's office, deliberating on their meeting with Armstrong and working out a strategy for their part of the investigation, finding answers about Caroline Dixon.

'Where's Sergeant Cribbens?' asked Abigail. 'I expected to be suffocated by his pipe.'

'He's out checking on those banks in expensive areas which have a shop with a cellar next door.'

'That's a lot of shoe leather to be worn out,' commented Daniel.

Feather shrugged. 'We have to be seen to be doing something.' He looked inquisitively at Daniel. 'How sure are you that Caroline Dixon's behind the bank raids and the murders?' he asked.

'At the moment it's just a gut feeling,' admitted Daniel. 'But of all the people we've met so far on this case, she's the one who fits. She worked in wax, first at Tussauds then at Greville's. She's a rich woman, which fits with the bank clerk who was possibly seduced by a rich woman for information about when money was in the bank vault. We don't know where her money comes from. Her late husband was said to have left her wealthy, but looking at her house and her lifestyle, unless she's got additional money coming in, her wealth will soon start to disappear. And I believe she's very ruthless. And you know, John, I've met a few ruthless people in my time and can recognise that evil quality in people. She's one. And it would need someone very ruthless to account for all the people who've turned up dead in this case.' He ticked them off on his fingers. 'Eric Dudgeon. Walter Bagshot. Michaels. Your two bank clerks. Five people disposed of. And not just disposed of, but three of them killed in a gruesome and high-profile way to make sure the message went out: stop these tunnelling bank robberies.'

'The message intended for Gerald Carr, I assume,' said Feather.

'And anyone else who might have the same idea. Which brings us to the question: where is Gerald Carr? Where was he heading for when I saw him leaving his yard this morning?'

'Let's hope that Inspector Jarrett gets some clues to that when he brings in Carr's man, Foxy,' said Abigail. 'So, how do we go about this? We need to find out how well-off Mr Dixon left Caroline when he died. And also, where did his money come from? Was there some criminality involved?'

'If there was, there was no whisper of it at the Yard,' said Feather.

'That doesn't mean there wasn't something dubious,' pointed out Daniel.

'It's not going to be easy digging up that information without Caroline Dixon finding out what's going on,' said Feather unhappily.

'There always gossip,' said Abigail. 'Newspaper reporters always seem to know things.'

'But if we go down that road, don't ask Joe Dalton,' warned Daniel. 'As far as he's concerned, Caroline Dixon is a paragon of virtue.' He turned to Feather and said, 'The way I see it is you go through the official channels, see what the police have, if anything, while Abigail and I see what we can dig up unofficially.'

'Without anyone finding out,' Feather reminded them.

Foxy Wood plonked himself down on the chair in Inspector Jarrett's office and scowled at the Inspector and Sergeant Pick.

'You've got no right to bring me in,' he told them angrily. 'Mr Carr left me in charge of looking after his yard while he's out. There's precious stuff in that yard. You didn't even give me a chance to get someone else in to keep an eye on it.'

'Where is Mr Carr?' demanded Jarrett, ignoring Foxy's outburst.

'How should I know,' said Foxy.

'He's your boss. He must have said where he was going.'

'He didn't.'

'He must have said how long he'd be away for,' pressed Jarrett. 'An hour? Three hours? A day? Longer?'

'He never said.'

'Who were the dead men who were taken out of the yard on the back of a wagon this morning?'

Foxy shook his head. 'There were no dead men.'

'Two dead men, covered with a cloth,' continued Jarrett. 'Did Carr kill them?'

'There were no dead men,' repeated Foxy firmly, his eyes fixed on Jarrett.

'We have an eyewitness who saw the dead men on the wagon, and saw it drive out of the yard. This same witness saw Gerald Carr being driven off in a carriage with two other men about the same time. Who were the other men, and where were they going?'

'I don't know what you're talking about,' said Foxy defiantly. 'I don't believe there is such an eyewitness. And if there is, they're lying.'

'Why would anyone do that?'

'Because there's lots of people who've got it in for Mr Carr. They're jealous of him. So they tell lies about him.'

'Carr isn't going to be pleased when he returns to his yard to find it's been left open and unguarded,' said Jarrett.

'That's not my fault,' said Foxy. 'Like I said, you took me in without giving me a chance to make arrangements.'

'And Carr will believe that, will he?' sneered Jarrett. 'He won't hold you responsible for falling down on the job.'

Jarrett could tell from the uncomfortable look on Foxy's face that he'd hit a nerve. Carr was notorious for blaming his operatives when things went wrong, even if it wasn't their fault, and he exacted terrible punishments.

'Like I say, I don't know where Mr Carr went, and I certainly don't know anything about any so-called dead men,' said Foxy defiantly. 'And you can't keep me here!'

'Yes, we can,' said Jarrett. 'You're a vital witness in a murder enquiry who's refusing to answer our questions. That's obstruction of the police in the course of our duty.'

'I've answered your questions!' Foxy burst out.

'Not to our satisfaction,' snapped Jarrett. He turned to Sergeant Pick. 'Sergeant, take him down to the holding cells.' He looked at Foxy. 'You'll have time to think about your answers there. Maybe, when you decide to give us the truth, we'll let you go back to the yard.'

'I want a lawyer!' said Foxy.

'Oh yes?' asked Jarrett. 'Who is your lawyer?' He smiled. 'I bet that's done through Mr Carr, so when he comes back he can arrange one for you. Until then, you're staying in a cell here. As soon as you're ready to tell us what we want to know, you can leave.'

Daniel and Abigail walked away from Scotland Yard, discussing how best to delve into Caroline Dixon's finances.

'What we want is someone who *doesn't* like Caroline Dixon,' said Daniel. 'A muck-raking gossip.'

'Like that rag you brought home,' said Abigail, '*The Whistler*.'

'Yes,' said Daniel, his face breaking into a smile. 'I think a visit to their offices might be called for.'

'I can imagine nothing worse than consorting with the people who produce that.'

'When you're looking for information you have to try a

range of people and places,' said Daniel. 'Not all of them nice. Many of them, in fact, downright disgusting. But that's the nature of being an investigator. And you have to make them think you're sympathetic to them to get them talking. Do you think you can do that at the offices of *The Whistler*?'

'Of course,' said Abigail.

Daniel grinned. 'I'm not sure about that. At some point your facade will crack and you'll look down your nose at them and they'll see your disapproval.'

'You make me sound like a prig,' said Abigail. 'A snob.'

'No, I make you sound like a very honest person who is not a hypocrite, and however much you pretend to be on their side, the kind of rather sleazy people who write for *The Whistler* will see that. Because they know they're viewed as rather nasty people by the upper and middle classes and so they're watching out for hints and signs of condemnation so they can defend against them.'

'You seem to know a lot about these kinds of vermin,' sniffed Abigail.

'I've been a police officer and a private investigator for twelve years,' said Daniel. 'In my early days I learnt that if you wanted to get information it sometimes meant swimming in a sewer. The important thing was not to let it drag you down so that you forgot why you were doing it.'

'I imagine you're referring to those police officers who one reads about who are caught taking bribes and such.'

'Exactly,' said Daniel. 'Abigail, you know I have the greatest respect for your skills as an investigator, but in this case, I suggest I drop into this particular sewer on my own.'

'You don't trust me.'

'It's not that. The reality is that *The Whistler* will only be the start, and I'm fairly sure that will lead me into even murkier waters with even less desirable people than those at *The Whistler*.'

'Such as?'

'Anarchists. Radicals. People with a deep loathing for the rich, like Caroline Dixon, and also for figures of popular importance. Like Florence Nightingale.'

'Why Nightingale?'

'I'm thinking of using the Nightingale Fund as the basis for my investigation. We're after finding out the source of Caroline Dixon's money, after all, and she provides much of the money for the Nightingale Fund. Find some people who are seriously opposed to Nightingale and her work and they're sure to have some dirt on her, and the fund, and possibly Caroline Dixon, even if that dirt is only libellous, untrue gossip. There'll be a grain of truth in there somewhere.'

'And you're going to befriend these sorts of people?'

'If we're going to get the information we need. And honestly, I'll be able to do it better on my own. I just know that at some point your face or your silence will convey your disapproval of these people.'

Abigail looked unhappy, but she nodded. 'All right, but you need to teach me how to swim in the sewer, as you term it, if I'm to play an equal part in what we do.'

'I will,' Daniel promised her. 'But let's nail Caroline Dixon first.'

'You're really sure it's her?'

'I am,' said Daniel. 'But proving it is going to be another matter entirely.'

'So, what can I do?' asked Abigail.

'I suggest you return to Tussauds and update John Tussaud on what's happening: the link between the current bank robberies and the tunnellers, and the murders.'

'But without mentioning Caroline Dixon,' said Abigail. 'You want me to be deliberately vague.'

'Absolutely.' Daniel smiled. 'Talk a lot and say nothing. That's the trick.'

Abigail stood with John Tussaud in the cellar of the wax museum, looking into the hole in the wall. It was the first time she'd seen the tunnel.

'It's quite remarkable,' she said.

'One could almost admire it,' said Tussaud, 'until one considered what it was intended for. To rob a bank!' He gave an unhappy sigh. 'You must consider me very foolish, Miss Fenton.'

'Foolish?' said Abigail, puzzled. 'Why?'

'Because I employed the two men who did this!'

'In good faith,' said Abigail. 'And more than that, you had references to their good character. And they did not rouse any suspicions while they were here. There is no need for you to feel responsible in any way.'

'I still don't understand why anyone would want to kill them. And in such dreadful ways!'

'We're still looking into that,' Abigail told him. 'And working closely with the police. We're looking into the possibility that a rival gang of bank robbers were responsible, who objected to the fact that the men were copying their method for breaking into bank vaults.'

'Do you have any evidence that points to who this rival gang are?'

Abigail hesitated, then said, 'Not at this moment, but we are gathering information. There are a couple of likely suspects, but at the moment Scotland Yard have asked us not to say more until we have more information.'

'Of course.' Tussaud nodded. 'I understand. At least it doesn't appear that the murders were a deliberate attack on the museum, which was one of my major concerns.'

'No, I think you can be reassured on that point,' said Abigail. 'If there's nothing else, Mr Tussaud, I'll take my leave of you now and join Mr Wilson. He's making enquiries about possible suspects and I'm keen to see what he's uncovered, if anything.'

'Of course,' said Tussaud. As Abigail walked towards the cellar door and the stairs up to the ground floor, Tussaud gave a slight awkward cough, which brought Abigail back, and she looked at him inquisitively.

'I'm sorry,' she said. 'There *is* something else.'

Tussaud looked disconcerted, obviously weighing up what he had to say. *There's something difficult he wants to tell me,* realised Abigail. *Something bad.*

'Miss Fenton,' began Tussaud awkwardly. 'I hope you don't mind, but there's something I feel I ought to share with you. About Mr Doyle.'

'Oh?'

Where is this heading? wondered Abigail.

'He has told me about the expedition he plans to take to

Egypt next year, with you leading it.'

'Yes,' said Abigail. 'It is a great honour, and I only hope I shall be up to the task.'

'I'm sure you will,' said Tussaud. 'The thing is, as you know, he and I have spent some time together while I've been preparing his wax model, and on those occasions this expedition has featured much in his conversation.' He paused, and they both realised that his hesitancy was because he was unsure of how to continue.

'If there is anything that Mr Doyle has told you that you feel impacts on my role in the expedition,' said Abigail, 'I would be very grateful if you would disclose it to me. I would hate to be tasked with leading the expedition if Mr Doyle has doubts about me.'

'Heavens, no!' exclaimed Tussaud. 'Indeed, the exact opposite is true. No, it's just that in the conversations he and I have had, I get the feeling that his motives for undertaking this expedition are not from a purely archaeological interest.'

'Oh?' questioned Abigail.

'I'm not sure how much you know of his wife's health.'

'Nothing at all,' said Abigail. 'It's not a subject that has arisen between us.'

'Her name is Louise, although he calls her Touie, his affectionate nickname for her. About three years ago she was diagnosed with tuberculosis and she suffers terribly with her lungs. Early last year Mr Doyle moved them to Davos in Switzerland in the hope the air there would offer some relief, and it did. He then heard from a friend of his who had consumption that he'd been cured thanks to the air and the soil in Hindhead in Surrey. Mr Doyle immediately returned to

England and bought a plot of land in Hindhead and arranged for a house to be built there, before he returned to the continent to re-join Mrs Doyle, whereupon they headed to Egypt for the winter in the belief that the climate there would help Mrs Doyle's condition.'

'Yes, he told us they'd spent most of the past year in Egypt,' said Abigail.

'At first the climate seemed to help, but then she found the heat out there too much for her, and so they returned to England. But I know he worries for her. The reason I'm telling you this is because I've gained the impression that Mr Doyle's interest in the pyramids of Egypt is more to do with the restorative powers they are supposed to have. I may be wrong, but I feel that's his real motive in undertaking this expedition, to try and find out if there is truth in the idea of the life-enhancing properties of the pyramid, and if so that there might be a way of utilising it to improve his wife's health.'

Abigail nodded thoughtfully, before saying, 'Thank you for telling me this, Mr Tussaud, and I promise you I will not divulge what you've told me to Mr Doyle, nor to anyone else. I'd already come to feel that Mr Doyle's intention with this expedition stemmed not so much from archaeological interest, but from an interest in the occult religion of the ancient Egyptians.'

'Of course, I may be completely wrong and may have misinterpreted what Mr Doyle said in casual conversation,' Tussaud put in hastily.

'No, I don't believe you are, Mr Tussaud,' said Abigail. 'And I'm grateful for you having told me. It helps me to understand what Mr Doyle's aim is in this forthcoming quest. It also helps me to think about how I should address it with Mr Doyle.'

'Without mentioning our conversation, I trust,' said Tussaud apprehensively.

'I promise you, Mr Tussaud, that will never come into it. As I said, from things Mr Doyle has said to me I'd already become aware that his interest was more towards the occult rather than the archaeological. That's what I will use as the basis for any conversation I have with him.'

CHAPTER TWENTY-SIX

Daniel walked away from the offices of *The Whistler* in Bethnal Green, annoyed that his visit had been a waste of time. His hope that the staff of *The Whistler* would be radically minded and eager to dish the dirt on the elite of society had been wrong. In fact they had no political inclinations of any sort; their aim was to dig out sensational stories, the more lurid the better, and suitably exaggerate them to titillate their readership. The aim of the owner of *The Whistler* was to make money, not to educate the public, or hold the establishment to account. As soon as they realised that he was the same Daniel Wilson who'd been Abberline's sergeant during the Jack the Ripper investigations, that had been all they'd wanted to talk about, eager for him to name names, especially if they were titled, and particularly to give them suspects with royal family connections. He soon realised that to try to talk to these people about the Nightingale Fund was a waste of time, they weren't really aware of the existence of the fund, and they didn't care about it. What they wanted was gore, violence, and illicit sex; that was what sold, as far as they were concerned. The apparent political or social concerns that they espoused were just to give the impression that they were a caring newspaper.

He made his way back to Scotland Yard, relieved that he was no longer persona non grata, and was pleased to find that John Feather was still in his office, now accompanied by Sergeant Cribbens and his infernal-smelling pipe.

'Daniel.' Feather smiled. 'What can we do for you?'

'I need your help,' said Daniel.

'This is your digging into the – er – person of interest we were talking about?' said Feather. 'Don't worry, I've filled Sergeant Cribbens in on everything that came up at the meeting, so he knows all about your interest in Caroline Dixon.'

'I can't believe it,' said the sergeant with the shake of his head. 'You read about her in the papers and the good works she's doing.'

'Yes,' agreed Daniel. 'But not everybody is what they seem.' He turned back to Feather. 'Which is why I'm looking for a radical organisation who oppose the establishment, and especially loathe and despise the rich.'

'That's not my department,' said Feather. 'You need Special Branch.'

'But Special Branch are unlikely to talk to me. I'm an outsider. You're inside Scotland Yard. I know Special Branch are a difficult bunch, but there might be someone you know who'll talk to you.'

'There might be, depending on the mood he's in,' said Feather. 'What particularly are you looking for?'

'Anyone who has an axe to grind over the Nightingale Fund.'

'You're going for Caroline Dixon through the money?'

'I am,' said Daniel. 'Which is why I'm looking for some radical outfit who are opposed to the whole capitalist system, the rich in general, and Florence Nightingale in particular.'

'Well, that's specific enough.' Feather grinned. 'I'll see what I can do.'

Sergeant Cribbens puffed at his pipe, his face showing obvious disapproval.

'I still don't think it right,' he said. 'A good woman like that. If you ask me, we need more like her.'

'And if you're right, Sergeant, I shall make amends in some way,' said Daniel. 'But right now I'm following the doctrine that Fred Abberline drummed into me: trust no one, suspect everybody.'

Abigail was reading through her diaries of her previous expeditions to ancient Egypt when Daniel arrived home.

'Preparations for the big trip?' asked Daniel.

'Yes,' said Abigail. 'Although there might be some doubt about it.'

'Why?' asked Daniel. 'Have you seen Mr Doyle again

and he's expressed doubts?'

'No. I talked with John Tussaud.' And she told him about her conversation with Tussaud about Doyle's wife.

'So you were right,' said Daniel. 'You said you felt that Mr Doyle had his own motive for wanting to mount this expedition, one based on the supernatural. Now we know why. It must be awful for them, her suffering such a dreaded illness in this way, and both of them wondering how long she has. It may not be scientific, but when someone you care for deeply is suffering from something with no cure, people will turn to anything to find a solution. It's no different to those who follow Mary Baker Eddy and practise Christian Science, believing that all illnesses can be cured by the power of prayer. Or those stories of voodoo practitioners and other forms of magic.'

'But the stories about the pyramids having supernatural powers of restoration have no basis in reality,' said Abigail. 'If that is why Mr Doyle is going, I feel I need to tell him the truth. He needs to know that he won't find the answer to his wife's illness in the pyramids.'

'You'll take that hope away from him?' asked Daniel.

'It's a false hope,' said Abigail. 'It would be cruel to lead him along that path without being told.'

'And if he decides as a result to cancel the expedition?'

'Then so be it,' said Abigail. 'I hope he doesn't, but I couldn't live with myself if I gained this as a result of not advising him of the reality. It would be wrong of me to encourage his delusion in order to achieve the leadership of the expedition.'

'Unless there is something to it,' said Daniel. 'Many

people attest to the power of prayer. And that includes some highly intelligent people: scientists, thinkers. How certain are you that you're right and they're wrong?'

'You sound like Mr Doyle. He told me that he's a member of the Society for Psychical Research, that he's attended seances, and seems to hold all manner of supernatural beliefs.' She looked at Daniel accusingly. 'I thought you felt the same as I,' she said, annoyed. 'I've never heard you say anything to suggest you have a religious belief.'

'I don't,' said Daniel. 'But I've learnt that it helps to keep an open mind. After all, who's to say that a strong belief in something can't in itself make things happen? There are stories about holy men in India who achieve amazing feats simply by thinking. Levitation. Walking across a pit of burning coals.'

'And that's all they are: stories,' said Abigail dismissively.

'Can you be so sure?' asked Daniel.

Abigail regarded him, curious. 'Are you suggesting I should say nothing to Mr Doyle about my concerns?' she asked.

'No,' said Daniel. 'All I'd suggest is that you temper it, give your own view, but don't destroy any hope he might feel. After all, she might live longer than others for a variety of reasons.'

'And if he attempts to do something, like perhaps recreate a pyramid at their house in Surrey, and she still dies?'

'Then he tried. What's the harm in that?'

Abigail fell silent for a while, before replying, 'Perhaps you're right. We all need hope in our lives. I'll raise it with him, but in a diplomatic fashion.'

Daniel chuckled. 'You? Diplomatic?'

'I can be,' said Abigail indignantly. 'The difference is I don't need to be diplomatic with you. With you, I'm honest. Because I love you and I know that you love me, warts and all.'

There was a knock at the door, and Daniel opened it to find John Feather standing there.

'John,' he said. 'I thought there was no need for subterfuge any more.'

'This isn't subterfuge, it's the information you were after from Special Branch.'

'Special Branch?' asked Abigail as Feather joined them in their living room.

'I asked John to enquire about anarchist organisations who might be able to let me have any dirt on Caroline Dixon's finances.'

'I thought you were going to ask the people at that rag, *The Whistler*,' said Abigail.

'I went there and it was a waste of time,' said Daniel. He turned to Feather. 'So Special Branch turned up trumps?'

'They keep tabs on all of these radical outfits, however small and mad they might appear, because they're never sure which one might suddenly start bombing or shooting people. The one they suggest that fits the bill for what you're looking at is an organisation called the Pure of Heart. Actually, "organisation" might be an exaggeration. I get the impression they're just a handful of disenchanted radicals who operate out of a room in Whitechapel.'

'An area I know well from my time with Abberline,' said Daniel. 'Thankfully, this time I won't be confronted with the mutilated bodies of women. Who are the Pure of Heart?'

'Despite the name, they seem to be a bunch of very angry anarchists. The clincher was that they certainly have no love for the Nightingale Fund. They think the money should go first to the poor and needy. Also, from what my contact inside Special Branch tells me, if they had their way, they'd slaughter the rich and privileged and have their blood running down the gutters of Park Lane.'

'And yet they're still free and on the loose?'

'I gather Special Branch prefer it that way. They can keep an eye on them and people they mix with.'

'So my visit to them will be reported.'

'I suppose so. I assume you won't be using your real name.'

'No, I shall be Joe Dawkins, a carpenter who has been robbed of his living and his meagre inheritance by the ruling classes.'

'My contact suggests that if you want to get any dirt from them on the Nightingale Fund, you mention Mary Seacole and compare her favourably to the revered Florence.'

'Who's Mary Seacole?' asked Daniel.

'She was a nurse in the Crimea at the same time as Nightingale,' put in Abigail. 'She's dead now, she died in 1881. She was originally from Jamaica.'

'White Jamaican or black?' asked Daniel.

'Black,' said Feather.

'She must have stood out in the Crimea.'

'She stood out in many ways,' said Abigail. 'By all accounts she was an excellent nurse, but when she applied to the War Office to be included in the second contingent of nurses being sent to the Crimea, following Nightingale and her first lot of nurses, the War Office rejected her. They also rejected her request for financial assistance to travel to the Crimea from Panama, which is where she was then living. So she paid her own passage.'

'How do you know all this?' asked Daniel.

'Because, as a woman who had to battle to be accepted in a man's world such as archaeology, I'm always interested to hear of other women who overcame similar obstacles in their own chosen paths. Mary Seacole was a very determined lady and became hugely popular among the soldiers, but there was a noticeable lack of warmth towards her from Nightingale.'

'Why?' asked Daniel. 'Are you suggesting some kind of racist bias from the Florence?'

Abigail shook her head. 'No, I think it was more about social manners. Seacole came from a very different background to Nightingale, who was the product of an upper class, very English background. The stiff upper lip, that sort of thing. Mary Seacole spent her life in the West Indies and Panama, where attitudes were very different, with much less emphasis on class distinctions. Nightingale was caring but relatively austere, as opposed to Mary Seacole, who was more liberal in her approach to the wounded men. Nightingale insinuated that Seacole drank and acted improperly with the soldiers. Not that there was any evidence ever given to back up the accusations. Seacole herself felt this attitude towards her came about purely because she was black. There have always been elements of racism in the British upper establishment.'

'So when I talk to the Pure of Heart, it's Nightingale bad, Seacole good,' said Daniel.

'That's about the size of it,' said Feather. He hesitated, then added, 'But do take care, Daniel. They might appear to be just a bunch of radical idiots, but there are some dangerous elements among them.'

'I'll be careful,' Daniel assured him.

After Feather had left, Abigail looked at Daniel with concern. 'Are you sure you're going to be all right with these people? The Pure of Heart? From what John said, they sound like they could be dangerous.'

'I'll be careful,' Daniel reassured her. 'What are your plans while I'm digging for dirt among the revolutionaries of Whitechapel?'

'I thought I'd seek out Mr Doyle.'

'About his wife's illness?'

'I can't say anything about that because I promised John Tussaud I wouldn't. But I thought I'd try and say something indirectly. I'll tell him, from my own experience of the pyramids, that there is no truth in the idea that a pyramid can actually restore the dead back to life. Without actually saying so, I'll let him know that a pyramid, along with the whole business of Egyptian religions about raising the dead and healing the sick is not a real option.'

'And if he decides to abandon the expedition as a result?'

'As I said, so be it. But he's too decent a person, with too good a heart, to be taken advantage of, which I'd be guilty of if I didn't make that clear to him.'

Daniel pulled her close to him and kissed her.

'You are the best person I've ever known, Abigail,' he said. 'You talk about Doyle having a good heart. No one has a better heart than you.'

'You do,' she countered.

He shook his head.

'No,' he said. 'I wish I had, but there's too much of the policeman in me. It keeps me austere. You're Mary Seacole, and I'm Florence Nightingale.'

CHAPTER TWENTY-SEVEN

John Feather sat in a luxurious leather armchair in the bar of the private Burlington Club. He always felt slightly awed and intimidated in surroundings such as these, the dark oak woodwork of the walls, the waiters who moved silently about serving drinks, collecting empty glasses and ashtrays. His companion, Hector Bullard, a writer on the *Financial Times*, held his glass of whisky aloft to Feather in a toast. Feather responded by raising his own glass and taking a sip.

'This place is better for any meeting than the members' room,' said Bullard. 'In there is a rule of absolute silence, which has to be maintained. Even rustling the pages of a newspaper is received by disapproving frowns.' He looked at Feather enquiringly. 'Walter said you needed some advice on financial dealings, but not your own.'

Walter was Hector Bullard's brother, a senior civil servant who Feather had once helped escape from an embarrassing situation in Whitehall, when one of his juniors had been accused of embezzlement and he had tried to implicate Walter Bullard. Feather's investigation had cleared Walter Bullard of any involvement and exonerated him completely. 'If I can return the favour in any way, you only have to ask,' Bullard had told Feather at the time. And so, on learning that Walter Bullard's brother was a writer on the *Financial Times* and privy to inside financial information, Feather had asked the civil servant for his assistance in some enquiries he was making into the dealings of a certain Charles Dixon.

'Yes,' said Feather. 'It's part of a wider enquiry we're conducting.'

'The recent bank robberies,' said Bullard.

Feather looked at him in surprise, and Bullard chuckled.

'If anyone wants to meet me, I like to know who they are and what they might want, so I make enquiries. I discovered from the newspapers that Inspector Feather is currently investigating the recent spate of bank robberies. It's very simple. As you can imagine, those of us interested in financial matters are also keen to find out why this recent outbreak of bank robberies is happening, especially as they appear to involve very large sums indeed, which will have an impact on the country's economy if they continue.' He took a further sip of his whisky. 'Walter mentioned that you are interested in the financial affairs of Charles Dixon, but I can't believe that he would have had any involvement in these robberies as he died before they started.'

'I'm interested in the source of his wealth,' said Feather.

Bullard nodded thoughtfully, then said carefully, 'Of course, the term "wealth" is relative. To a pauper, ten shillings is wealth. To the very rich, a million pounds is barely adequate.'

'And where did Mr Dixon sit on this scale?' asked Feather. 'Everyone I've spoken to describes him as very rich.'

'He was well enough off to afford a very good lifestyle,' said Bullard. 'But that was when he was a single man. Before he married. Running an establishment can be quite expensive.'

'So Mrs Dixon's financial demands were a drain on his resources?'

'She was – is – a woman with ambitions, mainly social. But to support those ambitions – especially to be seen and be highly respected as a major sponsor of something as high-profile as the Nightingale Fund – calls for lots of money.'

'I understand she holds fundraising events to raise the money.'

'But those fundraising events themselves need capital if they are to be the sort of glittering occasions that attract the rich and famous.'

'So Mrs Dixon needs more money than she had when she first married Charles Dixon.'

'In my opinion, as a mere observer,' said Bullard. 'But I am not privy to her financial affairs. For all I know, she has private investments.' He paused, then said, 'I believe the insurance money she received on the death of Mr Dixon was not as much as she'd hoped for.'

'But you would describe her as rich now?' asked Feather.

'Oh yes, certainly,' said Bullard. 'I know she has deposits in various very reputable banks. None of which, interestingly, were victims in the recent bank robberies. I believe most of her money is kept in branches out of town.' He smiled. 'Mrs Dixon is a very canny financial operator.'

Daniel mounted the stairs of the house in Whitechapel, aiming for the second floor after spotting the hand-written sign in the entrance which informed callers that the office of the Pure of Heart could be found there. He was wearing a set of old clothes he kept as a disguise for when he had to circulate among the poorer elements of society without creating suspicion. The jacket and trousers were worn and patched, but neatly to show a man who was poor but careful about his appearance.

The smell of damp and decay pervaded the air as he continued up the rickety wooden staircase, which creaked and gave slightly under his weight. This whole place could come down and collapse in a heap of brick dust and rotting timbers. He reached the second floor and saw the handwritten sign saying 'The Pure of Heart' on a door which the green paint was flaking off, exposing the wood beneath.

Daniel knocked at the door and stepped inside.

Two men were in the office, one in his twenties and the other in his late forties, sitting facing one another at a desk that overflowed with papers. They both looked at Daniel suspiciously.

'Yes?' demanded the older man.

'A friend of mine said he thought you might be able to help me,' said Daniel.

'Who is this friend?' asked the older man.

Daniel hesitated, then said, 'He would prefer not to have his name bandied about. But my name is Joe Dawkins. I have a grievance, and I hope you can help me right a wrong.'

The older man gestured for Daniel to join them and pushed a chair forward for him to sit with them at the desk.

'Where are you from?'

'Camden Town,' said Daniel. Apart from his false name and occupation, he'd decided to keep everything else as it was. It was always safer, when going undercover, to keep your story as near the truth as possible to avoid being caught out. Camden Town was known to be a slum area of north London, which would go down well with the Pure of Heart. 'I have told you my name; will you give me yours so I know who I'm talking with?'

'Smith,' said the man.

A lie, thought Daniel, but that didn't matter.

'Thank you, Mr Smith.'

'Brother Smith,' the man corrected him.

'Brother Smith.' Daniel nodded apologetically.

'What is your grievance, Brother Dawkins?'

'My father had always promised me that when he died he would leave me his gold watch.'

'A gold watch?'

'Well, it may not actually be real gold, but it looks like it. It's one he was left by an uncle. It has a chain and everything and is certainly worth four pounds. Possibly five. But now my father tells me he's changed his mind and is going to leave it to the Nightingale Fund.'

'The Nightingale Fund?'

Daniel nodded. 'I have found out it's an organisation set up by Florence Nightingale to train nurses. Personally, I suspect some trickery has taken place here to persuade him to bypass me and leave the watch to them.'

'A watch?' repeated Smith, weighing up the question.

Again, Daniel nodded, the very picture of a man injured by injustice. 'When I told my friend about it, he told me that if there was ever a fund to be set up for the Crimea nurses it should be in the name of Mary Seacole. I don't know her, but according to my friend, Mary Seacole did just as much for the soldiers in the Crimea as Nightingale, if not more.'

'Your friend is right. Did he serve in the Crimea?'

'No, but his brother did, and he said that Mary Seacole saved his brother's life.'

'What is your friend's name?'

Daniel shook his head. 'As I said before, he has asked me not to put his name about. He believes there are forces in this country that would dearly like to get evidence against him of his political opinions and put him behind bars again.'

'He has already been in prison?'

'He has, but some years ago, when he was younger. Since then he's been . . . careful.'

'And you yourself, Brother Dawkins? Have you been a prisoner of this state?'

'I have been apprehended, but never jailed,' said Daniel warily.

'Apprehended? Why?' asked Smith.

'A neighbour overheard me talking badly about the way we poor are treated by the rich and powerful.'

'You were questioned?'

'I was.'

'Who by?'

'They did not tell me who they were, but I could guess. Special Branch.'

'And they let you go?'

'There was no proof against me.'

'How long ago was this?'

'Four years,' said Daniel. 'Since then, I've been careful to guard my tongue when amongst strangers.'

'And now you come because of a watch.'

'Because I am to be cheated out of my watch, my rightful inheritance, all that my father has of any value.'

'And how do you think we can be of help?'

'My friend suggested that you might know of the truth of this Nightingale Fund. That the money it has might not all be gained honestly. If I can show my father that there have been dark dealings by those who provide its funding, he may well change his mind about leaving them his watch.'

'Did your friend mention any examples of dark dealings?'

'He only mentioned some names of people he said were financing the fund for their own ends, and in some cases to hide money that was the result of ill-gotten gains, and that by putting it into the fund they avoided awkward questions about where the rest of their money might have come from.'

Smith nodded thoughtfully. 'And whose were the names he mentioned?'

'Lord Cairns,' said Daniel. 'Admiral Yelland. And

Jeremiah Case, a businessman.'

Again Smith nodded. 'Examples of the brutal rich hiding behind fake auras of respectability, living off the backs of the poor. Jeremiah Case makes his money from slum housing in which mothers and babies die from cold and starvation.' He frowned. 'But I'm not sure if he gives money to the Nightingale Fund. I haven't heard it to be so. And we keep a close watch on the Fund and its subscribers, because one day we will call them all to account when we raise Mary Seacole to her rightful place in history and point the finger at these arrogant people for deliberately downplaying her role in the care of the sick.' He scowled as he added, 'I despise all this reverence for Nightingale. Nightingale was from a wealthy elitist family, with palatial homes in Italy and across England. Grand places, mansions. Mary Seacole, on the other hand, was a woman of the people.' And he fell silent, fuming with indignation.

'There was another person my friend mentioned,' said Daniel. 'A woman called Caroline Dixon, who has a house in Lowndes Square. I believe she's the widow of a wealthy man called Charles Dixon, who made his money on the backs of the poor.'

'Ha!' burst out Smith scornfully. 'Your friend has been misinformed. Charles Dixon made his money by crime.'

'Crime?'

'Robbery. Blackmail. Extortion.'

Daniel stared at Smith. 'You're not serious!'

Smith scowled. 'I knew someone who worked for Charlie Dixon. Dixon was always a thief, but he enlarged so that he had a gang working for him.'

'Including your friend?'

'At first,' said Smith. 'But then there was talk among the gang that there was an informer among them, and for some reason, my friend was named. Wrongly.'

'What happened to him?'

'He died,' said Smith bitterly. 'They said it was an accident; he fell from a roof during a break-in. But I know better. Dixon's men killed him.'

'Why were no charges made?'

'Dixon had the police in his pocket.'

'And his widow? Was she involved?'

Smith shook his head. 'I don't know. I feel she must have known how he made his money, but since he died I've had nothing to do with her or anyone associated with Dixon.' He looked intently at Daniel. 'They were always dangerous people, Dixon's gang. If you are asking questions about them, or about Dixon's widow, I would advise you to watch your back.'

Abigail sat, unable to really concentrate as she scanned her old diaries of previous expeditions, along with her treasured books on the religions and histories of ancient Egypt, because her mind was filled with how to raise her concerns with Conan Doyle when she next met him without upsetting him. Doyle was worried about his wife, that was clear, and worried people when faced with the unthinkable will turn to almost anything in order to find a solution. Had she the right to crush his beliefs?

A knocking at the front door interrupted her thoughts, and when she opened it she was surprised to see the figure of Maurice Greville standing there, looking distinctly unhappy.

'Miss Fenton,' he said apologetically, removing his hat. 'I am so sorry to call on you at home, but is Mr Wilson here?'

'I'm afraid not,' replied Abigail. When she saw his deeply crestfallen expression at hearing this, she offered, 'But if it's to do with the case we're working on, the murders at Tussauds, I'll do my best to help, if you'll let me.'

'Yes, please,' said Greville.

'Perhaps you'd like to come in.' And Abigail ushered him into the nearest thing they had to a parlour, the one comfortably furnished room reserved for special visitors. Greville sat himself down on one of the armchairs, while Abigail settled herself on another. She could tell that something was troubling the wax museum owner deeply and she was intrigued by what it could be. It had to be something of great concern to lead him to call on them at home.

'It's about Mr Michaels,' he said, but she noticed that he kept his gaze averted from her face, looking down instead at the carpet.

'The Mr Michaels who was killed?' asked Abigail.

Greville nodded. 'And whose body was left facing my museum.' He looked up at her and Abigail saw the fear in his face. 'I'm sure it was deliberate, and I'm concerned that I could be next.'

'To be killed?'

He gulped nervously and nodded. 'Someone must have found out that . . . that I did some business with Mr Michaels.'

'What sort of business?'

'It was a year ago. I was having difficulty finding people

302

good enough to work on my models. And then Michaels came to me with a proposition. Tussauds were getting rid of some of their older mannequins, Michaels knew one of the attendants at Tussauds, and, for a price, he told me he could get me some of the ones they were getting rid of. What happens is, when a model has served its time, the wax gets melted down and re-used. It seemed a great waste of some marvellous work. So, although the majority were taken and melted down, Michaels was able to pass on six of the heads and arms to me.'

'Just the heads and arms?'

'As you'll have seen, the bodies are hidden beneath clothes, so they are bulked up with wooden frames, with the heads and arms fixed to the frame.'

'And you used the heads that Michaels sold you.'

'With some subtle changes. I swear, it's the only time I've ever done anything like that, and only because we were desperate for new models to put on display quickly.'

'Why would that be a reason to kill you?' asked Abigail, puzzled.

'I don't know,' said Greville nervously. 'But something is happening, and these murders are to do with wax. The two nightwatchmen were killed in ways that indicated wax was involved, certainly in the case of the second man, encased as he was. And then Michaels being suffocated with plaster of Paris. Again, something which is used in the wax business.'

Abigail noticed that this time he called it the wax *business*, as opposed to the artistry.

'And it hinges on Tussauds. And Michaels sold me the wax models he'd stolen from Tussauds.'

'Which were going to be melted down anyway,' said Abigail.

'Yes, but these people *know*,' insisted Greville.

Abigail shook her head. 'Mr Greville, I think I can assure you that the murders are nothing to do with anything unorthodox happening in the wax business. Mr Wilson has ascertained that they are connected to the recent series of bank robberies that have been taking place. You may have read about them in the newspapers.'

'Bank robberies?' repeated Greville in bewilderment.

'Mr Wilson discovered the beginnings of a tunnel in the cellar at Tussauds, which had been dug out by the two nightwatchmen who were killed. It was intended as a way of breaking into the vault of a bank a few doors away, and Mr Michaels was instrumental in arranging for the tunnel to be dug.'

'But . . . the wax?' said Greville, baffled. 'One nightwatchman beheaded, one encased in wax, and Michaels suffocated?'

'Done, I expect, to throw any investigators off the scent. They are connected with the bank robberies. As long as you had nothing to do with those . . .'

'No! I swear!' exclaimed Greville passionately.

'Then I don't think you have anything to fear.'

'You're sure of this?' asked Greville desperately. 'Mr Wilson thinks so, too?'

'And Scotland Yard,' said Abigail. 'Mr Wilson is out with some of Scotland Yard's detectives following that exact line of enquiry.'

'Then I have nothing to fear?' And Greville looked at her, his mouth open, hope replacing the miserable haunted look he had worn when he arrived.

'No,' Abigail assured him, though inside she cautioned it with *I certainly hope not. But if I'm wrong . . .*

'Thank you!' said Greville, leaping to his feet. 'I cannot tell you what a weight has been lifted off me!'

Abigail rose. 'Rest assured, Mr Wilson and Scotland Yard are as one in that opinion. You will not be a target for whoever committed these murders.'

Greville almost crushed her fingers as he took her hand in gratitude and thanked her profusely all the way to the front door, and then out into the street.

Across the road from the house, Marion watched as the portly man shook Abigail's hand and then walked away, a happy smile on his face. Abigail went back inside and closed the door.

Where is Daniel? thought Marion. *Who was that man? Is he Abigail's lover?* Her heart lifted at this thought. If Abigail had a lover then Daniel would abandon Abigail and be free for her. Daniel and Marion.

Once again, she mentally kicked herself for being stupid and pushing Abigail into the road. The way to get Daniel for her own was to keep Abigail safe and alive and gradually persuade him that she was the wrong woman for Daniel, and Marion was the right one. He'd see that soon enough, especially once she went to Egypt on this expedition. *How could she?* thought Marion, shocked at the idea. If she really loved Daniel she couldn't go far across the world and leave him on his own.

But he wouldn't be on his own. Marion would be there for him, always ready, always waiting, and he'd gradually come to see her and become fond of her, and then love her as she wanted to be loved.

As she watched she saw a carriage pull up outside Daniel's house and two men get down from inside it and walk towards the door. Who were they? More men come to see Abigail? Or were they friends of Daniel's?

Suddenly, with a shock, she saw that both men were carrying pistols. Why? Who were they going to shoot? Daniel wasn't there, just Abigail. She couldn't let them shoot Abigail; that would destroy Daniel and Marion would lose him, possibly for ever. What was she to do?

Abigail heard the knock at the door. It must be Greville returning again, she decided. But why?

She walked along the passage to the door, opened it, and was stunned to see two men pointing pistols at her.

'What . . . what . . . ?' she stammered in shock.

'Get in the carriage,' snapped one of the men. 'Someone wants to talk to you.'

Abigail stared at them, and at the waiting carriage with the driver on the top seat, her mind in a whirl. What was happening? *I need to gain time*, she thought. *Slam the door on them and lock it and run out the back.*

'I need to get my coat,' she said, and began to retreat into the house, but the man scowled and thrust the pistol at her.

'No coat,' he barked. 'Get in the carriage. Now.'

CHAPTER TWENTY-EIGHT

Marion watched in shock as Abigail was pushed into the carriage and the two men climbed in after her. They were going to kill her!

Suddenly she knew what she had to do: she had to go with them, follow them, find out where they were taking Abigail and tell Daniel so he could save her. He would be grateful to her for ever, and when Abigail left for Egypt he would spend all his time with her because he'd be so grateful, and gradually – with Abigail gone – he'd come to love her.

As the driver flicked the reins, Marion ran across the road to the rear of the carriage and hauled herself up on the rack at the back. It was something she and her friends used to do back in her home village, going for a ride and then jumping off when the carriage pulled to a halt. She gripped the rack firmly with both hands, and planted her feet on the bottom of it as the carriage began to move off.

Vera Feather was on her knees in the living room sweeping the ashes from the grate when Marion rushed in in a state of panic.

'Aunt Vera!' she yelled. 'Daniel's Abigail has been kidnapped.'

Vera stared at her, bewildered. 'What?'

'I was outside their house when two men arrived. They had guns and they took her and put her in a carriage. I jumped on the back and they drove to a big house in a posh part of town. They took her into the house. I jumped off and came running all the way here. We have to tell Daniel and Uncle John!'

Vera regarded her niece with a stern look of deep disapproval. 'Marion, your uncle and I have told you before about telling stories . . .'

'It's not a story!' shouted Marion, her voice desperate. 'Men with guns! They took her in a carriage to this posh house.'

Vera studied her niece, so obviously distressed. She'd told stories about made-up events before that she said had happened to her, but Vera had never seen her this distraught before. 'We have to tell Uncle John and Daniel!'

Feather and Sergeant Cribbens listened as Daniel related to them what he'd learnt at the office of the Pure of Heart.

'If what they told me is true, the late Charles Dixon made his money from crime.'

'What sort of crime?' asked Feather.

'I didn't ask for details, but according to them it involved robberies and extortion. And, again, if what they said is true, Charles Dixon and his gang were a very dangerous crowd, who killed people suspected of informing on them.'

'And Caroline Dixon?'

'They didn't have anything specific against her, but she must have known what he was up to, and what sort of man he was. It wouldn't surprise me to find she continued his criminal activities after his death, using his gang.'

'I don't believe it,' burst out Cribbens. 'They're just trying to smear the reputation of a fine and generous lady.'

'But generous with whose money?' asked Feather. He looked at both his sergeant and Daniel, then said, 'I've been asking questions of a well-connected financial journalist. He admitted he didn't know where Charles Dixon got his wealth from, but he has questions about Caroline Dixon. It seems she didn't inherit a great deal of money from her late husband, and the insurance payout following his death wasn't as great as she'd hoped it would be. In fact, it's been suggested that Charles Dixon struggled to support his wife in the grand manner in which she desired to be kept. And, since his death, she seems to have amassed a lot of her own cash, though no one seems to know from where.'

'She does good works!' insisted Cribbens. 'She raises money from social events.'

'Oh come on, Sergeant,' said Daniel. 'We know that Caroline Dixon's main interest has always been in money, where it comes from and how to get her hands on it. Her late husband obviously did a good job of hiding the source of his wealth from the people in society that he cultivated, and I'm fairly sure that she would have done the same.'

'By robbing banks?' snorted Cribbens disparagingly. 'I don't believe it!'

The three men looked towards the door as they heard a frantic knocking at it.

'I expect Superintendent Armstrong wants us,' sighed Feather wearily, getting up and walking to the door. He opened it and they were stunned to see Vera Feather and Marion enter.

'I'm so sorry to trouble you at work,' began Vera, but she was interrupted by Marion, who burst out, 'Abigail has been kidnapped! By men with guns!'

Daniel and Feather stared at her, then at Vera, then back at Marion.

'You have to do something!' begged Marion. 'They're going to kill her!'

She then told them about how she'd been going towards the house when she saw the two men with guns take Abigail from the house and put her in a carriage, and how she'd climbed on the rack at the rear of the carriage to see where they were taking her, and she'd followed them to a big house. She saw them take Abigail into the house, then she'd jumped down from the back of the carriage and run home.

Feather looked questioningly at his wife, who said, worriedly, 'I think this time she's telling the truth.'

'I am!' howled Marion.

'Tell me about the house?' urged Daniel.

'It was big,' said Marion. 'A big white one.'

'Where?' pressed Daniel. 'What was the name of the street?'

Marion struggled to think. 'It began with an L,' she said.

'Lowndes Square?' asked Daniel.

Marion nodded eagerly. 'Yes! At least, I think that was it. It was Lowndes something, I'm sure.'

'Caroline Dixon's house,' said Daniel.

'We'll get some men and head there,' said Feather, getting to his feet and pulling on his coat. 'We'll take Marion with us to make sure it is the right place. Vera, you'd better come as well. You can take care of Marion and bring her home afterwards, if this is what we think it is.'

'No!' said Marion agitatedly. 'I want to be there!'

'We'll talk about that later,' snapped Feather. 'Sergeant, get three men while I fix us up with a van.'

Abigail sat on the bed in the small back bedroom, her hands and ankles firmly tied with stout rope. Caroline Dixon sat on a chair in the bedroom, the pistol held unwaveringly in her hand, pointed at Abigail. The two men who'd brought Abigail to Dixon's house sat in chairs by the window, watching.

'Why are you doing this?' demanded Abigail.

Dixon gave a cruel smile.

'Because I can,' she said. 'And because this way I can bring everything to a safe conclusion. I currently have Mr Gerald Carr locked safely in my cellar. When I am ready I shall kill you, and then kill him. Your bodies will be dumped at Carr's yard in Somers Town. He will have a suicide note in his pocket in which he admits to killing you, and himself. He will say that he was responsible for killing the two men at Madame Tussauds, and the other man, Michaels. He will also admit he was responsible for the bank robberies. He will say he killed himself because he knew the net was closing in on him and he could not face the thought of being hanged.'

'But why kill me?' persisted Abigail.

'Because your death will destroy your partner, Daniel Wilson, and he will feel responsible for it because he didn't move sooner to stop Carr.'

'Daniel won't let you get away with it,' said Abigail.

'He won't have any choice. The evidence that it was Gerald Carr who killed you will be overwhelming. The suicide note will clinch things. The police will stop investigating the murders and the bank robberies.'

'Carr won't write a suicide note,' said Abigail firmly. 'He knows he's going to die. He won't give you that pleasure.'

'You're right, he won't write it. I will. I've been sending him notes since he's been in my cellar, demanding written responses. Failure to reply means a beating.' She smiled again. 'Carr is a very stupid man. He doesn't understand why I really want those examples of his handwriting. Remember, I was – and still am – an artist. Making copies was my speciality. Wax and ink are similar mediums.'

'It won't work,' said Abigail. 'Word will get out. Someone will talk.'

'Who?' asked Dixon. 'Those who know anything are either dead, or – in the case of you and Carr – will be dead very shortly. All the crimes will have been solved to the police's satisfaction. I admit it's been an inconvenience to my business, but one that will resume after a suitable break.' She looked at the two men sitting watching. 'And my excellent helpers can't talk without incriminating themselves. So, you see, it's the end for you.' And this time her expression became even crueller, all traces of her smile gone as she said with great venom, 'And you want to know the real reason why I chose you to do this with, and not your partner, Wilson? Because you are everything I loathe, Fenton. You had everything handed to you on a plate. A glittering university education. Your prestige as one of the world's leading archaeologists, so I'm nauseatingly told by so many people I meet when your name is mentioned. Class and status, everything gained so easily. I had to work like a dog for whatever I've got.'

Daniel, Feather and Sergeant Cribbens squashed into the back of the police van alongside Vera and Marion and two uniformed constables. A third constable sat with the driver on the seat at the front of the van. Feather had authorised a pistol each for himself and Cribbens and the two men cradled the guns carefully in their hands. As the van rumbled over the cobbles, Daniel asked the question that had been puzzling him since Marion and Vera had burst into Feather's office.

'What were you going to our house for?' he asked Marion, curious.

'I wanted to make sure she was all right,' said Marion, lowering her head and averting her face from Daniel.

'Who?'

Marion was silent for a moment, then she said, 'Abigail. After what happened with her falling into the road.'

Daniel looked at Feather, inquisitively, who shook his head in reply, then asked Marion, 'How did you hear about Abigail falling into the road?'

Marion looked up at him, distressed, and stammered, 'I

can't remember. Someone must have said about it.'

Feather looked at his wife, who shook her head. 'I didn't know about that,' she said. 'What happened?'

'Someone pushed Abigail so that she fell in front of a horse in Oxford Street,' said Daniel. Puzzled, he asked Marion, 'Were you there? Did you see it happen?'

'Let's talk about it later,' said Feather suddenly, sounding very awkward, and he cast a look at his wife, who closed her eyes and pursed her lips as she tried to conceal her distress.

'I didn't mean to hurt her!' Marion cried miserably, and then she burst into tears.

'You haven't hurt her,' said Sergeant Cribbens gently. 'It's the men with the guns who are the danger here, not you.'

Vera put her arm around Marion and pulled her to her, but there was an emotional distance between the two of them, and suddenly Daniel realised what had happened. And a look at John Feather showed that he knew, too. Daniel was grateful that at that moment the van pulled to a halt and the driver called down to them, 'We're at Lowndes Square, sir.'

Feather opened the door and helped Marion out onto the pavement, Vera, Daniel and the others following.

'Is it one of these houses?' Feather asked his niece.

Marion looked along the terrace of large, white, expensive-looking houses, then pointed to one.

'That one!' she announced.

'Caroline Dixon's,' said Daniel grimly.

Feather rapped out a command and the constables jumped down to join him, while Vera took the unwilling and still distressed Marion back inside the police van. As they neared the house, they heard the unmistakeable sound of a gun being fired, twice. Daniel and Cribbens broke into a run as Feather turned and told one of the constables, 'Bring a sledgehammer from the van. We might need it.' Then he ran after Daniel and Cribbens, who were already at the front door of the house, banging urgently on it and pulling at the bell pull.

'Police!' shouted Feather. 'Open up!'

They pushed at the door, but it was a heavy one that refused to budge. Feather took the sledgehammer from the constable and smashed it hard against the lock, splintering the wood and sending the brass lock and door handle flying in shards of broken metal. He gave the door another smash with the sledgehammer and this time it swung inwards. Feather threw down the sledgehammer and pulled his pistol from his pocket. Daniel had already rushed in and he collided with a dishevelled man holding a smoking gun.

'Drop the gun!' shouted Feather, pointing his own pistol at the man.

The man threw his gun down, and Daniel recognised him as Gerald Carr.

'Where is she?' he shouted, grabbing Carr by the collar.

'It wasn't me!' said Carr desperately. 'I didn't do it!'

'Where is she?' shouted Daniel again.

Carr gestured towards the door to the living room.

'In there,' he said. 'She's dead.'

CHAPTER TWENTY-NINE

Daniel threw himself into the living room and stumbled over the body lying face down just inside the door. It was a woman, but it wasn't Abigail. He lifted her head. It was Caroline Dixon, and she was definitely dead.

He rushed back out into the hallway where Carr was being held by two constables.

'Where's Abigail Fenton?' he demanded angrily.

'Who?' asked Carr.

With a roar of rage, Daniel reached for him, and Carr cringed away from him, squealing, 'I don't know!'

'Constable, handcuff him and keep a close eye on him,' ordered Feather crisply. To Cribbens and the other two constables he said, 'Search the house.'

Daniel was already racing upstairs and Feather ran after him, gun in hand.

'Abigail!' shouted Daniel desperately. 'Abigail!'

They kicked open doors and rushed in and out of rooms. It was in the fifth bedroom they found her, bound and gagged on a bed, with two nervous-looking men standing guard, holding pistols, the same two men who'd attacked Daniel. Feather pointed his pistol at the nearest man.

'Police, Scotland Yard,' snapped Feather. 'The house is full of my men. Use those guns and you'll hang for sure.'

The men threw their guns down and put their hands up. Feather called for Cribbens.

'Get the others and take these two into custody. Handcuffs, and leg shackles from the van. Same for Carr. I'm not taking any chances on any of them trying anything.'

Daniel was hard at work untying the ropes that held Abigail prisoner and removing the cloth tied round her mouth to gag her.

'How did you know where to find me?' she asked.

'It's a long story which we'll tell you later,' said Daniel. He turned to Feather. 'You're going to need the van to get this lot back to the Yard. We'll find a cab and see you back there. And we'll drop Vera and Marion off first.'

'Vera and Marion?' said Abigail, bewildered. 'What are they doing here?'

'That's part of the long story,' said Daniel.

After Carr and Dixon's two henchmen had been deposited, handcuffed and shackled, inside the police van, where they were chained to the interior bars, Feather, Cribbens and one of the constables began a search of the house, while Daniel went in search of a hansom cab, leaving Abigail waiting with a grim-faced Vera and a tearful Marion on the doorstep of the house. Abigail wanted to ask Vera and Marion how they came to be there, but the hard expression on Vera's face told her that this was not the right time to ask that question.

Daniel reappeared with a hansom, at the same time as Feather and his police colleagues exited the house. Sergeant Cribbens gestured at the broken front door.

'We ought to do something about that, sir,' he murmured to Feather, concerned. 'If the place gets robbed while no one's here, we'll end up getting the blame. And there's a lot of expensive-looking stuff inside.'

'Good point,' said Feather. 'You stay here and guard the house. I'll send a carpenter over, along with a van to pick up Caroline Dixon's body. You can ride back to the Yard with them.'

He walked over to Daniel and Abigail.

'You sure you're all right?' he asked Abigail. 'You don't want to go to a doctor or anything?'

'Absolutely not,' said Abigail.

'In that case, I'll see you back at the Yard.' Feather then walked over to Vera and Marion, and held his wife close to him. 'Don't be too hard on her,' he whispered.

'Why not?' whispered back Vera, with an angry glance at Marion.

'If she hadn't been watching the house, Abigail might have been the one who died.' He hugged her and kissed her gently on the forehead. 'We'll sort it all out when I get home.'

With that, Feather headed for the police van. Daniel opened

the door of the hansom and helped Vera and Marion clamber in first; then he did the same for Abigail.

'Right,' he said. 'Let's get you home.'

The first part of the journey to the Feathers' house was in a strained and very awkward silence, with Vera doing her best to appear calm, and Marion hiding her head, unable to look anyone in the eye. It was only as they continued their journey to Scotland Yard that Abigail asked, 'What was all that about? How did Vera and Marion get involved?'

'It was Marion who saw the men with guns put you in a carriage,' said Daniel. 'She jumped on it and found out where they were taking you, and then reported it and what had happened.'

'But what was she doing watching our house?'

'I think she's a confused and troubled young woman,' said Daniel.

'It's about you, isn't it,' said Abigail. 'Remember, I said she had her eyes on you.'

'You did,' acknowledged Daniel.

'That's what it was all about. She was there to see you.'

'Possibly,' admitted Daniel. He hesitated. 'There's another thing. I think it might have been Marion who pushed you in front of that horse.'

Abigail stared at him, stunned. 'What?!'

'I think John and Vera think the same as well,' said Daniel.

'But . . . why would she do something like that? Is she mad?'

'I'm hoping that John and Vera might be able to enlighten us,' said Daniel. 'But forget that for the moment; tell me about you being taken to Caroline Dixon's. And how does

Gerald Carr fit into the picture?'

'She sent two men with guns to collect me from our house. She was going to shoot me and lay the blame on Gerald Carr. She told me she had him prisoner in her cellar.'

'She told you all this?'

Abigail nodded. 'I think she did it to boast how clever she was. She told me that she was going to shoot me, then shoot him and take our bodies to his yard in Somers Town and dump them there. She'd written a suicide note claiming to be from him, in which he claimed responsibility for the murders of the two nightwatchmen at Tussauds museum and Harry Michaels, and also the bank raids that had taken place, and finally my murder. She'd write that he couldn't live with the thought of being hanged, so he was ending things this way.'

'And she thought she could get away with that?'

'She kept sending notes to him while he was in the cellar asking questions to which he had to write the answers. If he didn't give them he was beaten at gunpoint so he couldn't fight back.'

'She was getting samples of his handwriting,' said Daniel.

'Exactly,' said Abigail. 'Remember, she was an artist and a very good copyist. When the authorities compared the suicide note with Carr's documents at the Somers Town yard, they'd see that the writing was the same.'

'And the men who were sent to warn me off, the ones holding you prisoner, made a point of telling me they were from Gerald Carr as extra evidence to point the finger at Carr.'

'And it might have worked if Carr hadn't shot her,' said Feather.

'But how did that happen?' asked Daniel. 'She had her men

in the house protecting her; how did Carr manage to get free and kill her?'

'For that, we have to listen to what Carr has to say.'

With the necessity of organising a van to return to Lowndes Square to collect Caroline Dixon's body and Sergeant Cribbens, and also to arrange a carpenter and a locksmith to secure the house, by the time Inspector Feather was ready to undertake the questioning of Gerald Carr alongside Superintendent Armstrong, Daniel and Abigail had arrived at Scotland Yard.

'You can sit and observe,' Armstrong told them firmly, 'but you don't say anything. If you have any questions you'll pass them to Inspectors Feather and Jarrett, and they'll decide if they want to ask them.'

He then gestured for Daniel and Abigail to take their seats behind him.

'We're like the unwanted children at school, sent to the back of the class,' Daniel whispered to Abigail as they sat down.

'We should count ourselves lucky to be allowed into the room,' Abigail whispered back. 'It was only a few days ago we weren't even allowed in the building.'

'Bring in the prisoner,' commanded Armstrong.

A constable appeared, ushering the handcuffed Carr and pushed him down onto a chair facing Armstrong, who was flanked on either side by Feather and Jarrett.

At least we can see Carr's face as he answers the questions, Daniel thought.

'You shot and killed Caroline Dixon,' said Feather, opening the session.

'It was a case of self-defence,' said Carr. 'She was going to have me killed, the same as she'd had Harry Michaels and the two nightwatchmen killed. She was stark staring mad! I wasn't safe as long as she was alive.'

'Tell us about the tunnel at Tussauds museum,' said Jarrett.

'That was Michaels' idea,' said Carr.

He's keen to talk, thought Daniel. *He wants to be seen as cooperating, hoping it'll get him off.*

'Michaels had seen how this gang had been robbing banks by breaking through into their vaults from the cellar next door. "Mr Carr," he says to me, "there's an opportunity here to make big money." I told him no. I said it was too dangerous doing the same thing; they could well end up bumping into the gang in the same shop and it'd all be over.

'"It will all be over for them soon enough, Mr Carr," he said. "Think about it: there's only so many banks with a vault next door to an empty cellar. The banks will get wise to it. Every one with a vault next to a shop with a cellar with no one living there will be guarded. No, my idea is we stick to the same principle, but we break in from further away."

'"What d'you mean?" I asked him.

'"We tunnel in. We find somewhere with a cellar that's two or three doors away from a bank that's got a vault in the basement, with solid earth in between, and we tunnel through."

'"Rubbish!" I said. "You can't dig a tunnel like that overnight."

'"I don't intend to," he said. "What we do is find a place that needs nightwatchmen. We put a couple of blokes in who've got tunnelling experience, and they can spend a week, maybe two, even three digging a tunnel. No one'll be expecting that so no one'll be guarding against it."

'"Where are you going to get the tunnellers from?" I asked.

322

'"I've got 'em," he said. "Two blokes who used to dig tunnels when they were in the army. I've also got the perfect place for our first job. Madame Tussauds wax museum. They've got a cellar and it's two doors away from a bank. And they need nightwatchmen."

'He then told me the rest of his plan: to pay off the existing watchmen and get these two ex-army blokes in. He'd done his research about the bank vault as well. He reckoned there was about a million quid in cash and valuables in it. What he was looking for was a financial backer, someone to put up the money to get the job done: paying off the nightwatchmen who worked there already, and paying the two tunnellers.

'In the end, we made a deal: I'd put up the cash he needed for seventy per cent of the take.'

'And he agreed to that?'

'I was the one taking all the risk,' said Carr. 'Say they got through to the vault and there was nothing there, or hardly anything. I'd be out of pocket. Anyway, Michaels set it all up and we got the tunnellers installed at Madame Tussauds, and they set to work at nights. They were good, too. They were making lots of headway, and then . . .' He scowled bitterly. 'Somehow the Dixon woman found out about it.'

'Did you know Mrs Dixon already?'

Carr shook his head. 'But I knew Charlie Dixon. Her husband. He was a crook, and very successful. We knew about one another but our paths didn't really cross, so to speak. He worked mainly in the richer parts of town: Mayfair, Knightsbridge, Belgravia, classy places.'

'Doing what?'

'Jewellers, money-lenders.'

'Break-ins?' asked Feather.

'Break-ins, sometimes threats of what would happen if they didn't pay up to have their shop protected. These were rich people; the last thing they wanted was trouble. Charlie and his boys did well out of it. He had a big house with a big garden at the back of it, all very swell. I think that's why she married him: his money. But she wanted more. It turned out that she was the one who came up with the idea of breaking into bank vaults through the cellar of the shop next door. Clever stuff.

'And then Charlie died. Heart attack, they said, but if you ask me it was her doing him in so she could get all the money.'

'You got any proof of that? That she bumped Charlie off?'

'Proof?' Carr shook his head, then added, 'But you've only got to look at how she did for those two watchmen and Joe Michaels. One with his head cut off, Michaels having plaster of Paris poured down his throat. She was ruthless. Cold and hard. When I found out what had happened to the watchmen, and then to Michaels, and the word on the street was that she was the one who did it. Maybe she didn't do the killings at the museum, but she certainly did the wax job on the second watchman, and killed Michaels the way she did. She used to do waxworks, you know, so they were the tools of her trade.'

'Yes, so we've been told,' said Feather.

'Anyway, I knew at once what was going on, the message she was sending. She didn't like the idea of anyone treading on what she saw as her territory, doing the bank jobs the way she was doing 'em.'

'But Michaels' way was different, tunnelling not breaking through a cellar wall.'

'Think I'd try telling her that? Like I said, she's mad. And vicious. No, I could see the writing on the wall. She'd done for the watchmen, and for Michaels, and I bet she made Michaels tell her who he was in it with.'

'So you decided to kill her.'

'No, I decided to see if I could do a deal with her. I'd tell her I'd back off and leave her with the banks, and I'd make it worth her while. Sort of, pay a fine, that sort of thing. I thought she'd see reason. But she didn't.'

'What happened?'

'Me and the boys went to her house at Lowndes Square. I took them because I knew she had her own people there, so I thought I'd be safe. I didn't expect her to do anything stupid in her own house. But as we walked in, she suddenly pulled out a gun and shot Iggy and Joe right there. Then she told her blokes to put me in the cellar. I ask you, what sort of woman pulls out a gun?'

'Did you know that Miss Fenton was being held prisoner in the house?' asked Feather.

Carr shook his head. 'No. All I knew is she wasn't going to let me go. She was playing with me. All this business of sending me notes. So I set to work on the lock, and at last I got it open. I was going to sneak out, but when I got upstairs, there she was.'

'On her own?'

Carr nodded. 'This time, when she pulled out her gun, I was ready. I jumped on her and tried to grab it off her, but she hung on. We was fighting for it, when it went off.'

'She was shot twice,' said Feather.

'I couldn't take the risk she might get up again. Like I said, she's the most dangerous person I've ever met. Anyway, I was worried the sound of the shots would bring her blokes running in, so I decided to leg it.'

'Taking the gun.'

'Of course. I didn't know who I'd run into. Lucky for me, it was you, not them.' He looked at them, begging. 'It wasn't murder. It was self-defence.'

CHAPTER THIRTY

The interview over, Carr was taken down to the cells in the basement.

'I think we've already got enough to hang him just for killing Caroline Dixon,' said Armstrong. 'The second bullet will be the clincher. But I'm pretty sure there's more to be got on him.'

'I agree,' said Feather. 'I suggest some serious questioning of everyone involved in his outfit, along with talking to everyone in Somers Town. Once people know he's going to hang they won't be afraid of him any more, and they'll start to talk.'

Armstrong nodded. 'It's going to be a big job. I suggest you and Inspector Jarrett work on it together.'

'It'll be good to clear the streets of Carr and his gang,' grunted Jarrett. 'Bring some decency to the place.'

'Until some upstart comes to take his place,' said Feather ruefully. 'That always happens.'

'But this time we squash it before it gets out of hand, like it did with Carr,' grunted Armstrong. 'Right, next let's have those two scumbags you picked up at Dixon's house and talk to them.'

'Can I suggest that Miss Fenton leads the questioning of them,' proposed Daniel.

'Why?' demanded Armstrong.

'Two reasons. First, she was the one they kidnapped at gunpoint, so they're going to find it difficult to lie about that. Second, they've been bossed around by a strong woman, Caroline Dixon, so it's likely they'll react the same way to another strong woman, in this case Abigail.'

Armstrong looked at Feather and Jarrett inquisitively for their opinions. Jarrett looked unimpressed by the suggestion, but Feather – as Armstrong expected – nodded to show his agreement. Armstrong looked at Abigail and asked, 'Do you feel up to doing this?'

Calmly, Abigail replied, 'These men kidnapped me at gunpoint and were undoubtedly going to kill me. If I had my way, I'd rip their throats out. I think you can trust me to handle the situation.'

'Very well,' said Armstrong. 'But I'll still be in charge of the interrogation. I'll start, and then hand them over to you.' He looked at Daniel, Feather and Jarrett. 'Feel free to pose any questions that may arise.' He looked at Abigail and added, 'With your permission, of course.'

'That's fine with me,' said Abigail.

Armstrong looked at the uniformed constable on guard at

the door. 'Bring in the two prisoners.' As the constable left to collect the men, he told Abigail and Daniel, 'Their names are Ralph Abbott and Sam Wallace. Abbott is the one with the scar on his cheek. Both have criminal records, although there's been nothing against them for the last eighteen months.'

'Since Caroline Dixon took over her husband's gang,' commented Daniel. 'She was a very careful woman.'

The door opened and two constables ushered in the two men who'd abducted Abigail and sat them on chairs facing Armstrong. Abigail had now taken the place of Inspector Jarrett on Armstrong's right, Jarrett moving to join Daniel in what Daniel termed 'the back row'. Feather retained his seat on Armstrong's left.

'Ralph Abbott and Samuel Wallace, you are facing various charges of murder,' began Armstrong.

'We never killed anyone!' burst out Abbott.

'Quiet!' stormed Armstrong, banging his fist hard on his desktop. 'You will talk when answering questions, that's all. I repeat: you are facing various charges of murder, along with a charge of abducting Miss Abigail Fenton, who is sitting here alongside me, and with holding her prisoner with intention to kill her. We will start with that one before we move on to the other charges.' He turned to Abigail. 'Miss Fenton, you may question the prisoners.'

Abigail glared at the two men; her intense look of loathing and disgust, along with her deliberate heavy silence as she looked at them, caused the men to exchange looks of extreme fear and uncertainty.

Good, thought Daniel. *She's got them.*

'You admit that you came to my house with the intention

of abducting me?' said Abigail, not so much a question as a statement of fact.

The two men hesitated, crouching down in their chairs as if hoping to be invisible, then they nodded, Wallace especially swallowing hard.

'You will answer with words, not just nods!' barked Abigail. 'And sit up straight!'

Intimidated, both men shifted back in their chairs, then sat up straight.

'Yes,' croaked Abbott.

Abigail turned her glare on Wallace, who managed to say, 'Yes.'

'And you were both armed with pistols.'

'Yes,' said both men again.

'You would have shot me if I had refused to go with you.' Again, it was a statement, not a question.

'No!' burst out Abbott.

'Then why the guns?' demanded Abigail.

'To . . . to put pressure on you,' said Abbott. 'To make you think we would.'

'Why did you abduct me?'

'It was on Mrs Dixon's orders,' said Wallace. 'She was the boss.'

'The boss of what?' asked Abigail.

Abbot swallowed hard, then said, 'Everything. She was the boss of everything.'

'The bank raids?'

Abbott and Wallace hesitated, then both men nodded. 'Yes,' admitted Abbot in a faint voice.

'You robbed the banks,' said Abigail.

330

'Yes,' repeated Abbott, and he looked at Wallace, who added his own 'Yes.'

'You killed the two nightwatchmen at Tussauds wax museum,' continued Abigail.

'No, that wasn't us!' bleated Abbott. 'That was Mrs Dixon!'

Abigail gave a snort of disbelief. 'You're trying to tell us that Mrs Dixon killed Eric Dudgeon and cut off his head in the Chamber of Horrors.'

'Yes!' Abbot nodded. He looked at Wallace. 'Tell her, Sam.'

'It was her who did it,' said Wallace. 'We didn't know what she had planned. We thought she was just going to do some damage to the place. Beat up the watchmen. That sort of thing. She told us to knock 'em out and bring them to the Chamber of Horrors. And then she told us to put one of them on this block thing beneath the guillotine, and she produces this really sharp knife, more like a saw. The sort that butchers use. And she just . . . sawed his head off.' He shook his head, as if sickened at the memory. 'It was horrible!'

'What about the other nightwatchman?'

'She hit him hard on the head again to finish him off. Then she told us to take him down to the carriage.'

'Who was driving the carriage?' barked Abigail.

'Ernie,' mumbled Abbott. 'Ernie Richmond. He's her regular coachman.'

'Was he the one who drove the carriage when you abducted me?'

Abbott nodded. 'Ernie does all the driving.'

'Where is he?'

'I don't know,' said Abbott. 'He left after he delivered us to Mrs Dixon's.'

'Where does he keep the carriage and the horse?' asked Feather.

'At a stable in Green Park,' said Abbott. 'He's got a room there over the stables.'

Feather pushed a piece of paper and a pencil to Abbott. 'Write down his name and the address of the stable,' he said.

They waited while Abbott wrote the address and pushed the paper back to Feather. Feather called the constable over and handed him the paper. 'Take this to Sergeant Cribbens in my office. Tell him to locate this man and bring him in.'

The constable nodded, and left. Feather turned to Abigail. 'Yours again, Miss Fenton,' he said.

Abigail looked at Abbott and Wallace. 'You took me to a bedroom in Mrs Dixon's house, tied and gagged me and put me on a bed, while you sat watching over me, both of you with your pistols at the ready. Mrs Dixon had informed me that I was to be shot dead. Which of you was to kill me, or was it both of you?'

'No!' protested Abbott and Wallace simultaneously.

'Not us!' continued Abbott. 'That wasn't our job.'

'No, we was just there to keep an eye on you,' added Wallace.

'So who was going to kill me?'

'Mrs Dixon,' said Abbott.

'And you were going to be accomplices to my murder,' stated Abigail.

Both men looked uncomfortable.

'We don't do murders,' mumbled Abbott, averting his eyes from Abigail's stern gaze.

'Taking part in any murder carries the same penalty,' said Armstrong. 'Hanging.'

'No!' howled Wallace. 'We haven't killed anyone!'

'What about the two bank clerks?' asked Feather. 'Derek Parminter and Arthur Crum?'

Abbott and Wallace looked at him, at first bewildered, and then in fear, gulping nervously and now sweating.

'They were accidents,' mumbled Abbott.

'And young Thomas Tandry?' put in Daniel. 'The thirteen-year-old boy.'

'That was Dixon!' cried Wallace. 'She did him! We only got rid of the body.'

'Where?' asked Daniel.

'There's an old cesspit at the bottom of her house,' said Wallace. 'It's not used any more since they put the main drains in, but it's still there. We used to tell her she ought to fill it in, in case anyone fell in it, but she said she still had a use for it.'

'Who else went in it?' asked Armstrong.

The two men looked even more uncomfortable, and Wallace mumbled something.

'Speak up!' barked Armstrong. 'Who else went into the cesspit? How many more bodies will we find there?'

'We don't know,' said Wallace.

'If there are more, we didn't put them there!' defended Abbott. 'We only know about the boy. And she did for him. Mrs Dixon.'

'What about Harry Michaels?' asked Jarrett, speaking for the first time.

'Who?' asked Abbott nervously.

'The gent found dead in Piccadilly Circus with plaster of Paris stuffed down his throat.'

Abbott suddenly pulled himself up in his chair, all resistance gone, although he tried to show defiance. 'I'm not saying any more,' he said. 'It was her, not us. We was just her helpers.'

'Yes,' said Wallace. 'That's all we were. Her helpers.'

Abigail turned to Armstrong.

'I'm finished with them for now, Superintendent,' she said. 'If you or your inspectors would like to question them?'

'No,' said Armstrong. 'I think we've got enough to be going on with. We'll talk to them more later. Constable, take them down to the cells.'

CHAPTER THIRTY-ONE

After Abbott and Wallace had been taken away, Armstrong turned to Daniel and Abigail. 'I think we can take it from here,' he said. 'If there's anything more you can think of that will help us prosecute, let us know, but I think we've already got enough to get our convictions.'

Daniel and Abigail nodded and rose to their feet.

'Perhaps you'd show our guests out, Inspector Feather,' said Armstrong. 'There are one or two things I need to go over with Inspector Jarrett.'

'Certainly, sir,' said Feather.

As Daniel, Abigail and Feather walked away from the superintendent's office, Feather remarked wryly, 'He doesn't trust me. He thinks I'm too close to you.'

'We're glad you are,' said Abigail.

'Actually, this gives me an excuse to talk to you,' said Feather. 'In private.'

'Your office?' asked Daniel.

Feather shook his head. 'Sergeant Cribbens could return at any moment with Ernie Richmond, if he's found him. Or the superintendent could decide he needs to have a word with me. We'll go to the stables. Less chance of interruptions.'

They walked down the stairs to the main reception area, then out the back way into the yard where the police vans were parked and the horses that pulled them were stabled. A strong smell of horse manure hung in the air.

'I'm guessing this is about Marion,' said Abigail.

'Yes,' said Feather with a sigh. 'Sooner or later the superintendent is going to ask me why my wife and niece were at the raid on Caroline Dixon's house.'

'And what will you tell him?'

'I'll say that Marion was making a social call on you at your house, and when she arrived she saw the two men taking you away at gunpoint. So she ran home and told Vera what she'd seen.'

'And he'll believe that?' asked Abigail.

'What's there to question?' asked Feather. 'He's just glad that it turned out all right, and a coup for Scotland Yard.'

They stopped by a police van parked close to the exit. Feather stood in thought, silent, weighing what he was going to say.

'So, Marion?' prompted Abigail.

'Yes,' said Feather. 'My sister, Emily, sent Marion to us because she was having problems with her.'

'What sort of problems?'

'Emily's a widow; her husband died two years ago and Marion was really upset by his death. About six months ago she began to get besotted with the vicar at their local church in their village.'

'Besotted?'

'It didn't seem that way at first. In fact, initially Emily encouraged Marion to go and talk to the vicar about her grieving over her father. She thought an older man, someone in that position, might be able to help her. And at first it appeared he had helped her. But then she began calling at the vicarage to see him more and more, and it was as if she chose the times when she knew his wife would be out. Emily discovered later that Marion used to watch the vicarage and wait for the vicar's wife to leave. And it wasn't just to talk about her father; she wanted to talk about everything . . . especially about love.'

'She was in love with him?'

'She told Emily she was. And she also told the vicar.'

'How did they take it? Though I guess I know the answer to that already: that's why she's here with you.'

Feather nodded.

'Did anything happen with the vicar? You know, between him and Marion?'

'No. Nothing like that, although it might have if he hadn't been a decent sort of chap. The Reverend Wattle is a good man. He expressed his concerns to Emily that Marion was becoming too – as he put it – forward, and he'd be happy to talk to her, but only in the company of his wife, or Emily, and that he would be telling Marion that.'

'I'm guessing that didn't go well.'

'No.'

'Rages? Anger?'

'No, Marion took to her bed in floods of tears, refusing to eat. She blamed Mrs Wattle, said the vicar's wife was determined to destroy the relationship that she and the vicar had.'

'Relationship?'

'In her mind he and she were in love. Soulmates.'

'Even though nothing had happened between them?'

'Once, when she was distressed, he put his arms around her to comfort her. That was all.'

'According to him,' commented Daniel.

'I believe him,' said Feather. 'As I said, he's a good man, devoted to his wife. They've been married for over twenty years and there's never been a hint of scandal about him.'

'Any children?'

'They had two, both of whom died in infancy. When I saw the way she was looking at you, Daniel, I worried we might have the same problem, It was the same way she used to look at the Reverend Wattle. And older man, kind, caring. I didn't expect her to actually physically attack Abigail in the way she did to try to get rid of her.'

'We don't know for sure she did,' said Abigail.

'Yes, we do,' said Feather. 'You know it, I know it, Vera knows it.'

'But if her aim was to get rid of Abigail, why did she come to her rescue?' asked Daniel, puzzled.

'Because reality was intruding on her fantasy,' said Abigail.

'I think the reality might be more mundane,' said Feather. 'If she saved you, or at least tried to, then Daniel would be for ever grateful to her. And, with you going away to Egypt . . .'

'I see.' Abigail nodded. 'Yes, it makes sense. What will you do now, about her?'

'Warn her off Daniel, and you,' said Feather. 'I think Vera will be more watchful of her after this. And I think we've got to talk to my sister about Marion going back home.' He looked at them apologetically. 'I'm so sorry this happened. After what happened with the Reverend Wattle, I should have been more on my guard.'

'You can't be everywhere,' said Daniel. 'And Vera's got a lot to handle with the household, let alone having Marion to deal with. We'll stay away from calling on you for a while, see if things settle down.'

Feather held out his hand. 'Thanks,' he said.

They each shook his hand firmly, then Daniel gestured towards the rear exit from the stable yard. 'I think we'll head out the back way,' he said. 'That way we'll avoid running into Armstrong or Jarrett. Everything may seem harmonious at the moment, but somehow I feel it won't last.'

It was when they got home and were finally able to relax that Daniel asked, 'By the way, I meant to ask how Mr Doyle reacted when you told him the pyramids don't have life-giving powers. With everything that's happened, all other thoughts were driven out of my head. My only thought was to find you.'

'Yes, it has been rather fraught,' she admitted. 'And as for Mr Doyle, I never went to see him. I thought about what you said, and decided you were right. The only thing he and his wife have in regard to his wife's illness is hope. It would be wrong of me to take that away from them. And, I agree, sometimes hope can achieve the most astounding results that fly in the face of logic. When I was in Egypt once, there was a man who was so seriously ill his village prepared for his death, which was expected the very next day. But, to my surprise, but not to theirs, the next day he rose from his bed as if nothing was wrong with him.'

'Did he die later?'

'I don't know. He was still alive, and very active, when I left the site two months afterwards. No one explained how he'd come to recover; they simply said it was the will of Allah.' She looked at Daniel and sighed. 'So, in that case you and Mr Doyle were right.'

CHAPTER THIRTY-TWO

This time there was no William Melville in the room at 10 Downing Street, just Superintendent Armstrong with Lord Salisbury and Sir Matthew White Ridley. Even the secretary who had taken the minutes of the previous encounter was absent. *So this is an off-the-record meeting*, thought the superintendent. *Completely deniable.* Both the prime minister and the home secretary looked very uncomfortable, as well they might, thought Armstrong; one of their own was the villain behind everything that had happened.

'You're absolutely sure that Mrs Caroline Dixon was responsible for the bank robberies, and the murders at Tussauds wax museum?' asked White Ridley.

'Absolutely,' said Armstrong. 'My Inspector Feather found

the evidence at Mrs Dixon's home, including many of the documents that were taken from the safety deposit boxes from the bank vaults.'

'There is no chance that she was an unwilling and unwitting accomplice?' asked White, desperate to find anything that would exonerate her and her reputation.

'I'm afraid not, sir,' replied Armstrong. 'We have confessions from her accomplices who carried out the bank robberies stating that she masterminded them. And also from these same men detailing how she herself committed the murders, including the beheading of one of the nightwatchmen, and the suffocation of a man called Harry Michaels, who was also planning to rob banks. They also said that she had murdered a thirteen-year-old boy who helped her wrap one of the men she murdered in wax, the body of the nightwatchman that was subsequently found returned to Tussauds wax museum. There is also the evidence from Gerald Carr, the notorious gangster who shot and killed Mrs Dixon, claiming it was in self-defence because she was planning to kill him.'

The prime minister and home secretary exchanged deeply unhappy looks.

'This must never get out,' said Salisbury. 'Mrs Dixon was a pillar of the community, her support for the Nightingale Fund applauded through all levels of society, right up to the royal family.' He looked at Armstrong with mournful eyes. 'I assume that is where most of the money that was stolen went? To the Nightingale Fund?'

'Only a certain amount, we believe. It seems that Mrs Dixon kept much of the proceeds of the robberies.'

'Then we should be able to recover part of the money that

was lost,' said the home secretary hopefully.

'That will depend on her lawyers,' said Armstrong. 'Inspector Feather will be examining her bank accounts, but there could be some doubt as to whether it can be proved beyond question that the money deposited in her account came from specific robberies, and particularly whose money it was. Her lawyers have intimated that they will question any attempt to have that money removed from her estate. In which case, it may well result in a court case to decide the outcome, which would result in unfortunate publicity revealing her role in these criminal activities.'

Salisbury and White Ridley fell silent, an oppressive, heavy silence. Finally, Salisbury said, 'For the same reason, the man who shot her . . .' He struggled for the name.

'Gerald Carr,' said Armstrong.

'Yes, Carr.' Salisbury nodded. 'He cannot go to trial for her murder because his defence would reveal her involvement in the bank robberies and the murders.'

'I'm afraid so,' said the Superintendent.

'And the same applies for the men you say carried out the bank raids under her direction,' added Salisbury.

'It would seem that is the case, sadly,' agreed Armstrong.

'So what is the answer?' appealed White Ridley. 'What explanation can we offer to tell the public that the bank robberies have been stopped and the villains apprehended, and the murders at Tussauds caught, whilst at the same time maintaining Mrs Dixon's reputation as one of our finest citizens?' A horrifying thought struck him because he suddenly blurted out, 'What about these Museum Detectives? Daniel Wilson and Abigail Fenton. Do they know the truth of the situation and the extent of Mrs Dixon's guilt?'

'Sadly, they do. We have a statement from Miss Abigail Fenton in which she says that she was held captive by Mrs Dixon, who told her she was going to kill her and then frame Mr Carr for her murder. And Mr Wilson was with Inspector Feather when they arrived at Mrs Dixon's house and it was he who found Miss Fenton being held prisoner at gunpoint.'

'They must be ordered to stay silent about those events,' stated Salisbury firmly. 'I shall tell them so myself, as their prime minister. I assume they are respectable and responsible persons who will agree.'

'If not, we will threaten them with imprisonment for treason,' spat White Ridley nervously.

'I'm sure that won't be necessary,' said Armstrong. 'They are, as you say, responsible people. Especially Miss Fenton.'

Although I'd quite like to see Wilson's face if he was threatened with imprisonment for treason, he decided. But no, he couldn't allow it. However much he hated to admit it, Wilson had been instrumental in solving this case. Both cases. The only satisfying aspect to the superintendent was that there'd be no publicity, so no chance for the so-called Museum Detectives to take the credit here. If there was to be a false story told, then he would make sure it was told the right way, to reflect the credit to where it should go. Scotland Yard would take the glory.

Next morning, Daniel and Abigail studied the newspapers over breakfast, with Abigail getting more and more irritated the more she read.

'This is all absolute bilge!' she burst out. 'According to all the reports, Mrs Caroline Dixon was brutally murdered by burglars at her own home. They then go on to wax lyrical about her achievements as a philanthropist. According to them, this woman – a vicious murderess and bank robber – was virtually a saint.'

'They daren't tell the truth for fear of smearing the reputation of the Nightingale Fund,' said Daniel. 'In fact, I doubt if people like Joe Dalton know, or would even admit it if faced with the evidence, that she could have been a criminal.'

'So who's decided to put out this false story?' asked Abigail.

'Someone very high up,' said Daniel. 'There are lots of very important and influential people who were involved with Caroline Dixon and her fundraising.'

'Superintendent Armstrong?'

'Oh, much higher than him,' said Daniel. 'He's just a cog in the machine.'

'But surely the truth will come out when Gerald Carr is put on trial for her murder.'

'I think that's unlikely to happen,' said Daniel. 'The last thing anyone at the top will want will be the truth coming out. There are reputations to be protected, and high among them will be that of Caroline Dixon, philanthropist extraordinaire.'

'So what will happen to Gerald Carr? And the two men who abducted me?'

Daniel shrugged. 'It wouldn't surprise me if they were offered lucrative employment abroad, possibly in one of the colonies.'

'But they are killers!'

'It wouldn't be the first cover-up that's taken place to protect the reputations of the rich and powerful.'

Abigail pursed her lips in annoyance as she scanned the papers and reported, 'I see that our names aren't included in any way. Instead, Superintendent Armstrong gets all the credit. Not even John Feather!'

'The superintendent is ambitious,' Daniel reminded her. A noise from the hallway caught his ear. 'That sounds like the post.'

He went out to the hallway and reappeared with an expensive-looking envelope, which he opened.

'Well, well,' he said with a smile, and he handed the letter to Abigail. 'It seems we have been invited to meet the prime minister. He requests our presence urgently today.'

Abigail looked at the letter, puzzled.

'Why?' she asked. 'Why does the prime minister want to see us?'

'I believe it relates to what we were just talking about,' said Daniel. 'If I'm right and Gerald Carr and Caroline Dixon's henchmen are to be offered immunity, providing they go to some distant land, under threat of execution if they ever return, and with Caroline Dixon, Harry Michaels, the two watchmen and various others involved in the case conveniently dead, that leaves just we two as members of the public with the knowledge of what actually happened. John Feather and the other police officers will be bound by a pledge of silence.'

'You can't mean we are to be offered sanctuary abroad in exchange for our silence?'

'No.' Daniel grinned. 'The importance of the country's reputation will be explained to us. And then you will be presented with a piece of paper which you will be asked to sign.'

'Why me?' asked Abigail. 'Why not you?'

'Because I've already signed the Official Secrets Act. I was required to sign it during the Jack the Ripper investigation, as was the rest of Abberline's squad, to stop us talking about certain prominent people who were under suspicion.'

'I've never heard of it,' said Abigail.

'Most people haven't,' said Daniel. 'It was passed by an Act of Parliament in 1889.'

'And if I refuse to sign?' demanded Abigail, annoyed.

'It's unlikely you will be allowed to leave the country ever again. So, no leading a dig in Egypt for Mr Conan Doyle. No future explorations anywhere. And you could well be jailed.'

'But that's an infringement of my civil liberties!' burst out Abigail. 'My rights as a citizen!'

'Yes,' agreed Daniel. He took the letter from her. 'So, what is it to be? Your signature, or martyrdom?'

'You may be completely wrong,' said Abigail. 'He could be asking to see us to congratulate us on our work on this case.'

'He *could*,' said Daniel. 'But I bet you he isn't. But, if I'm wrong, I shall take you for a meal at whichever restaurant you care to name.'

'And if I'm wrong?'

'Then you take me for a meal at my choice of eating house.'

Abigail eyed him warily. 'This is going to be Stevensons' Pie and Mash Shop, isn't it.' She gave a sigh. 'All right. But what does one wear to meet a prime minister?'

AUTHOR BIO

JIM ELDRIDGE was born in central London towards the end of World War II, and survived attacks by V2 rockets on the Kings Cross area where he lived. In 1971 he sold his first sitcom, starring Arthur Lowe, to the BBC and had his first book commissioned. Since then he has had more than one hundred books published, with sales of over three million copies. He lives in Kent with his wife.

jimeldridge.com